WICKED NIGHTS

A. D. JUSTICE

STEELE SECURITY SERIES

WICKED NIGHTS

Steele Security Series
Book 3

A.D. JUSTICE

1

CHAPTER ONE

Ten Years Earlier

"Eyes on target," Reaper whispered into his comm. The rest of the Delta Force team remained in place with their muscles tensed and ready to move when the command was issued.

"Big Eye, Reaper. Can you confirm friendlies are still in the southwest corner of the compound?" Reaper spoke into the handheld radio to the reconnaissance plane that flew overhead.

"Roger that, Reaper. Thermals show five stationary warm bodies, one in motion inside the room, and one stationary outside the door."

"Copy that. Going dark. Reaper out."

He pressed the microphone button on his neck to talk to his team on the ground. "Positions."

One word was all it took for Bull, Rebel, and Shadow to move quickly into their places. They moved silently across the grounds to surround the area where the hostages were held. The houses inside the compound were all connected by doorways or covered breezeways, obviously built over time as the need to expand arose. They were constructed of a mixture of sunbaked mud and clay brick, with flat roofs and very few windows. As they covered the major entryways of the house, each man alerted their leader when he was in place and ready to take control of the situation.

When the news first broke that hostile insurgents had taken five American contractors hostage, Reaper knew his team would soon be called to intercede. The terrorists were demanding the release of one of their leaders in exchange for the five American men they currently held. For every day the government waited to make the exchange, the extremists vowed they'd behead one of the hostages. Reaper's team specialized in getting in and out of secure places, safely extracting the hostages, and effectively disabling the resistance.

When everyone was in place, Reaper gave the one-word command. "Go."

With his weapon drawn, each man crept silently through the dark in his assigned hallway until the four met in the back corner of the house. As they reached the last turn, they prepared to meet the resistance waiting for them. Rebel took his position, crouching low to the ground, ready to cover Reaper when he bolted to the opposite wall. Shadow and Bull prepared to move into similar positions immediately after the initial foe was incapacitated.

Like the well-oiled machine they'd trained to be, they executed their plan flawlessly. When the guard saw Reaper step into the hallway, his brain barely had time to register the shock before Rebel's double-tap took him out. Shadow and Bull moved into the lead positions as they continued to the door. Shouting in Arabic, followed by painful yelps, alerted the team that their enemies inside the hostage room were aware of their presence. Three men took their places on either side of the door, and then Shadow hit the door with a well-placed kick. He quickly jumped to the right side of the door, out of the way before the men inside the room opened fire.

The location of the bullet spray in the mud bricks across the hall gave the men a good indication of the enemies' locations inside the room. Rebel and Bull faced each other before one took the high position and the other took the lower one. As the guys swung around the doorframe with their weapons drawn, the guards were disarmed with minimal effort.

The team moved fully into the room, completed their full sweep, and untied the hostages. "US Army," Reaper introduced himself. "Is anyone injured?"

"Not bad. I can walk," one man answered. The others replied that they weren't injured.

Reaper pointed to the man who was obviously stronger than the others. "You stay with him—" he pointed to the slightly wounded man "—right behind me. We move at the speed of the weakest person." He finished giving the instructions on how each hostage would follow them out so that a member of the team covered each man.

"Big Eye, Reaper," he said into the radio. "Recovered. Exiting with five."

"Copy that, Reaper," came the reply. "Eyes on you."

Reaper transferred the connection from the handset to the speaker in his helmet so the recon plane could easily communicate with him. The group of men formed a line and began their withdrawal from the compound. The echo of heavy footfalls and voices became louder from the direction in which they were headed.

The voice in his helmet alerted him. "Reaper, Big Eye. Multiple hostiles are blocking your current route. Turn left at the next intersection. Proceed to the window. Extraction team being relocated."

"Copy," Reaper replied and proceeded on the updated route. Slinging his gun over his shoulder by the strap, he picked up a chair and busted a pane of the glass of the small panel window. Once the shards were cleared, he placed the chair in front of the window and motioned for Bull to go first. "Cover."

Bull nodded and deftly moved through the open window to take his place outside. "Men approaching," he said quietly into his comm.

"Big Eye, Reaper. Confirm extraction team location."

"Reaper, the team is less than half a klick from your current location."

"Copy," he replied.

He relayed the information to Bull as he helped the first hostage through the window. Rebel and Shadow remained in position with their rifles at the ready as Reaper fed the remaining men through the small opening.

"Your turn, ladies," Reaper said to Rebel and Shadow.

"Age before beauty." Shadow smirked at Rebel and jerked his head toward the exit.

"I'll be waiting on the other side of that wall to kick your ass," Rebel chuckled as he climbed out nimbly.

"You're up, big guy," Reaper said.

Shadow shouldered his weapon and followed Rebel. "Let's go, Reaper. Playtime is over," Shadow said from outside the window.

"Reaper, Big Eye. Multiple hostiles approaching your location. Take cover."

As Reaper started to turn toward the window, the first of the combatants turned the corner and spotted him. The hostile raised his rifle and took his aim at Reaper. A shot rang out and the man crumpled to the floor before he could squeeze the trigger. Reaper stepped on the chair and dove through the window, landed on his hands, and rolled in a somersault to lessen the force of his landing. Rebel simultaneously moved to cover the team, his rifle trained on the small opening.

As more men entered the hallway, Rebel squeezed the trigger

of his automatic rifle. One by one, one insurgent after another fell to the floor.

"Let's go," Reaper yelled to the hostages.

They began their trek across the compound grounds toward the back wall. Armed men began pouring out of multiple doorways behind them. The men yelled curses in Arabic as they ran toward the fleeing hostages. Rebel turned and began to fire his weapon, hitting his mark repeatedly as he covered the team and hostages. One man fell from Rebel's covering fire, but he was still determined to kill the American infidels who had defiled his residence. While lying on his stomach, he raised his rifle with his bloody hands and tried to steady his shaking arms.

He fired his gun and the bullet whizzed by Rebel's head, way too close for comfort. The close proximity of the bullet to his head only fueled Rebel's anger. He turned his gun back to the wounded man and returned fire. The bullet struck the man in the head and left a gruesome, gaping wound in its wake.

A portable tactical ladder suddenly appeared over the wall, and Reaper directed the hostages to it while he and the other men provided covering fire. Several members of the extraction team climbed over the wall and moved into position in the yard, helping deter more armed opponents from approaching them. Once everyone was safely over the wall, they ran to the waiting helicopters and were safely lifted out.

Tears of joy and gratitude flowed down the faces of the rescued men. Rounds of sincere "thanks" and "thank you so much" were repeated over and over as the weight of reality set in. They were so very grateful to be going home to their families. Happy, healthy, and largely uninjured, thoughts of what could have been played through their thoughts and sent shivers down their spines.

In the courtyard of the terrorist compound, two young boys left the safety of the darkness and approached the corpse of the man who had kept shooting even after he'd been injured. The eldest of the two dropped to his knees beside the body, then dropped his pistol as his knees struck the dirt. Tears formed tracks over his cheeks through the dust that had collected on his face.

"I'm sorry, Father," he said to the lifeless man. "I failed you. I'm your firstborn, and I failed to do my duty."

The younger brother placed his hand on the older one's shoulder. He was young, but he inherently understood the despair his brother felt. Family honor had been instilled in them since birth. Following orders, making their father proud, and taking a stand for their country weren't just ideals they talked about around the dinner table. The two boys had lived it every day of their young lives.

"Orphaned at barely thirteen," the older one said aloud. "It's all my fault."

2

CHAPTER TWO

SEPTEMBER
Current Day

The end of summer was marred by a different kind of ending. The rounds of chemotherapy and radiation therapy had begun to take their toll on the elder Steele man. The cancer that had weakened his body progressed rapidly, and the toxic treatments had a hard time keeping up with the new cell growth. The chances of improvement had begun to dwindle, and the doctors were forced to consider Steve's other options.

"Mr. Steele, it doesn't appear the treatment is working as well as we hoped we it would," Dr. Patel began. "It may be time for you and your wife to start discussing your final wishes, what lengths you're willing to go to for treatment, and at what point you want to stop treatment altogether."

Sara's soft whimpers were the only sound in the room. Steve stared at the wall straight ahead of him as he processed the bad news. Noah and Brianna sat beside Sara, both unable to string a few words together into a coherent response. Colton and Chaise sat on the other side of the bed, with Chaise holding Steve's hand while tears streamed down her face unchecked.

"Thank you, Dr. Patel. Sara and I will discuss it," Steve finally spoke.

Dr. Patel nodded and, before leaving the room, said, "Let me know if there's anything I can do to help. I'm sorry to be the bearer of such bad news. We will keep hoping for a significant change soon."

Steve and Sara both nodded at Dr. Patel in appreciation before Sara leaned over and laid her head on Steve's shoulder. Her tears dripped onto the sleeve of his hospital gown until it was soaked all the way through to his skin. She slowly started moving her head from side to side and muttering, "No. No. No."

"*No!*" she screamed before the sobs racked her body and her cries became long, guttural moans.

Steve maneuvered until his arm wrapped around her body, and he gently pulled her closer to him. Crawling up on the bed, Sara laid down beside Steve, wrapped her arm around him, and they simply held each other in their shared pain. Through all the ups and downs in their marriage and their family, one thing had remained constant: at the end of it all, their love was still as strong as steel.

"Dad," Chaise choked out, "we'll get a second opinion. Dr. Patel is great, but he could be wrong."

Steve shook his head. "He's the best, baby girl. He's not wrong. I had to stop my treatment a few days ago because of the severe reactions. They put me on IV rehydration for a while. If my body can't tolerate the treatment, there's nothing to keep the cancer in check.

"I plan on sticking around for a few more months anyway, so I can die a happy man. I'm going to hold my first grandbaby," he said as he looked at Noah and Brianna. Then he looked at Chaise and Bull, "And I'm going to walk my baby girl down the aisle to give her away to an honorable man who loves her. Most of all, I'll die a happy man knowing my family is whole again, and you'll all be at my side when I go.

"Sara." He paused as she raised her head from his chest. "I'm ready to get out of this hospital and go home now."

"Dad," Noah spoke then cleared his throat. "Are you sure that's really a good idea?"

"We've already talked about my options for home health care, son. I'll have around-the-clock nurses so your mom can still just spend time with me," Steve explained. "It's hard on her being at the hospital all the time."

"It's not just that, Dad. There has to be something else we can do." Noah's exasperation filled his voice.

Steve smiled at Noah. "I appreciate your concern more than you'll ever know, son. But, I'd rather spend my remaining days with my family, at home and comfortable. I'll still go for chemotherapy and radiation as long as I can, with home health care to help us out with the extra care at home."

Sara left the room to find Dr. Patel and arrange for her husband's discharge home. The weight on her heart was heavy as she walked the hospital corridor. Thinking that this could be their last trip home together threatened to knock her to her knees. She drew her strength from deep inside as her legs carried her forward until she found Dr. Patel. She approached him with a lump in her throat, inhaled deeply, and exhaled slowly.

"Dr. Patel, my husband has decided he'd like to go home. Can you arrange for his discharge and home health care as soon as possible, please?" Sara asked, rushing her words before she lost the courage to speak them.

Dr. Patel's kind eyes softened as the meaning behind her words took hold. "Yes, Mrs. Steele, I'll be glad to do it right away." Calling a nurse over, Dr. Patel gave her instructions on Steve's discharge and had her call social services to begin the paperwork for his home health care. Turning back to Sara, Dr.

Patel tried to reassure her. "This is very difficult, but you'll have a lot of help and support through it. I'm very sorry I didn't have better news to deliver."

Unable to stop the tears flowing from her eyes, Sara quickly whisked each one away, only to have it replaced by another. "It's not your fault, Dr. Patel. We both know you've done everything you can do. We'll just have to keep trying and pray for a miracle. Thank you for your help."

Turning to walk back to Steve's room, Sara thought the corridor had never seemed so long before. Each step was harder for her to take than the last. Each breath became harder to breathe as she felt she might hyperventilate at any moment. The makings of a full-blown panic attack were threatening to take over and put her in a fetal position, crying and rocking in the corner.

One thought kept swirling through Sara's mind as she moved slowly down the hall.

"How can I do this?"

Hours later, the family had moved Steve from the hospital back to his home just south of Miami. The beachfront estate had every amenity a first-class businessman could hope to surround himself with. Steve Steele had made his name and fortune as the CEO of a major insurance company.

His shrewdness in running large, complex organizations had turned him into a highly sought-after commodity. Since his official retirement, he'd realized the important things he'd missed out on in life. Instead of focusing so much on making a name for himself in the marketplace, he realized he should've focused on making a better impression with his children. He'd decided the most important project he could work on was repairing his family bonds.

Then one night he landed in the hospital with unusual stomach pains and a stomach so upset he couldn't bear another second of it, and everything changed. That was the night of his emergency surgery. The night the surgeon broke the news that he had cancer and it was already advanced. He watched his plans evaporate before his eyes. No way to reconcile with his children. No time to repair what he'd so thoroughly destroyed.

Then Noah and Chaise appeared in his hospital room. At first, he thought it was a reaction to his pain medications. A hallucination conjured by his mind there to taunt him. But then he realized his visions were real as he watched Sara hug them through her tears. His children had returned—two of them anyway. There was still one son unaccounted for, but he at least felt he had a chance now.

As he lay in his own bed, Steve reflected solemnly on Dr. Patel's words. "I've worked all my life, only to retire and learn I have cancer. Terminal cancer, for all intents and purposes." he whispered to himself. "How did this happen?"

Hearing voices approach, he cut his eyes to the door and waited for Sara and the home health nurse to appear.

"Is there anything I can get you, honey?" Sara asked sweetly as she walked in.

"Just you." He smiled.

"You have me. You've always had me," she assured him as she took her spot on the bed beside him.

"I'm a lucky man," he said as he kissed her head.

"Hello, Mr. Steele. I'm Hope, and I'll be one of your nurses." The nurse extended her hand and smiled.

"Hope," Steve said thoughtfully. "I need hope, too."

She nodded, understanding his meaning. "I need to get your vitals and do your initial medical assessment. It won't take long."

"I don't seem to have any other plans right now." Steve smiled. "Let's get it done."

Noah paced back and forth in the great room of the house he'd grown up in. "There has to be something else we can do."

"We'll figure something out, babe. We're not giving up yet," Brianna assured him.

Sara walked into the room and all eyes snapped to her. "Hope is going over his medical information and getting his vitals. I thought I'd come check on you while they're busy."

"Mom, we're fine," Noah assured her. "You need to rest. This is taking a lot out of you."

"I'm just trying to stay busy," she admitted. "It's easier than sitting and thinking about everything."

"What can we do to help?" Brianna asked Sara. "Just say the word and we'll do it."

"We're all doing everything we can right now," Sara replied, taking Brianna's hand. "Don't feel obligated to stay here. He's not dying today. It just wasn't the news we had hoped to hear."

Noah, Brianna, Chaise, and Bull stayed with Sara as Hope worked with Steve. A couple hours later, Hope joined the family in the great room. "Mrs. Steele, I've finished with my assessment. Mr. Steele is sleeping now. That's completely normal, so don't worry. All the moving, transferring, and people poking at him just made him more tired than usual."

"Thank you, Hope. Please call us Steve and Sara," she replied with a tired smile.

"I'll be back tomorrow with more help and we'll set up our schedules. Here's my contact information," she said, handing Sara her card. "If you need anything, call me at any time."

After Sara walked Hope out, she returned to her family. "It's so good to see you all here. You're welcome to stay, but you really don't have to. He'll sleep the rest of the night, and we'll start chemotherapy and radiation again tomorrow."

"We'll go and let you get some rest then, Mom," Noah replied as he kissed her cheek. "Call if you need anything."

Chaise stood and hugged Sara. "I love you, Mom. Do you want me to stay with you?"

"No, baby," she replied. "Go home with Colton and rest. I love you all. More than you'll ever know."

After they said their goodbyes, Sara climbed into bed with Steve and snuggled up next to him. Her hot tears slid slowly out of her eyes as she drifted off to sleep.

The mood in the Steele Security office was still somber a week after Steve's home health care started. His treatments had resumed and, with the help of medications and hydration treatment, he began to tolerate the side effects better than before. Concern for his health and future weighed heavily on the entire extended family.

"You know," Brianna began. "Your mom reminds me so much of my neighbor in Colorado. I didn't realize how much I'd depended on her to keep me sane while I was away from you. I miss her."

"I'd like to meet her," Noah replied earnestly. "With everything that's happened in the last few months, we've barely had time to slow down. We should take a week or two and go see her. You can show me around and tell me all about your life in Boulder."

"Really?" Brianna perked up. "Do you think your parents would be okay with us leaving?"

"Yeah, I talked to Mom this morning and she said we need to stop acting like Dad is dying tomorrow," Noah chuckled. "She's right, though. Everyone has called at least once a day to ask how he is feeling. If we need to come back early, we'll have the jet so we can leave at any time."

"Let's go," Brianna agreed. "I want to surprise Mrs. Stanton, and I guess I have a lot of explaining to do to her, too."

"We're going, too," Bull chimed in.

Noah's eyebrows rose in question.

"Don't look at me like that, Reaper. Brianna is my little sister, and I missed three years with her, too. If you two are going on a stroll down memory lane, I'm strolling with you," Bull demanded as he crossed his arms over his chest.

"Using that logic, Shadow and I are going, too," Rebel spoke up.

"Hell, yeah," Shadow added. "We're not sitting this one out."

"I'm with the guys on this one, Noah," Chaise added and winked at Brianna.

"Looks like you're outnumbered, big guy." Brianna smiled. "We're taking the whole family to Colorado."

Noah glanced around the room at the family that had been at his side for nearly every major event in his life. "Fair enough. I'll have them get the jet ready to leave first thing in the morning. We'll have to brief Roman tonight and let him know he's in charge while we're away. This should be an interesting trip."

"Of course it will be. Look who's going with you," Shadow quipped.

Noah groaned and the room erupted in laughter. "I'm taking my woman home now. Meet us at the airstrip at eight tomorrow morning."

"I'll call Roman on my way home and give him the rundown, Reap," Rebel offered as he walked to the door. "See you bright and early in the morning."

"I'm right behind you, man," Shadow replied. "Have a good night, everyone."

"Let's go, Chaise. You have womanly duties to perform," Bull commanded.

"Bull. Seriously." Noah gave him a disgusted look.

"What?"

"She's my sister," Noah complained emphatically.

"Yeah, I know," Bull spoke slowly. "It's her turn to make dinner tonight, and I need her to help me pack my suitcase. What did you think I meant?"

"Nothing. I don't want to think about it," Noah amended quickly.

"Oh, wait. You thought I meant…" Bull smiled broadly. "Good idea. She definitely has those womanly duties to perform tonight."

"Get out," Noah ordered. "Get out of here right now."

"Come on, Colton," Chaise laughed. "You have some manly duties to perform for me, too."

"I can't hear you," Noah replied as his hands covered his ears. "Can't hear a word. Get out."

Chaise and Bull walked out the door laughing together and left Noah and Brianna alone. Brianna walked over to Noah, straddled his lap as she faced him, and kissed his lips. When he opened his eyes, she pulled his hands down from his ears. "They're gone now. You're safe."

"Thank God. I'll never get used to hearing that," Noah admitted.

"She's grown and he loves her, Noah. You have to accept that." Brianna smiled. "Where is your brother? Have you heard anything yet?"

"Not a word. He's deep undercover and hasn't checked in with his handler in a while now. Shadow said that's completely normal, especially if he's gathering a lot of intel and can't risk blowing his cover," Noah sighed. "I just hope that's the case, and it's not because something bad has happened to him."

"You've had a long enough day," Brianna decided. "It's time for you to take me home and perform some husbandly duties for me."

"It sounds so much better when you say it, wife." Noah's eyes darkened. "It's all my pleasure to perform my husbandly duties for you."

"Not *all* your pleasure," Brianna quipped. "I happen to get a lot of pleasure from it, too."

"Time to go," Noah replied as he shut his laptop. "Now I can't wait to get you home."

He stood, taking Brianna with him as she wrapped her legs around his waist. Her baby bump at sixteen weeks was just big enough to be noticeable but not enough to get in the way. Noah held her close to him, and she took the opportunity to kiss and lick his neck as he carried her out to the car.

"You're killing me, woman," he growled.

"Maybe I'll give you a special treat while you're driving," she purred in his ear.

"Shit, you want me to wreck," he chuckled. "Not that I'll try to stop you or anything."

"It's a good thing our SUV is nice and roomy," she replied. "I have better access to you."

"That does it. We're not going anywhere until I'm done with you. We'll just have to pretend we're horny teenagers and climb in the backseat."

"If you insist," she agreed.

"Babe, I love your pregnancy hormones," Noah said as he opened the back door of the SUV. After he carefully placed Brianna inside, his take-charge personality emerged again. "Strip. We're taking advantage of these new black-out windows."

Wedged in the backseat of the car, Noah explored every inch of her body, relishing her eagerness to please and her penchant for adventure.

"Oh my gosh, that was so hot," Brianna panted. "We need to do this more often."

"Only if you insist." Noah smiled smugly and leaned over to kiss her softly.

"I love you, Noah," she said as she stroked his face.

"I love you, Brianna. More than life itself."

3

CHAPTER THREE

"Colton, are you ready, baby?" Chaise asked.

"That depends," he replied as he leaned against the doorframe. "Ready for what?"

"I know that smirk," Chaise laughed. "The answer is no. It's not happening, so don't even think about it. We don't have time for another round."

"Chaise." He grinned mischievously as he stepped toward her. "We both know I can change your mind. Don't make me prove it."

He reached his hand out and ran his finger down her arm, barely making contact but leaving chill bumps in his wake regardless. Her eyes lit with desire as his smile covered his face. "And you're mine now."

"Get out of here!" She swatted his hand away playfully.

Bull chuckled and picked up their suitcase. "Don't feel bad, baby. You can change my mind just as easily."

"I'll keep that in mind," she promised. "Let's go or we'll be late and Noah will be mad at us both."

When they reached the private airstrip, the jet was ready and waiting as Noah promised. They rushed to the stairs and entered the plane, hoping they weren't the last, just as Shadow and Rebel took their seats.

"Nice of you two to join us this morning," Shadow quipped. "What took you so long?"

Chaise blushed pink as she tilted her face downward, letting her long hair partially hide her face.

"We're right on time," Bull retorted as he and Chaise took their seats.

The flight attendant closed the cabin door and strolled through the cabin to ensure all seat belts were fastened for takeoff.

"We'll be there in about four hours," Noah announced. "The hotel rooms are taken care of, so we'll each have some privacy while we're there."

Rebel and Shadow laughed openly. Brianna also laughed before quickly coughing to cover her outburst. Taking Noah's hand in hers, she squeezed it as she beamed up at him. "Still can't get used to the fact that your sister is all grown up now, can you?"

"I realize she's grown. I just don't want to be in the same house with them while they're…" He paused, his face struck with disgust. "You know what."

"Suits me just fine, Noah. This way we can have privacy, too." Brianna grinned as she lightly stroked his arm.

"Thanks for that visual. I needed it." He leaned over to kiss her.

"I know you did," she laughed as she leaned toward him.

Four hours of razzing, threats, and mocking laughter later,

the group of friends and family had deplaned, hauled their luggage into the waiting rental cars, and checked in to their hotel rooms. When they met in the lobby after getting settled in, Shadow started with the most important question.

"When do we eat?"

Brianna laughed. "I thought that was my line," she replied as she rubbed her pregnant belly.

"You're too slow. I'm hungry *now*," he laughingly replied.

"Let's go by my old place. I can introduce everyone to my neighbor and maybe we can talk her into going out to eat with us," Brianna offered.

"Sounds good to me. Lead the way, little sister," Bull chimed in.

On the ride to her former townhome, Brianna talked animatedly about the area, like a good hostess on a guided tour. As Noah passed by the lantern-lined pedestrian mall, Brianna smiled. "I spent a lot of time at this outdoor mall, just people-watching and not much else. A few streets over was where I used to work when I lived here."

"Where did you work?" Noah asked. "I just realized I have no idea what you did for a living while you were away."

"I worked at a pottery store, actually making the ceramic pottery on a spinning wheel." She smiled.

"Like in that movie?" he asked.

"Yes, just like that. It was so glamorous and sexy just like they portrayed it. I wasn't covered in water and sculpting compound from head to toe every single day or anything. I didn't have the mud-like clay stuck under my fingernails, in my hair, or even in my ear at all," she quipped.

"I guess I just assumed you worked for another newspaper," he mused.

"No, I couldn't. My degree and all my credentials were under my real name. I had to take a job where they didn't ask too many questions. It wasn't that bad, really. It was a small mom-and-pop store. The owners were more about making original pieces with character than turning a profit. And by character, I mean flaws, because I really sucked at it for the first six months," she explained.

When Noah pulled into the driveway, he sat motionless for a moment as he took in the townhouse where she'd lived during the three years they were apart. "So this is it, huh? This was home," he said, a spark of pain lingering in his tone.

"This was never home, Noah," she replied softly. "Home has always been with you. This was a place for shelter until I could find my way back to you."

He raised her hand and kissed the back of it, letting his lips linger on her skin as he inhaled her sweet scent. "I thank God every day that you did," he told her, his brown eyes melting to dark chocolate. "You'd better introduce me to your friend before I decide to take you back to the hotel room right now."

Giggling, she opened her car door and began to slide out. Noah still held her hand in his and stopped her with a slight tug. "I thought I'd make a clean getaway," she laughed.

"A clean getaway? Never. I'll never let you go again," he said sincerely. "I just want to make sure you're really okay with being here again."

"Noah, as long as I'm with you, I'm good anywhere we are. Bringing you and our family here chases all the old, painful ghosts away," she assured him. "It also brings new life here."

"Let's go meet Mrs. Stanton, then." He smiled.

"She was my one bright spot here. I feel bad about how I left her, too." She pursed her lips ruefully.

Exiting the vehicle, they walked hand in hand to Mrs. Stanton's front door. Brianna rang the doorbell and waited patiently. When she heard the door being unlocked, she grasped Noah's hand tightly and prepared for Mrs. Stanton's reaction to seeing her again.

When she swung the door open, Mrs. Stanton was taken

aback at first by the large figure who filled her doorway. Behind him stood three more men every bit as large and intimidating. Her eyes roamed across the unfamiliar faces as she struggled to find her voice, until they landed on Brianna and recognition dawned on her.

"Kris!" she exclaimed and jumped into Brianna's arms. "I've been so worried about you. Where did you go? What happened to you?"

"Mrs. Stanton," Brianna said as she hugged her tightly. "I have a story to tell you that you'll have a hard time believing. The first thing is, my name is really Brianna Steele."

As Mrs. Stanton leaned back to look Brianna in the face, her puzzled look was impossible to hide. "Brianna?"

"Yes, ma'am. This is my husband, Noah. Noah, this is Mrs. Elizabeth Stanton."

"It's so nice to finally meet you, Mrs. Stanton," Noah said warmly.

"Call me Liz, please." She looked around at the rest of the group. "Where are my manners? Come in, all of you. I can't wait to hear this story."

The group chuckled at her honesty as they filed into her small living room. After they were all comfortably seated, Brianna introduced everyone before she began explaining everything that happened before the first time she'd arrived in Boulder. The gasps, *oohs*, and *ahhs* from Liz were the only sounds that punctuated Brianna's story. Liz's hand occasionally flew to cover her mouth as she pictured the scenes that Brianna described.

When she finished the entire story, all the way up to her current state of pregnancy, Liz's eyes were filled with tears of happiness. "Oh, Brianna." She paused. "It feels so strange to call you that, by the way. But, I'm so happy for you both. You found your way back together through all the tragedies life threw at you."

Turning to Noah, she gave him a stern look. "Don't you ever

take that for granted, young man. This girl lived beside me for three long years. No matter how hard I tried to set her up with a nice man, she wouldn't have it. Now I know why—she loves you. You better take care of my girl. In all my sixty-six years, I've never met anyone like her."

"Yes, ma'am. I have every intention of loving and taking care of her for the rest of my life." Noah smiled at Liz before turning his gaze to Brianna. "She's my whole life, and soon our baby will be, too."

"He's a keeper, Brianna. I know good stock when I see it." Liz's playfulness danced in her eyes as she spoke, reminding Brianna how much she'd missed her.

"Noah is definitely a keeper." Brianna smiled. "He brought me back here because I've missed you and I owed you an explanation in person. You kept me sane while Noah and I were apart. We're here for a few days, but we'd love to take you out to eat today and spend time with you."

"I get a date with all these handsome men?" Liz asked playfully. "You there—Shadow? Are you married?"

"No, ma'am." Shadow gave her his most enticing smile. "Are you going to propose to me?"

"You're a little too young for me, son. But I'll let you take me to lunch today. Give all the people in my neighborhood something to talk about." She returned his mischievous grin.

"My kind of woman," Shadow said as he stood and offered his hand.

"I like these boys, Brianna. You have my approval," Liz said as she stood, hooked her arm in Shadow's, and walked out her front door.

The rest stood and followed them outside. When the others were safely out of earshot, Bull pulled Chaise to him and whispered in her ear. "Just so you know, even watching Grandma Liz hit on Shadow doesn't dampen my libido. I can't wait to get you back to the hotel room."

"I'm looking forward to that myself. I love the garden Jacuzzi tub in our room. Maybe we should put it to good use while we're here," Chaise challenged him.

The heated look in his eyes was the only response she needed to know that he was in full agreement. "You're playing with fire," he murmured.

"I thought I was taking the bull by the horns," she joked.

"You'll be taking Bull by something later tonight," he growled.

"Lock the door, will you, dear?" Liz called over her shoulder. Bull nodded as he pulled the door closed behind him.

As they approached the car, another car pulled into the parking spot for the neighboring townhouse. "Is that your new neighbor?" Brianna asked.

"Yes, he moved in not too long ago. He's such a nice young man—quiet, keeps to himself, doesn't have wild parties till all hours of the night." Liz shook her head. "Boring."

As her new neighbor slid out of his car, Liz called to him. "Lee, can you come over here and meet my friends?"

Lee's smile was outwardly friendly, but Noah immediately noticed how he swiftly schooled his features to hide his true annoyance. Had it simply been due to irritation with his older neighbor, Noah may have dismissed the burst of suspicion that flashed in his mind. Since he'd never been one to tamp down his instincts, he reasoned he wasn't about to start now.

When he locked eyes with Bull, Noah recognized his friend's suspicions matched his own. Quick glances at Rebel and Shadow assured him they were all on the same page. Lee was definitely hiding something. Noah silently vowed as long as Brianna and Chaise were around this guy, he'd also be there. The vibes Lee emanated were unmistakable and far too familiar to Noah, but the fact that his brothers also picked up on them solidified his resolve.

"Lee, this is Brianna. I told you about her before, but at the time her name was Kris." Liz tried to explain, but failed miserably.

Confusion flashed across Lee's face, and he opened his mouth to ask for clarification, but he shook his head slightly instead. "Brianna?" he asked to confirm when he held out his hand.

"Yes," she chuckled. "I'm Brianna, and it's a long story, so I'll spare you the details."

"And this is her husband," Liz continued, motioning to Noah.

Noah recognized the immediate change in Lee's demeanor when their eyes met. Noah narrowed his eyes slightly as he extended his hand toward Lee. The Middle Eastern accent was hidden to the untrained ear, but it was there nonetheless. The fact that Lee consciously hid his descent was very concerning. "Hey. How are ya?" Noah asked casually.

Lee's eyes swept across Noah's face as his top lip began to snarl unconsciously. He cut his eyes to Bull, then to Shadow, before finally resting on Rebel. He remained silent, not responding to Noah or accepting his hand for an uncomfortably long time. The second hand ticked away on Noah's watch as Lee stood rooted to his spot, his eyes sweeping back and forth between them.

Reluctantly grasping Noah's hand with his, he gripped it firmly and gave it a manly shake. The hatred burning in Lee's eyes was palpable, and the venom dripped from his lips when he finally replied. "I have never been better."

"Good," Noah answered. "These are friends of mine. They're just along for the ride."

Noah intentionally skimmed over the rest of the introductions. He wanted to test Lee, but he also didn't want to give him more information than they already had. He'd just decided Lee was on a strictly need-to-know basis, and he didn't need to know anything else about them.

When he released Noah's hand, Lee turned to stare down the other three men again. For someone who was roughly half his body size, Noah had to admit that Lee was brazen and bold. However, he wouldn't add intelligent to that list of characteristics just yet. His black hair, thick black eyebrows, deep brown eyes, and olive-toned skin gave him more of a Mediterranean appearance than Middle Eastern.

"It's very fortunate that I arrived home when I did," Lee replied. "Do you live around here?"

The abrupt subject change wasn't lost on Bull. "No, we don't," he replied matter-of-factly.

"Visiting Mrs. Stanton, then." Lee nodded. "Are you family?"

"I claim Brianna as my own," Liz replied. "But they're not family. She used to live in your house, Lee."

"Ah, yes. Mrs. Stanton has told me many stories about you." Lee turned to Brianna, slid his hand into hers, and lifted it toward his lips. "She's been very complimentary of you."

Noah smoothly took her hand from Lee's just before his lips touched her skin. "How nice. We need to get going. Good to meet you, Lee."

"I'm sure we'll see each other again soon," Lee replied.

"Of that, I have no doubt." Noah nodded.

As they piled into the large SUV, Noah kept his eyes on Lee. But it seemed that Lee only had eyes for Rebel.

"Rebel, you catch that?" Noah asked.

"Couldn't miss it, Reap. A flashing neon sign would've been better disguised," Rebel replied.

"Recognize him?"

"He definitely reminds me of someone from a long time ago, but I've never met *Lee* before," Rebel replied.

"You don't have to be jealous, Noah," Liz chimed in. "He was flirty with Brianna, but we can't blame him for that. I'll bet he would've been the same with Chaise if I'd had a chance to introduce them."

Liz turned to Chaise. "I'm so sorry about that. My mind must really be slipping in my old age. That was so rude of me."

Chaise chuckled easily at Liz's words. "It's fine, honestly. I'm not upset at all."

"That's right. She only wants *me* to flirt with her," Bull replied with a wink.

"Young man, I can't blame her for that. You are one handsome man," Liz replied, emphasizing her final words. "If I were thirty years younger, I'd give her a run for her money."

Laughter rumbled through the vehicle and increased at Bull's reddened face. "I'm sure you would, Liz." Chaise grinned widely. "You're still feisty now. Do you flirt with Lee?"

"I tried at first," Liz admitted. "But he's definitely an old fuddy-duddy to be so young. I've managed to get him to join me for breakfast a few times. He didn't like my store-bought honey, though. Said it wasn't as good as the kind he's used to having."

"He eats a different kind of honey?" Rebel asked.

"That's what he said. I only know of one kind—from honeybees. But whatever. Enough about him. Where are you taking me on our date, handsome?" Liz reached up and tickled Noah's ear as he drove.

"Wherever you'd like to go," Noah chuckled. "You name it, you got it."

"No wonder you ran off for this one," Liz said to Brianna. "But since he's taken and so is Bull, I guess I'll have to flirt a little harder with Rebel and Shadow."

"Oh yeah, I like her," Noah announced to the group. "It's about time that Rebel and Shadow got to be thoroughly embarrassed."

"Won't happen, man," Shadow replied. "We're the *cool ones* of the group. We're not like you and Bull—we don't get embarrassed. But we'll gladly flirt with a pretty lady." Shadow waggled his eyebrows at Liz suggestively but kept his playful grin intact.

She giggled like a schoolgirl with her first crush. "I'm sitting beside him."

When they arrived at the restaurant Liz chose, the group filed inside and appeared outwardly oblivious to the stares and gawking women who leered after the hulking men as they passed. Rebel seemed genuinely distracted and the other men knew he was deep in thought, but what caused his state wasn't clear. When Rebel finally met Noah's gaze, Noah slowly raised his eyebrows at his friend. Rebel shook his head almost imperceptibly and immediately joined the conversation.

They both knew a detailed discussion would occur later.

4

CHAPTER FOUR

"M rs. Steele?" Hope approached her.

"Call me Sara, please," she replied. "Yes, Hope?"

"Steve is sleeping now, but I wanted to alert you to a slight change in his condition. He seems to be more confused by everyday tasks than he was when I was last here. That's a known side effect of chemotherapy that a lot of people call 'chemo brain.' But if it gets any worse, the doctor may want to do an MRI of his head to make sure nothing else is going on," she explained.

"Are you saying it could've already spread to his brain?" Sara whispered.

"I'm saying it's something we need to watch and catch early if we can," Hope clarified. "I'm on my way out now. If you need anything, feel free to call me."

"Thank you, Hope," Sara replied absently.

Sara started her trek down the hall, and each step was more painful to take than the last. The long corridor seemed stifling as Hope's words reverberated in her mind. She just needed to see him, watch him sleep, and reassure her frantic mind that her Steve was still there. That he was still fighting to get through this and come out stronger on the other side.

Sara reached her hand out, placed her palm against the door, and pushed with light effort. The door moved in slow motion as she waited for him to come into view. As she stood in the doorway, she saw him as he currently was and not by the picture she carried in her heart. His large, strapping form had deteriorated to the point that he appeared gaunt. His skin's normally healthy glow had dimmed to a dull, flat pallor. His typically thick muscles had begun to atrophy from minimal use.

Sara's fears were becoming reality. Steve was slipping away from her. It was happening a little at a time perhaps, but steadily increasing nonetheless.

"What are you staring at, woman?" Steve smirked.

"I'm staring at my husband. You got something to say about that?" she retorted with a grin.

"You should be over here in the bed with me. Not all the way across the room."

She sighed heavily in mock contempt. "If I must. But you have to quit hogging the bed if I do."

"I've never promised you that, woman," he chuckled.

Sara crawled into their bed, laid her head on his chest, and wrapped her arms around him. She hid her worry when she felt how cold his skin was to her touch. She swallowed the tears that threatened to overtake her when the thoughts of losing him crept in. The knowledge that Steve faced his circumstances with a new attitude helped give her the strength to push it aside and simply enjoy spending time with him. She ran her fingers lightly through his thinning hair, massaging his scalp as she did.

"That feels so good," he murmured. "It's been too long since you've done that."

"You can have this every day if that's what you want," she promised.

Steve chuckled. "I won't turn it down if you're offering."

"How are you feeling today, babe?"

"Chemo is rough," he admitted. "But I'm hanging in there. Hope gave me some medicine before she left."

Within minutes, the medicine took effect and Steve drifted off to sleep. His arm was still draped around Sara. It was symbolic to her of how they'd held on to each other through so many ups and downs throughout their life together. An overwhelming feeling of anger unexpectedly hit Sara.

"Fuck you, cancer," she whispered. "You're not taking my family when we just put it back together. I've spent enough time worrying and being sad. We'll fight you every step of the way."

A sense of peace and calmness settled in her chest, bringing her hope for the first time in too many weeks. With a newfound determination, Sara allowed her muscles to relax as she closed her eyes. For the first time in a very long time, she wasn't concerned that bad dreams would cause another sleepless night. Taking a nap with her husband would become a welcome treat again.

When Steve woke from his nap, his heart filled with love when he looked down at his wife. She was curled up at his side, her arm draped across his body, and she was actually sleeping instead of staring at him. Since Dr. Patel delivered the news that the treatments weren't working as well as they'd hoped, his whole family seemed to stare at him, waiting for him to keel over in front of their eyes.

It was unnerving to Steve, to say the least. He'd always been the strong, domineering patriarch, and now he was quickly becoming a frail, pitiful shell of a man. This was one turn in his life he'd never seen coming. He mused to himself how the cancer that was killing him was the very thing that had brought his family back together. His family was his life, and he'd let them slip away from him once before.

"Never again," he muttered. "Dying to live."

Sara stirred in his arms before her eyes fluttered open. "Steve, are you okay?"

He gently stroked her cheek with his thumb. "That's the first thing you ask me every day when we wake up. Do you realize that?"

"I guess you're right," she chuckled. "I can't help it."

"Sara, I haven't done enough to deserve the love you've always given me. But I promise you, that's changing right now. For the rest of our lives, you'll never doubt how deep my love for you is," he murmured. "No more worrying about me, baby. I'm too mean to die."

"We've been together nearly forty years, Steve. You can't expect me to stop worrying about you now." Sara smiled warmly through the tears that glistened in her eyes.

"That is asking a lot, huh?" Steve winked. "I'll make a deal with you. I'll tell you if I'm feeling especially bad as long as you stop asking me how I feel every day. Unless I tell you otherwise, just assume I'm as good as I can be."

"Deal," she agreed. "But only because you asked nicely. Don't hide anything from me, though, Steve. I mean it. If you actually feel worse but don't tell me because you're trying to power through it, you could end up worse off."

"Yes, ma'am," he replied contritely. "I promise—no secrets."

"It's a deal then." Sara leaned up and placed a lingering kiss on his lips. "Sealed with a kiss."

"I'm going to shower and then we're going out for dinner," Steve decided. "I haven't taken my wife on a date in a long time."

He slowly quirked his eyebrow up at the dubious expression on her face, silently daring her to question him. Her features softened and she nodded her concession. "Where are we going?"

"Somewhere nice. Get all dressed up for me."

An hour later, Steve and Sara entered the upscale restaurant hand in hand. The music played softly in the background as the maître d' showed them to their table. Steve pulled out Sara's chair for her before taking his own. The normally welcome aroma of the various dinners quickly became a source of discomfort. As Sara looked over her menu, Steve held his breath, swallowed hard, and slowly exhaled. He inwardly vowed that he'd finish this meal with his wife or die trying.

When Sara glanced up at him, she immediately knew that the scents had intensified his nausea. Her resolve to keep her word to him was all that kept her from blurting out that they should leave. After she waited a couple of minutes, watched as he sipped on his ice water and pretended to stare at the menu longer, she was relieved when his color improved and his tense muscles relaxed.

"Have you decided what you want?" Steve asked.

"Yes. I'm ready when you are." She smiled through her worry.

Signaling for the waiter, Steve and Sara placed their orders and settled into comfortable conversation. Neither brought up the cancer, the chemotherapy drugs, the radiation treatment, or the prognosis they didn't want to face. That night was all about the couple who'd been in love for more years than not. Steve managed to consume his bland meal without incident. Even though food didn't taste the same as it had before, he felt like he was regaining some of his old strength with his body properly nourished.

"Thank you for dinner out tonight," Sara said as they walked toward the car.

"My pleasure," Steve replied. "I know you're thanking me because you're worried about me, but I appreciate that you haven't mentioned it."

"Are you going to leave me hanging here?"

Steve laughed out loud at her forwardness. "No, I know it's pure torture for you. Dinner was hard at first, but I controlled my breathing, sipped a lot of water, and chose bland foods. I actually feel better since I made myself eat."

"You know I plan to take advantage of this information." Sara grinned.

"I have no doubt of that, my love." Steve stopped walking. "In fact, I'm counting on it."

~

"Chaise, you're a dirty, dirty girl," Bull chided her softly.

"I don't know why you're blaming me. It's your fault," she retorted playfully.

"How can you say such a thing about me?" Bull feigned hurt and offense at her declaration.

"Colton Lanier, are you honestly going to stand there and deny it to my face?" Chaise's hand rested on her hip, she cocked her head to the side, and she narrowed her eyes at Bull. Her foot tapped lightly as she waited for his reply.

"I guess I need to get you out of those clothes." His voice dropped an octave as his eyes darkened with desire.

"If you think you're getting lucky while I'm standing here drenched to the bone and covered in mud, you're crazy," Chaise replied dryly. "Don't even try your moves on me, mister."

"You love my moves, though," Bull replied, emphasizing the double meaning his words held. "Let me remind you."

"Bull." She pointed at him, emphasizing the double meaning her reply held. "You are the cause of this mess. I'm trying to stay mad at you right now, so you have to let me."

The corner of his mouth lifted involuntarily as he fought to hold back his laughter. Chaise could never stay mad at him for very long. and they both knew it. Bull often used it to his advantage. "The timer on the sprinklers in Mrs. Stanton's flower beds is not my fault. It's also not my fault that you happened to be standing directly over the top of one of the sprinklers when it went off."

"Remind me again, Colton. Who was it that ran while the sprinklers soaked me?"

"Now, wait a minute—"

"Then who was it who didn't come to help me when my heels sank into the ground and I couldn't move? Then continued to stand on the sidelines when one of my heels broke off in the ground? Then laughed his ass off when I'd finally dug my heel out of the ground and slipped in the mud when I tried to run? Who was that, Colton?" she demanded.

"Reaper. And Rebel. And Shadow. Oh, and Brianna," Bull replied, his naughty grin fully in place. "Let's not forget Mrs. Stanton, the sly little lady who knew how to turn them off but didn't."

"Let's not forget Bull, my fiancé, my personal bodyguard, my big, tough soldier, who *ran from the water*," Chaise emphasized.

"I don't like wearing wet clothes," Bull explained with a single shoulder shrug.

Chaise's mouth dropped open and her eyes widened. "Are you freaking kidding me right now?"

"Not at all. I had to wear wet clothes in the Army sometimes, but I didn't have a choice," Bull started to explain.

"I'm not talking about your clothes!" Chaise yelled before stomping off to the bathroom.

Once the door was shut, Bull doubled over in laughter as the sight of Chaise angrily marching toward the bathroom replayed in his mind. One high-heeled shoe on, one off, but she still held her head high and her shoulders back. All while she tried to portray an air of authority and indignation at his insult.

When he heard the water start, he immediately stopped laughing. On the other side of that door stood a naked Chaise, whose skin begged to be lathered in soap, thoroughly washed, and meticulously worshiped. There was only one man who was up for the job. Bull unbuttoned his shirt on his way to join her. When he twisted the doorknob, he shook his head before leaning against the door.

"Chaise, unlock the door," he called.

"Nope."

"Baby, please let me in."

"Nope."

"Chaise, let me in or the hotel will have to replace the door and we'll have to go stay in the room with Noah and Brianna after they kick us out of here."

"You wouldn't dare."

"You know damn well I will," Bull replied.

He heard Chaise's huff of contempt as she unlocked the door but didn't open it for him to enter. Bull slowly turned the knob and walked into the room just as Chaise stepped into the shower. He shed his clothes and quickly followed her inside the generous shower stall. She stood under the stream of hot water with her eyes closed, soaking in the warmth and washing away the remnants of her mishap.

His eyes followed the small rivers of water that flowed over her body. His hands ached to feel the silky smoothness of her skin. His lips were drawn to the fullness of her breasts and the tautness of her nipples. His tongue longed to taste her, to lap up her essence, and bring her exquisite pleasure.

But first, he knew he had to make amends.

"I'm sorry if I hurt your feelings, baby," he said softly.

She opened her eyes and met his gaze but remained silent.

"I'm sorry I didn't help you when you were obviously having a hard time," he continued.

She still waited.

"I'm sorry I laughed at your misfortune."

Chaise picked up the shampoo and began lathering her hair but still didn't speak.

"And I'm sorry I said you looked like a frog when you were flailing around in the mud."

Bull dropped his chin to his chest, his outward display that he'd been appropriately chastised. Actually, he was attempting to hide the smile that threatened to cover his face as he envisioned the scene yet again. After a couple of seconds, the memory of the sight of Chaise sprawled out on Mrs. Stanton's front lawn, soaked to the core from the sprinklers and covered from head to toe in mud as she screamed obscenities at Bull was more than he could keep in. The repeated slips and slides from the slick mud ensured that every part of her body was thoroughly covered in dirt and flower bed mulch.

When his shoulders began to jump from his laughter, Chaise picked up the handheld showerhead, quickly turned the hot water off, and covered Bull with ice-cold water. He yelped and reached for the sprayer, but Chaise had already anticipated his moves. She ducked to the side and kept the spray of cold water centered on him.

"Chaise..." Bull's tone threatened. "When I get to you..."

"What? Think I'm scared of you?" she goaded as she continued to spray him.

Charging through the cold water, Bull wrapped his thick arms around her and pulled her to him. He smiled when she screamed because the handheld sprayer was trapped between them with the cold water still flowing strong. "You never have to be scared of me," he said softly as he adjusted the water temperature with one hand. "I'm sorry, baby. I shouldn't have laughed. I should've helped you."

Chaise shook her head and began to laugh herself. The more she laughed, the more hilarious it became. "Okay, maybe I overreacted. I'm sure it was a pretty funny sight."

"It was, but I left you when I should've helped you instead. That'll never happen again," he promised. "Now we need to finish cleaning you up, my dirty girl."

After he replaced the showerhead, Bull massaged his fingers in her hair to wash away the grime and gave her extra special attention. He gently pushed her under the spray of water, and she leaned her head back to rinse out the shampoo. After he'd repeated the process with the conditioner, he lathered her mesh travel sponge with shower gel and took his time washing every inch of her body.

"Colton?" Chaise huskily breathed his name as he gave her foot extra attention.

"Yeah, babe."

"I've waited long enough."

Bull lifted his eyes to meet hers and instantly recognized the hunger in her eyes. With a smirk, he moved deliberately slowly to increase her anticipation. "Well, if my lady is impatient, I guess I'd better do something about that."

"Colton, don't make me—*aaahhh!*"

Before she could issue her threat, the leg that had been in Bull's hand was thrown over his shoulder. Chaise stumbled back against the shower wall while her hands searched for something hold on to. Finding nothing but the slick tile walls, she clenched her fingers on Bull's shoulders, her fingernails digging into his skin. With every flick of his tongue, graze of his teeth, and pull of his lips, Chaise saw brilliant flashes of light and stars. Moans of pleasure escaped her lips of their own accord.

"Babe, I love hearing that noise more than you'll ever know," Bull said as he stood.

"I'll never get tired of yelling at you for that." She smiled alluringly.

"Let's test that theory."

He turned the water off, threw Chaise over his shoulder, and sprinted toward the bed. After he deposited her in the center, he resumed feasting on her body. The multiple sensations his ministrations elicited in Chaise's body increased her sensitivity. Every scrape of his five-o'clock shadow pushed her closer to the edge again.

When they at last joined as one, his guttural growl of appreciation echoed through the bedroom. "I'm so lucky you're mine," he told her. "*Always*. You'll always be mine."

Chaise knew Bull well enough to read between the lines of his outward bravado. At times like this when he expressed his feelings, he showed his vulnerability. "I'll always be yours," she whispered in reply. "And you'll always be mine."

"Always," he confirmed.

5

CHAPTER FIVE

"They've been in and out of her townhouse for the past week. I'm positive it's them," Lee stressed into the phone. His Middle Eastern accent slipped back into the tone and inflection of his voice unconsciously when he was especially upset. "Just send me the package like I said and don't second-guess me again."

Lee hung up the phone and settled back in his chair. As he absently rubbed his chin, his mind strayed back to the moment he'd laid eyes on the four men. There was no mistaking them for anyone else. Their builds aside, the fierceness they projected, along with the carriage and confidence from their military days, was hard to hide. The way they quickly sized him up and assessed his threat level impressed Lee, but the hatred he harbored ran much deeper than any respect he could've had for them.

He pushed up from his reclining position and paced the floor, walking quickly from one end of the small room to the other. After several minutes of it, he realized he'd reverted back to his old training. He'd been twisting quickly on his heel as he prepared to turn around. "Old habits die hard," he mused to himself.

"They've visited the old lady every day this week." He abruptly changed his thoughts, going back to his original topic. "She's obviously very special to Brianna. I heard her tell Liz that they'd come back to see her soon."

His mind was on overdrive as he contemplated all the possibilities of revenge. That train of thought was dangerous, he knew, because it reduced his ability to focus on the task in front of him. But he couldn't pass up the opportunity when it presented itself so beautifully and effortlessly. It would be a sin not to take advantage of the opportunity that was so obviously a divine sign. Before he realized it, his hand had curled into a fist and he was knocking on Mrs. Stanton's door.

"Why, hello, Lee. I'm surprised to see you today," Liz greeted him.

"Hi, Mrs. Stanton." He smiled, hoping his expression didn't betray his thoughts. "How are you?"

"I'm good. Would you like to come in?" Liz stepped out of the doorway to give him room to enter. "And if I've told you once, I've told you a hundred times. Call me Liz," she laughed.

"Okay, Liz," he conceded. "It's a sign of disrespect in my family to call a lady by her first name, so it's purely out of habit."

"I can understand that." Liz nodded. "But it's also a sign of disrespect if a lady asks you to call her by her name and you don't."

"Touché," Lee laughed.

It really is unfortunate that the old lady has to die, Lee thought. *I was actually just starting to like her.*

"Would you care for some coffee or hot tea?" Liz asked.

"Hot tea would be great. Thank you."

Liz smiled and nodded. "I'll train you right eventually."

"You keep trying." He flirted playfully.

"Honey?"

"What?" Lee asked, confusion marring his attempt to be suave.

"Do you want honey in your tea?" Liz clarified.

"Yes, please," Lee replied.

After making their drinks, Liz sat at the table with Lee and they chatted amiably for a while before he brought up her recent visitors.

"Having visitors this week seems to agree with you," Lee commented.

"It was so nice having them here. I've missed Brianna so much, and I worried about her every day," she said solemnly. "I reported her as missing, and I never did understand why the police couldn't get any leads on her. Now, I understand."

"Why was that?" Lee asked.

"She was in witness protection. Whatever they were told about her was enough to keep them from looking for her. Broke my heart, though. I just thought they didn't care about her. But, she explained everything, and I can't blame her for running back to Noah. Don't think she didn't get a good tongue-lashing for not calling me as soon as she was able, though."

"I'm sure you put her in her place." Lee smiled. "Are they coming back over today?"

"No, they've all gone back home now. They promised they'd be back in a few weeks. Noah is looking into expanding his business, and he found a place here that will work out well."

"Wouldn't that be nice, Lee?" Liz exclaimed suddenly. "You know, my kids don't ever come see me. At least this way, Brianna and her family would come see me regularly."

"Why wouldn't your kids come to see you?" Lee took a sip of his tea and kept her talking.

"They're too busy with their own lives and don't have time

for an old lady. My son is a doctor and his patients need him. My daughter has plenty of activities to keep her busy." Liz shrugged.

"Where do they live?"

"My son is in Texas and my daughter is in California."

"It's too bad they don't live closer to you," Lee lied. "Have you considered moving to be nearer to one of them?"

"Oh, it's crossed my mind," Liz explained as she kept her eyes trained on the table. "But I couldn't pick one over the other. Besides, it's time for them to live their lives and not worry over me. Their kids are in their early teens now and off doing their own thing. My son and daughter are enjoying just being married couples and having some time to themselves again. I'd be a third wheel to either of them."

Lee made an exaggerated show of checking the time on his watch as he quickly rose from his chair. "I'm sorry to rush out like this, Liz, but I'm late for an appointment. If you don't mind, I'd like to come by again soon. It seems we're both alone here."

"That'd be great, Lee." Liz smiled. "I have to admit, I never really thought you liked me much."

"What's not to like?" His charm oozed out of him as if it were natural. "I've had my own problems lately and I've been preoccupied. My mind is clear now."

"Glad to hear that. We don't need any muddled brains around here," Liz laughed good-naturedly.

As Lee left, his smirk covered his face. His plan would work out even better than he'd originally thought. With her only family members living multiple states away, she'd be a much easier barrier to remove. She'd become very familiar with him and could too easily identify him. That wouldn't matter after he'd exacted his revenge, but he had to eliminate any possible hindrance ahead of time.

"Say goodbye, Mrs. Elizabeth Stanton. Your time here is drawing to a close," Lee said smugly to himself as he got into his car.

Keeping up appearances would be important now. He had to appear to leave for work at the same time every day, come home after work at staggered times, and begin planting the story around the nosy neighborhood of his upcoming required business travel. Once his alibi was firmly set, the neighbors would be less likely to implicate him during the aftermath.

He could picture the neighbors' dumbfounded replies when the police finally found Liz's dead body in her townhouse.

Lee will be so upset when he gets home. He loved Mrs. Stanton.

No, officer, I don't have his cell phone number. He said he'd be back in a few days.

"By the time these idiots realize I'm not coming back, my trail will be as cold as ice," Lee said aloud.

"Where have you been for the last two weeks, young man?" Liz playfully chastised Lee.

"Work has been just crazy lately." He shook his head. "I finally took some time off to get a break."

"What do you do?" she probed.

"Nothing I want to talk about on my off day." He winked.

She patted his cheek in her motherly way. "One day, you'll tell me all about yourself. You think you're hiding that pain you carry around, but I see it."

He was taken aback for a few seconds. He'd never allowed anyone to get close enough to get a read on him before, but her words made him second-guess what he thought he knew. Was she really that intuitive, or had he slipped and revealed more than he realized?

"The only pain I have is that I wasn't born with a silver spoon in my mouth, independently wealthy, so I don't have to work."

He attempted to play it off, avoid her directness, but the look she shot him was unmistakable. She wasn't buying it.

No matter, he thought. *It'll soon be over.*

"I hate to trouble you on your off day, but I need some help unloading bags of mulch for my flower beds. Do you mind helping me?"

"Not at all," he lied. "Lead the way."

His sole purpose was to see his plan through, and he'd planned the perfect time. At that time in September, schools in the area were starting back. Most of the parents in the neighborhood were away from home, taking their young children to school, and preoccupied with all the first day activities. In their distracted state, they wouldn't pay attention to a single man and an elderly lady.

Liz walked out the front door and toward her car. Popping the trunk open, she motioned to the bags stacked in the back, one on top of the other. "We can just put them here on the grass," she pointed. "That'll make it easier for me to put them out in the beds."

A mountain of unopened mulch bags waiting in her front yard would definitely draw attention. The whole neighborhood knew Liz loved working in her flower beds. She bragged about them to anyone within earshot who would listen. Every single day, she could be found pulling weeds, meticulously making them perfect. Lee knew there was no way he could leave it unfinished without calling attention to them both.

"Let's go ahead and spread the mulch," he suggested. "Working outside will do me good after being stuck inside behind a desk all the time."

"You're sure you don't mind?" She raised her eyebrows in disbelief.

"I don't mind at all."

For the following two hours, Lee split one of the plastic bags open, poured the mulch into the beds to Liz's exact specifications, and grabbed the next one to repeat the process. When he finally reached the last bag, the buildup of tension had him wound as tightly as a metal coil. Purposely maintaining his outward cool, he completed his task and waited for Liz to make the offer he knew was coming.

"Everything looks beautiful, Lee," she gushed. "Thank you so much for helping me."

"It's my pleasure."

"Surely you had something better to do than spend your off day with an old lady. Don't you have a nice young lady in your life?"

"No, no one like that." He shook his head.

"A wild, free-spirited girl, then?"

The twinkle in her eye almost made Lee laugh. Liz had a way of getting under his skin in a way that made him wish he still had his mother. The way she tried to mother him made a part of him long to be cared for, nurtured, and have someone he could depend on. Those feelings and sentiments had frequently been the source of fights and harsh disappointment from his father.

His father had been very traditional and had expected Lee to be the man of the family from a very early age. He'd ruled his house with an iron fist and a thick rod for the backs of children who didn't meet his expectations. When Lee remembered his father, he couldn't recall ever feeling like he'd had his father's approval. It was that feeling that drove his need for revenge. He'd been robbed of achieving his father's blessing, leaving him as only half a man.

It was this fact that helped Lee keep his eye on the goal when he was tempted to give in and just live a normal life. "No wild, free-spirited girl, either," he laughed and shook his head. "What about you? Do you have a secret man in your life?"

"There is no man who could fill the shoes my husband left behind," Liz said sadly. "I have friends. I have hobbies to keep me busy. But my heart will always belong to my husband. I'll be with him again one day."

Lee chose to take her words as a confirmation that he was doing the right thing. "My throat is getting scratchy." He rubbed his neck. "I'd better go get something to drink. Can I bring you anything?"

"Young man, you know cold drinks won't help get rid of a scratchy throat. You need some hot tea to soothe that. It's probably from all the pollen after working in the flower beds. Come inside and I'll fix our tea," Liz offered.

"Are you sure I'm not imposing?" he asked, feigning concern.

"Of course not," she insisted. "I enjoy your company. Come on in and let's talk about where you can find a free-spirited girl these days."

"Oh, I have something for you to try. Let me grab it first."

Lee jogged to his townhouse and rushed to the kitchen. He grabbed the jar from the counter and hurried back to Liz before she put that awful honey of hers in his tea. "Liz, are you in here?" He cracked the door.

"In the kitchen. Come on in," she answered.

As he stepped inside, he realized that Liz was cooking a meal for them to share. "What are you making?"

"Thought we'd have some croissants and tea. I saw this recipe on a television show and it looked delicious," she replied animatedly. "You get to be my guinea pig and try them out for me."

"Only if you'll try something for me, too. It'll actually go perfectly with your croissants." He attempted to entice her.

"I'm not scared of trying something new." She placed her hand on her hip as she cocked it to one side. "You got a deal, young man."

Lee smiled smugly, pleased with how flawlessly everything was coming together. As Liz worked on creating the perfect homemade croissants, he planned his next move. Waiting weeks for her friends to return so he could kill them all at once was not an option. His pride, his honor, and earning the respect of his father forced his hand and his timetable. He suffered through the tedious conversation until the oven timer rang.

Death for whom the bell tolls, he thought.

When Liz served the hot pastries, Lee took the opportunity to open the jar. "Now it's time for you to try a real delicacy. Put some in your tea and slather it all over your croissant. You'll love it," he promised.

He dipped a small drop of honey into his tea and put another drop on his plate beside his pastry. He patiently sipped his tea while he watched Liz spoon the large blob of honey into her tea and then generously drizzled it across the top of her pastry. Lee's eyes followed the stream of honey, knowing her sweet tooth wouldn't allow her to stop when most other people would. That was exactly what he was counting on.

With every couple of bites of her pastry, she'd stop and take a drink of her tea. Lee patiently pretended to sip on his tea, raising the glass to his lips but not actually drinking it any longer. The pastries were delicious, he had to admit, and Liz had quickly scarfed hers down. When she reached for a second one, Lee sat back in his chair and watched as the intense reaction started.

The first sign was her unsteady hand as she stretched her arm across the table. When her hand dropped to pick up the croissant, she completely missed the plate. Lee lifted his eyes to hers and smirked as the bewilderment in her expression increased. She attempted to pick it up again and at last managed to succeed.

As she brought her arm back toward her body, she began to sway back and forth. Her eyes became more vacant as she started having a harder time staying upright in her chair. Her eyes swung to Lee's, fear now mixing with the confusion, knowledge that something was terribly wrong had settled in, and the uncertainty of how to convey her predicament crippled her.

"Lee?" she pleaded with one word.

He remained silent, still, and emotionless as he watched as

her body succumbed to the toxins. She attempted to stand and move toward the phone, but Lee knew it was fruitless for her to even try. Her small frame crumpled to the floor as her heart rate slowed. He stood over her and watched as the life faded from her eyes.

"Goodbye, Liz," he whispered as he stepped over her, locked the door behind himself, and drove away.

6

CHAPTER SIX

Noah was fully engrossed in planning a complex security detail when his cell phone on his desk rang. He absently held the phone to his ear and answered. "Steele."

"Is this Mr. Noah Steele?" the man asked.

"Speaking. Who is this?"

"I'm Special Agent Landry with the FBI in the Denver office. I need to ask you a few questions in regards to a case that landed on my desk."

Noah's curiosity was piqued enough to put the security detail to the side and focus on the phone conversation. "I'm glad to help if I can."

"Did you visit the Boulder area in late August?"

"Yes, I did. Why do you ask?" Noah replied, his senses immediately on alert.

"Did you visit with a Mrs. Elizabeth Stanton while you were in town?"

The fact that Special Agent Landry had just completely

ignored Noah's question didn't go unnoticed. "Landry, right?" Noah asked, his tone of voice sharp.

"Yes," he replied, clearly not pleased that his hard-earned title had been omitted.

"Since you're calling me, I'm sure you've already been briefed on my background. There's no need for a pissing contest, because I guarantee my security clearance is higher than yours. Cut the bullshit where you try to establish your authority so we can get to the part where you tell me about the case you're working." The intent of Noah's direct and demanding tone was impossible to misunderstand.

Noah waited patiently through the few seconds of silence on the other end of the line. He could tell Special Agent Landry was fighting to keep his cool, wishing he could just hang up, but Landry knew he had called Noah called for a reason. "Mrs. Stanton was found on the floor of her home. If her son hadn't shown up exactly when he did, she would've died. Fortunately for her, he's a doctor and kept her alive until the paramedics got there to transport her to the hospital."

"Is she all right?" Noah jumped up from his desk as he asked. His first thought was to make sure Brianna was safe.

"She is now. Her heart rate dropped dangerously low and led to a heart attack. She spent a few days in CCU," Landry explained.

Noah picked up his keys and quickly moved toward the door. There was no reason for the FBI to call him to tell him about Mrs. Stanton's health scare. "Let's hear the punch line."

"The paramedic noted in his report that she had what's called widened QRS complex. The initial thought was that she'd had a bad reaction to a toxin in her system, possibly an overdose of medication. But when she regained consciousness, she was adamant that she's not on any medications."

"So, are you thinking it was an environmental accident or an intentional poisoning?" Noah climbed into his truck, intent solely on getting to Brianna, but he already knew what the agent's reply would be as he transferred the call to Bluetooth.

"Her son insisted that the medical staff figure out what had happened to his mother, so a couple of technicians went back to her townhouse with him to have a look around. There was evidence that someone else had been there with her and that they'd eaten just before her heart attack.

"The techs took the plates, food, and drinks back for testing. The results came back positive for something called grayan-otoxin. It comes from *deli bal*," Landry paused.

Noah's heart also paused before racing at breakneck speed.

"Mad honey," Noah muttered disbelievingly.

"So you're familiar with it," Landry replied with a chuckle. "Why am I not surprised?"

"I spent enough time in the Middle East, Landry. Mad honey is found in a certain area of Turkey," Noah said as he pressed the gas pedal harder.

"That's right, and it's lethal in large doses. People in that area know to take it in extremely small amounts. Mrs. Stanton had a large amount in her teacup and even more left over on her plate. The second plate had a small amount that appeared to be untouched. The second cup had a miniscule amount in it, but whoever was with her didn't drink enough of it to make a difference," Landry explained.

"It was obviously someone who knew exactly what an overdose of mad honey would do. Intentional poisoning, since he was careful with how much he consumed but probably watched her use way too much." Noah envisioned the event in his head in many different scenarios, but he saw Lee in every one.

"Sounds like you have a suspect in mind," Landry probed.

"There was a weird vibe from her neighbor," Noah replied. "His name is Lee, but I didn't get his last name."

"Actually, his name is Ali Babek Turan. Mrs. Stanton positively ID'd him from a photo we showed her. He's been on an FBI Watchlist for some time, but we apparently lost him," Landry explained.

"Do you think I'm on his shit list since I was there with Mrs. Stanton?"

"I think you're on his list, but not for that reason. After I searched your name and Turan's name in a federal database, I was suddenly locked out of it completely. Spooks showed up in my director's office and took the whole case file right out of my hands. Something's obviously up, and with your impressive service history, I thought I should give you as much of a heads-up as I can."

"Thanks, Special Agent Landry. I really appreciate it. I'm sure the CIA will be waiting for me when I get home," Noah replied.

"Best of luck, Steele."

When Noah pulled into his driveway, he immediately spotted the nondescript cars on his street that hadn't been there before. Since CIA analysts needed to blend into the background wherever they went, their clothes and vehicles had to blend in as well. Most people wouldn't notice the compact car parked next to the house two doors down or the family van against the curb. But then, most people weren't trained to spot them for a living either.

The gate began to open, and he shook his head as the van moved toward him. He pressed his quick dial option for Shadow on the truck's Bluetooth.

"You're losing your touch, man. I'm already here," Shadow chuckled.

"Get your ass out of that compact car in my neighbor's driveway and get over here before the gate closes," Noah retorted. "You're too big to fit in that tiny car anyway. You'll break it."

"On my way, boss," Shadow laughed.

Noah stopped at the front door and watched Shadow climb out of the compact car with a bemused expression. Rebel and Bull pulled in the driveway just after Shadow and just before the soccer mom van that narrowly beat the closing gate.

Chaise came out of the house and walked over to stand next to Bull, her concern written on her face. She laced her fingers with his as they joined Noah. Bull gently squeezed her hand as he leaned into her. "Don't worry, baby. It'll be fine."

Two men exited the van and started walking toward the waiting crew. The front door opened and Brianna stepped outside, looking first at her family and then at the approaching men who tried a little too hard to be casual. Noah slid his arm behind her and gently pushed her until she was completely shielded by his body. "Stay there, Bri," he said over his shoulder.

"What's going on, Noah?" she whispered to his back. Her fingers gripped his shirt as she stepped closer so their bodies were touching as much as possible.

"CIA, babe. I'll tell you the rest in a minute."

"Noah Steele?" one of the men called.

"That's right," Noah replied.

"I'm Joe Brown. This is Bill Smith. We'd like to talk to you."

"Very imaginative names. What exactly can I do for the CIA? You boys here for some covert surveillance training?" Noah grinned.

Joe smiled good-naturedly as his gaze floated from one man to the next. "We've been briefed on all of you—Reaper, Bull, Rebel, and Shadow. Figured if we tried to hide too well, they'd never find our bodies."

"You'd be right about that," Shadow replied, the typical gleam of wit in his eyes.

"Mind if we talk to all of you inside?" Bill asked. "It's fortunate you're all here. Saves us a lot of time."

Noah nodded and motioned toward the door. "Come on in." As he turned, he took Brianna's hand in his and raised it to his mouth for a kiss. "You're staying with me," he said quietly.

"Just let them try to tell me to leave," Brianna replied as she opened the door.

Everyone followed Brianna into the spacious den. "Have a seat, guys," Brianna offered.

Noah sat first and pulled Brianna into his lap. She willingly took her seat, wrapped her arm around his neck, and flashed an obstinate look at Bill and Joe. Bull pulled Chaise down beside him, their thighs touching. The message was clear—this family intended to stick together no matter what was thrown at them.

Joe sat on the edge of the seat, his tense energy palpable. He clearly knew the group wouldn't be receptive to the news he had to deliver. He cleared his throat and repeated the story Special Agent Landry had already told Noah. The men remained stoic as they listened and took in every detail. The only exception was when Joe explained Liz's emergency. Noah's fingers tightened on Brianna's hip when she attempted to jump up from his lap, and a slight smile played on his lips as he shook his head.

When Joe finished, he looked at Noah. "Why does it seem like you already knew all of this?"

Noah shrugged. "Life is full of mysteries. Like why the CIA has taken over a domestic case of civilian poisoning."

Bill smiled knowingly. "It's a little more complicated than that. As Joe said, Turan was on the FBI Watchlist, but he disappeared for a while. We think he's working with someone else in the US. He probably stole someone's identification and started a new life. We've checked every aspect of Mrs. Stanton's life and his cover as Lee Clover while he lived next door to her. He'd never been late for work, never missed a day, and never even had a parking ticket."

Joe chimed in. "The only trigger point we've identified is your visit to Boulder a few weeks ago. He abruptly quit his job without giving even a day's notice. He closed his checking and savings accounts. Then he poisoned Mrs. Stanton and left her for dead."

Joe and Bill paused, looked at Brianna, and then watched as Noah covered her and their baby with his free arm. Joe recognized the protective gesture and carefully weighed his next words. "Right now, the only connection we've found is Brianna's visit to the Middle East. After what happened with US Marshal Stevens, we can't discount the possibility that another member of the same international crime ring is after her."

"You think he's coming after me?" Brianna asked. Her hand flew to her stomach and joined with Noah's to shield their growing baby. "I was in Boulder every day for a week. Why not try something then?"

"There's no cause for alarm yet. We just want you to be extra vigilant about your surroundings. We're still looking at other leads and connections." Bill tried to assure her.

"But you don't know where he is or why he's here or why he tried to kill Liz. That doesn't sound like no reason to be alarmed to me," Brianna shot back. "You're in my home for a reason, aren't you? You obviously know we have every reason to be alarmed. Don't patronize me, and don't lie to me."

Noah smiled proudly at Brianna. "There's my tiger." He winked. His expression changed when he met Joe's and Bill's gazes. Noah and Reaper could be two different men at times. The man before them was definitely Reaper. "Don't disrespect my wife like that again."

"How about one of you just man up and spit it out?" Bull challenged, irritation lacing his tone.

"He has several aliases and our intel on Ali Babek Turan isn't complete, but we know that he's a merciless killer. He's never left anyone alive before, so chances are high that he thought Mrs. Stanton was dead when he walked out. Had her son not been a doctor, she probably would've been classified as another heart attack case and we would've never known about the toxin.

"Our lab guys confirmed that it came from a bee farm in Turkey from the type of rhododendron pollen in it. It was fresh, too, so he recently acquired this batch. Our computer techs are currently scouring Customs' databases for package tracking info, but I don't expect to find anything. He's been smart enough to avoid us so far, so I don't see him making that kind of mistake."

"Babek Turan doesn't make sense," Rebel interjected.

"What do you mean?" Noah asked.

"Babek is a Persian surname. Turan is a Turkish surname. It's another alias, and he's saying he identifies with both cultures," Rebel explained.

"Have you figured out why he's so familiar to you yet?" Noah asked.

Rebel shook his head from side to side, but Bill immediately picked up on the comment.

"You think he's someone you've encountered in the past?"

"No. But something about him reminds me of someone I've come across before. I've been racking my brain, going through the details of our operations, but nothing has clicked yet." Rebel stood and began pacing the room. Like a caged tiger, restless and irritated, his display of aggravation was apparent and uncharacteristic.

Joe's phone buzzed and he quickly checked the message. "Another death has just been linked to Ali Babek Turan," Joe said. "It was a sudden, unexplained death, and the circumstances too closely matched Mrs. Stanton's close call. We had it double-checked and the word just came back."

"Who was it?" Shadow asked.

"Tom Nash, a former civilian contractor for the Defense department."

Rebel's head whipped around when he heard the name. His eyes met Noah's and immediately knew what the other thought.

"What? You know something. What is it?" Joe asked.

"Tom Nash was one of the hostages we rescued from a compound in Iran, just across the border from Turkey, ten years ago," Noah answered.

"Were you detected?"

"Yeah, it ended in a firefight just as we extracted the hostages," Noah replied.

"Not that he isn't somehow part of that group, but Ali is young right now. He would've had to been just a boy ten years ago. I didn't see any kids there that night," Rebel said.

"Neither did I," Shadow confirmed. "There were a lot of grown men, but I'd remember if any kids had been part of that group. It was a close call to get some of the hostages out of there without getting shot. One thing I never wanted to face was deciding whether or not to shoot a kid."

"I don't think he's after Brianna," Rebel said and gave Brianna a reassuring smile. "I do think he's here for us, though."

"You're right. He could very well be here for all of us," Bull replied. "But killing our loved ones in the process could be an added bonus for him."

"Men, this is a matter of national security. There's more we need to brief you on, but we have to be in secure quarters." Joe retrieved four envelopes from his inside coat pocket. "By special order of the President of the United States and Commander Adkins of the United States Special Operations Command, you are all hereby served with your orders. You've been fully reinstated as Delta Force operators to assist with the capture of Ali Babek Turan, by any means necessary."

Whatever reaction Joe and Bill had expected, it was not the reaction they received. The team's faces remained expressionless, but their eyes held fire and ice. The trained killers were no doubt still lurking just beneath their civilized exteriors. Bill attempted to break the tension in the room with a moment of levity. "It's a little unnerving to have the four of you staring at us like that."

"Like what?" Bull asked.

"Like, if I look away for a second, I'd never wake up again," he replied.

"I must be losing my touch, then," Bull replied. "You shouldn't be able to tell exactly what I'm thinking."

"We need you guys. The country needs you. We could very well have an activated sleeper cell on our hands. On American soil. We have a chance to stop whatever he has planned," Bill urged.

"But the CIA doesn't have jurisdiction on American soil," Chaise interjected.

Bill and Joe both smiled. "Sure, we don't," Joe replied, intentionally cryptic.

"It's not like you have a choice, since in a way you're being drafted. But we'd much rather you join us willingly," Bill added.

"I'm in, but I have conditions," Noah spoke first.

"Let's hear them," Bill replied.

"I'm not leaving the country. We have a baby on the way, and I'm not getting stuck out on assignment somewhere and missing the birth. Or anything else that Brianna needs me here for," Noah replied.

"Deal. You stay stateside. What else?"

"If I have to leave for more than a couple of days, Brianna comes with me. I won't leave her safety in anyone's hands but these three men here with me."

"Agreed."

"Since Brianna and Chaise are in as much danger as the rest of us, they're privy to any information we get. Their safety isn't up for discussion or debate."

Joe and Bill exchanged glances, knowing that some of the information they had was classified at above top secret. Noah sensed their hesitation and chuckled humorlessly.

"Guys, you can't tell me you've never divulged a little top secret information in exchange for even better intel from a confidential informant. You're spooks. It's what you do." Noah leveled his gaze on them. "I'm not asking, gentleman. I'm telling you this is how it will be."

"You know you can agree to this, gentleman. These two civilians are under our protection and can't leave our sight," Shadow added. "It's the right thing to do."

"Fine," Joe conceded.

"What about Liz?" Brianna asked.

"She's been moved to a safe place. The neighbors don't know if she's still alive or at her son's house, and we've intentionally left it vague. With the medical laws, the hospital can't give patient status, so there's not much risk there. She's asking about you, though." Joe smiled at Brianna. "It's been hell to convince her you and the baby are safe."

Brianna chuckled. "That sounds like her."

"We have a couple of different ways we can play this to draw him out. While we're strategizing, it's probably best if all of you move to a safe location, too," Bill suggested.

"I'll beef up security around here. Chaise can stay here with Brianna if we're away, and I'll add my best security guys to the grounds. Otherwise, I don't want to hide anywhere." Looking at his brothers, he silently confirmed their agreement.

"Your mail will be scanned and packages opened by a trained team. No delivery trucks or unknown vehicles are allowed inside the gates. Every man on your payroll has already been vetted. We're not taking any chances with this," Joe admitted.

"Good to know," Noah nodded.

Before Joe and Bill left, Joe reluctantly promised he'd have Liz contact Brianna through a clean cell phone from her safe location. "That's against every protocol on record, you know."

"I doubt you'll lose any sleep over it, Joe," Brianna deadpanned.

~

Later that evening, Noah and Brianna settled onto the couch together. "Is this how you felt when you were an operator all the time? A constant ball of stress in your gut?" Brianna asked as she laid her head on his chest.

"Not really stress, babe. After all the training, it becomes almost second nature. There's always a surge of adrenaline mixed with a little nervousness. That's what kept us on our toes, though," he replied. "You have nothing to be stressed about. I'll never let him get close to you."

She raised her head to look him in the eye before she spoke. "I'm not worried about me nearly as much as I'm worried about you, Noah."

"Bri, this is my job. This is what I have done for years. You don't have to worry about me. I can take care of us. I've tried to convince you of that before." He raised an eyebrow at her.

"You're never going to let me live that down, are you?"

"Nope. Not if I can use it to get what I want." He grinned slyly.

"Let me rephrase what I said to be more accurate," she said dryly. "I'm scared of losing you because I know what it's like to live without you. I don't want to do it again."

Noah's face softened as he threaded his fingers through her hair. "I feel exactly the same way. Baby, I promise we'll never know what that's like again. The security here will be thoroughly overhauled. Owning a security firm, I should've already handled that, but after you 'died,' I really just didn't care about anything. Nothing mattered except my business and protecting others, because it took my mind off what I'd lost here.

"Now I know I can't take a single thing for granted or take any chances with you and our baby. Several big enhancements will be immediately installed, so we'll both be as safe as we can possibly be," he assured her.

"You know," she purred. "All this talk of being my big, strong protector is really turning me on."

"Oh, yeah?"

"Oh, yeah," she confirmed before she lifted the hem of his shirt and pulled it over his head. "Definitely."

7

CHAPTER SEVEN

"Do you think you'll have to leave?" Chaise asked Bull on their way home.

He heard the worry in her voice, saw the concern in her eyes, and knew that her question ran deep. As much as she worried about his safety, she also worried about the anxiety that plagued her when he wasn't around. "If I have to leave you, it'll only be for the night, and you'll stay with Brianna while I'm gone. Otherwise, you will be right with me. I won't leave you for longer than that, Chaise. I promise."

She'd diagnosed herself with post-traumatic stress disorder after her ordeal with the Cordova family. She woke after having terrible nightmares at night and often had tears streaming down her face. Bull's arm would tighten around her and he'd whisper soothing words in her ear until she'd calmed down enough to fall asleep again. Her refusal to seek medical help had been the source of arguments, but Bull was often silenced when she reminded him of how he'd previously coped with stress.

"I know you think I'm weak," she half-whispered.

"No, I don't think that at all. I'm amazed at how strong you are and how well you're dealing with all the stress you've been under in the last few months."

"Colton, I depend on you way too much. It's like I can't even let you do your job without panicking over you being away. That's not who I want to be," she said solemnly.

"We depend on each other," he emphasized. "As much as I love protecting that hot body of yours, I don't want you to completely shut down if I'm away. What do you suggest we do?"

"I think taking self-defense classes may help," Chaise admitted. "Maybe my real problem is a feeling of helplessness."

"That's a great idea. You already know how to shoot and handle a gun. I can give you the names of a few places, and you can pick which class you want to go to," Bull offered.

"You're pretty slick, ya know?" She smiled playfully.

"Me? How's that?"

"The whole 'pick which class you want to go to' part. I know you did that to make me feel like I'm in control."

"You are in control. I'll even let you pick all the positions for our sexual acrobatics tonight," Bull replied.

"I think I like this 'being in control' thing."

"Yeah, don't get too used to it," Bull warned playfully.

"I'm stressing a little over planning our wedding, too," Chaise admitted.

"What's stressing you about it?"

"Several things, honestly. Not knowing what's going to happen with my dad, if he'll be able to give me away, or…if he'll even still be with us. Trying to coordinate everything around Noah and Brianna's baby. Now this guy is after us and could be part of a terrorist sleeper cell. All of this on top of the normal stress of planning a big event like this is just a lot," she explained.

"Baby, if you want a big wedding, we'll have the biggest wedding ever imagined. If you'd rather run away and elope, we'll still have the loudest honeymoon anyone's ever heard. As long as you're mine forever, I'll do this however you want," Bull replied.

"You're right," Chaise decided.

"About?"

"Everything. Starting with the acrobatics tonight. Hurry up and get me home."

"Yes, ma'am." Bull saluted.

~

The next morning, Bull and Chaise met the others at Noah's house to begin the assessment, strategy, and planned reconnaissance part of their mission. Bill and Joe rejoined them and brought the files they'd collected on Turan. Each man began by reviewing every page in an attempt to identify any other ties to past missions they'd been on.

"Here you go," Joe said and handed Brianna a plain, black cell phone. "Liz will call you in a few minutes. That woman is a handful. She hasn't let her guardian have a break since we told her she can call you."

"Thanks, Joe. I appreciate this. She was my only friend for a long time, and she's very special to me," Brianna replied.

Brianna and Chaise retreated to another room in the house to wait for Liz's call. When the phone rang, Brianna immediately put it on speaker and answered excitedly. "Liz! Are you okay? Chaise is here with me, and we've been so worried about you," Brianna exclaimed.

"I'm fine now, sweet girl. I felt like I'd been run over by a semi when I first woke up in the hospital, but all the side effects are gone now," Liz assured her. "How are you and my beautiful Chaise doing? How's my baby?"

Chaise laughed at Liz's reply. "I'm fine, Liz, and I'm glad you've healed now."

"The baby's fine, too," Brianna replied. "What do you remember about the attack, Liz?"

"Not much at all," Liz said disappointedly. "This was before the poisoning, but I remember Lee coming to see me more often than he had before. Now I know why—he was studying me closer so he could pull this shit on me. I hope Shadow finds him and kicks his ass."

Chaise and Brianna both laughed at Liz's reply. "I'm sure he will, Liz. He's pretty easygoing until you rile him up, then he's lethal," Brianna said.

"Good. Just how I like my men," Liz giggled. "Do you know where I am? These damn men won't tell me anything."

"No, Liz, I'm sorry. We have no idea where they're keeping you. But, if I can arrange it, would you want to stay here with Noah and me?" Brianna asked. "Chaise will be here with us whenever the guys have to leave for the night."

"That would be heaven. This place is nice, but these guys are boring as hell. They won't even play strip poker with me," Liz huffed. She raised her voice to ensure they heard her when she continued. "It's because they know they'd lose!"

"Okay, let me see what I can do," Brianna laughed. "But, Liz, we're not playing strip poker here either."

"Fair enough. Unless everyone else leaves and Rebel or Shadow has to babysit me. Then we never had this conversation," Liz replied.

The three ladies continued talking and catching up, with Brianna asking the probing questions she'd learned as a reporter in her attempt to gather anything that could help them. After they disconnected with Liz, Brianna and Chaise rejoined the men in the den to share her suggestion. With the team on her side, she knew there was no way the CIA would stand a chance.

"We just hung up with Liz. She's doing great. Bragged on her son a lot for saving her." Brianna smiled. "We have a great idea."

All eyes swung to her, and they waited for her to continue.

She met Noah's gaze and held the connection to him as she spoke.

"I'd like for Liz to come stay here with us until this is over. I think it'd be best for all of us. We'd all be in the same house to help each other. Maybe talking with us can help jar her memory of that day. She also wouldn't be there to harass the agents guarding her, even though Rebel and Shadow would have to bear the brunt of it." Brianna smiled.

"I think that's a great idea. She can flirt with me all she wants." Shadow grinned. "It's good for the ego."

"If that's what you want, I'm fine with it. We have plenty of room," Noah agreed.

"We had just decided that Reaper and I would stay here for the recon that requires more than a couple of days of travel. If that frees up two agents to help travel, it only makes sense to do it," Bull interjected.

"If you're sure you two don't mind, I can have her here tonight. She has to be in full disguise to leave the house, though. So if she goes to a doctor's appointment with you—" Joe motioned toward Brianna "—she has to be completely incognito. Turan can't know that she's still alive until we want him to know."

"We can handle that," Chaise agreed and Brianna nodded in agreement.

"Okay, it makes sense. It'll be late tonight when we move her. But if you're willing to live with her, who are we to deny you?" Bill deadpanned.

"Have you boys solved all of our other problems yet?" Brianna asked jokingly.

"Absolutely," Rebel replied. "Right down to the country's deficit."

Easy laughter rolled through the room. "We're developing a plan. One step at a time so we don't get ahead of ourselves."

Chaise's cell phone rang and she glanced at the screen. "It's

Mom," she said as worry instantly infused her tone. "I'll be right back."

When Chaise left the room, Noah looked at Joe. "You have eyes on my parents right now, right?"

"Yes. He won't get to them," Joe replied confidently.

When Chaise rejoined them, her color had paled and her hands were shaking lightly, though she tried to hide it. "That was Mom. She wanted us to know they're admitting Dad back into the hospital because he's not eating enough. She said it's just a precaution and for us not to worry."

"That means she's not telling us everything," Noah replied.

"Exactly. He must be in worse shape than she's saying."

"And he must feel pretty bad to agree to go back inpatient," Noah guessed.

"We'll put extra surveillance in the hospital. We have a few agents who used to be nurses who can take a few shifts and watch over your father," Bill said and retrieved his phone from his pocket. After a clipped conversation, he had everything lined up as promised. "Everything's being put in place as we speak."

"Okay, let's get back to work and put an end to this," Rebel spoke up. "Turan needs to be stopped before anything else happens."

"Damn straight," Shadow said, and the men began their discussions again.

"Where's the file that has his work history in it?" Noah asked.

Joe and Bill exchanged glances, and Noah quickly stood, knowing immediately that they were hiding information from him. "We told you we don't have much on him." Bill avoided answering the question.

"Where is the file?" Noah asked through gritted teeth. "So help me God. Withholding vital information from us is the fastest way to getting your ass kicked."

Bill retrieved a single sheet of paper from the stack and reluctantly handed it to Noah. He quickly scanned the page before advancing on Bill and Joe.

"You've got to be kidding me! Why didn't you tell us this before now?"

Shadow and Bull jumped up from their seats and physically restrained Noah when he suddenly lunged for Bill. Even as strong and muscular as they both were, it took all of their strength to hold Noah back as he continued pushing, intent on plowing through them until he reached his target. With the icy tone of a killer, the fiery eyes of a madman, and the low tone of seriousness, Noah issued his warning.

"This is my family you're fucking with. I don't know you, I don't like you, and I don't trust you—especially after this. If you know anything else, you'd better speak up now because I'll cut your tongue out if I find out later."

❧

"Lee Clover is now dead," Ali said as he shredded his fake license. "Good riddance."

Ali had driven to Miami and arrived undetected. He had no intentions of keeping his presence here hidden, though. On the contrary, he had every plan of letting the four men and their loved ones know that he was very much alive and well, right there in their city.

"I could be right behind any one of you, and you'd never even know," he sneered.

Retrieving his multiple suitcases, he began setting up his own network in the small, furnished house he'd rented. His numerous laptops had all of the most advanced features since he'd built them himself—from the hardware parts to the operating system and the software programs. He arranged each one in the exact optimum location. The self-designed models weren't traceable like store-bought systems were—the first rule of being a genius in computer science. They also didn't have the quirks and limitations that prevented him from carrying out his commands with the speed and precision he required.

When the first one was powered up, he located several close Wi-Fi signals and ran his decryption software to retrieve their passwords. "The second rule is never use your own Internet connection, always access someone else's, then bounce the signal all over the world. By the time anyone with any intelligence locates your area, you are long gone," Ali muttered to himself. He continued to make one connection after another, projecting his unique address into different countries and making the signal zigzag in a jumbled mess that more closely resembled a mass of cooked spaghetti noodles.

He repeated the process with each machine he set up so that no two machines had the same pattern and, therefore, wouldn't have the same signature. For the average computer analyst geek employed by the government, it would take years to unravel his schematic. Ali was positive that he had plenty of time to exact his revenge and have a little fun at the team's expense along the way.

"First, let's see if you were smart enough to change your cell phone numbers." Ali shook his head. With the stroke of a few keys, he located every cell phone that had been in their possession at Liz's house. "Idiots. How can you not know to change your cell phones?"

Tapping into the cell phones' cameras remotely, he switched between each of them until he found one that was out in the open. He then activated the microphone so he had complete video and audio. He was so pleased to know they were already talking about him.

"You didn't tell us he worked as an information tech for the Army Corps of Engineers," Noah bellowed. "You knew that he's had access to all of our confidential information this whole time and didn't tell us."

"You know as well as I do that your top secret information isn't housed in the same system. It's in a stand-alone, self-contained system that couldn't be breached, even by the most notorious hacker," Bill replied.

"My family's information has been accessible to that asshole. I'm not afraid of him—let him face *me* like a man and he'll run home crying to Mommy like a little whipped pussy. But he's had access to my family's information and that's not all right with me," Noah replied loudly.

Noah pulled his phone out of his pocket and angrily punched a few keys. "Roman, I need you, Blake, and Alex over here immediately with every security upgrade we have available and some we haven't even offered yet. It's past time to lock this place down tighter than Fort Knox."

"Yes, by all means, bring in your best and see if you can barricade yourself away from me. I love the challenge," Ali replied to his computer screen.

An idea sprung to mind that was simply too good to resist. Quickly killing them when they had no clue he was there wasn't a true test of his superiority. He would torment them first, keep them on edge and constantly looking over their shoulders as they feebly attempted to outwit him. With each step and every turn, he would show them that he was better than them in all ways imaginable. Then, when it was time, he would look them in the eyes and watch the terror fill their faces as they died alone, realizing he'd beaten them.

"Yes, I know you told me to do it years ago, Roman. Just get over here and spruce it up," Noah said into the phone. "Bring extra men if you need to. And Brad. Bring Brad with you."

"Okay, they're gathering the supplies and will be here as soon as possible. Bull, do we need to up the surveillance at your place for you and Chaise?" Noah asked as he turned.

"No, we're good. I already have the most state-of-the-art system there is. And I have a lot of big guns," Bull replied. "I also have Chaise. Any man who messes up her decorating touches should be more afraid of her than he is of me."

"Very funny, Bull." Chaise elbowed him in the ribs. "You'll pay for that later."

"See?" Bull laughed and pulled Chaise to him for a kiss.

"Rebel? Shadow? What about you two?" Noah asked.

Shadow smiled. "Nah, man, I'm good. I *hope* he comes to see me first."

"I'm good, too, Reaper. No way I'm hiding from that little sissy," Rebel replied.

Part of him was entertained at how they spoke so boldly about him when he wasn't there to defend himself. They would soon learn what he could do. But another part of him needed the rage that their insults fueled. It reminded him of why his mission was so important, why he couldn't let them have the upper hand even once, and why he had to remain patient until the time was right.

In the meantime, he would still have a little fun with them. Ali opened the cell phone's speakerphone to address his captive audience. "Yes, by all means, men. Call every security specialist you can find and have them fill your homes with their pathetic gadgets. It'll be all the more entertaining for me in the end. I'll walk through the front door of your homes as easily as if you left the light on for me and a key under the front door mat."

Ali chuckled at their confusion while they attempted to locate the source of his voice. When they followed the sounds and Noah picked up the cell phone, Ali continued with his taunts. "Aren't you the clever one? You found me in the cell phone, very impressive. Do you feel any safer yet?"

Noah's reply wasn't what Ali expected. He smiled at the blank screen of the cell phone. "Ali, I have no reason not to feel safe around a sorry little pussy like you. Picking on little old ladies doesn't take a big set of balls. How about you meet up with me somewhere? We'll see who feels safe then."

"That's a very tempting offer. Really. Alas, I will have to pass," he mocked. "However, I will accept a date with that sexy wife of yours. It may seem odd, but I've always been attracted to pregnant women. They just glow with radiant beauty.

"Or maybe your gorgeous sister? I'd bet my life that her beauty would rival the brightness of the sun if she were pregnant. Perhaps I can help her with that since your friend seems to be unable."

"What did that little piss ant just say?" Bull demanded as he jumped up from his seat beside Chaise. "I'll tear you limb from limb, you little piece of shit."

"As much as I'm enjoying our little chat, gentlemen, I'm afraid I have more work to do. But don't worry. You'll hear from me again very soon," Ali promised as he cut the connection.

He leaned back in his chair, laced his fingers behind his head, and smiled from ear to ear. This would be his favorite mission by a long shot. In fact, he was already looking forward to his next interaction with them.

He opened the image he'd saved from the live video feed of Brianna and Chaise standing side by side to stare at them longer. His smile crawled across his face before he spoke. "How about a nice game of cat and mouse, my beauties?"

8

CHAPTER EIGHT

"Where is he?" Brianna asked, staring out the window.

Ali had systematically sent packages to Brianna over the past few weeks. One arrived at the same time every week, but a different courier delivered each one. The first package had caused a major scene outside the gate. When the agents on duty scanned it and decided it was safe to open it, a flurry of activity quickly ensued. Cars swarmed in from every direction, agents and police cornered the deliveryman to interrogate him, and Noah moved Brianna as far away from the windows as possible.

Ali had sent her an early Halloween present—a fake finger that appeared to have been cut off. He added corn syrup tinted with red food coloring to make it look more realistic. When the package was finally delivered to Brianna, she cleaned off the extra "blood" and stuck it on her middle finger. She took a picture and posted it on her social media site, knowing he was most definitely monitoring it.

The second week, he continued the theme and sent a dozen

black roses to her. Not willing to be one-upped, Brianna carefully painted each one with a different color of nail polish before posting a picture of her "beautiful, multicolored roses." After the second delivery, she'd had a talk with Bill and Joe.

"Every time a package is delivered, it draws your men from wherever they're stationed. Ali's watching every one of them and waiting to see where they're coming from. You need to take the packages to them or get a new way to scan them here. Just don't fall for his games anymore," Brianna suggested after they'd opened the second one.

"You think we don't know that?" Joe asked, somewhat amused.

"You don't act like you know that, Joe," Brianna answered honestly. "You've played into his trap both times. See what he does when you change your response to him."

"Good idea. We'll try that," Joe answered.

"Why didn't you think of that before now?" Liz asked. "And the cell phones—why didn't you know about that?

Joe and Bill exchanged glances, but they'd already learned the hard way it was best not to engage Liz directly. They'd been embarrassed one too many times by the sweet, little old lady who wasn't afraid to put them in their place or call them out on their screw-ups.

"That's exactly why we aren't taking any chances with the next package. The armored van with a portable X-ray machine in the back will be parked at the curb so any package can be viewed remotely through our secure wireless connection," Joe replied.

When the delivery van pulled up to the gate with the third package, the agents were waiting to see what Ali had sent that time. They quickly took the package, secured it in the X-ray machine, and signaled to the technician inside the house that it was ready for inspection.

"Here goes nothing," Rob, the technician, uttered to himself.

The image lit up on the screen, and Rob cringed when he recognized a couple of the more obvious items. Rob knew Reaper would be out for blood when he found out what was in it. The screening didn't reveal any explosive or dangerous contents, so Rob approved for it to be opened. When Joe brought the package inside the house, Rob quietly moved away to avoid Reaper's wrath.

"What the hell?" Reaper bellowed. "Wait until I get my hands on him."

"What is it now?" Brianna asked.

"Baby presents. *Engraved* baby presents that have his last name on them," Reaper growled. "I'm going to kill him."

Brianna put her hand on his arm, her touch instantly calming him, and she rose up on her tiptoes to place a chaste kiss on his cheek. "You know he's just trying to rile you up. Don't give him the satisfaction."

"You know I've never been rational when it comes to you," he replied. "Definitely not when another man is trying to claim my baby." His hand slid across her stomach in his protective and possessive display.

"Yeah, we all know I'm yours, Noah," she cooed.

"He's definitely toying with you. This isn't the normal MO for a terrorist group. It's possible that he's a lone wolf, banking on his seventy-two virgins waiting for him when he takes out a few infidels. But this package is much more personal, whereas the previous ones were macabre," Bill said as he inspected the contents. "Mixed signals again."

"This guy is one big screwed-up mess," Liz chimed in. "That's my official diagnosis. I'll send you my bill. But I charge extra for house calls."

Bill stared at Liz for several moments while keeping his face expressionless. In return, she gave him a toothy grin, shrugged one shoulder, and flipped her shoulder-length gray hair as she turned away from him. He shook his head and chuckled lightly to himself. It took too much energy to be aggravated with her when she so thoroughly amused him.

"What's the plan now?" Noah asked. "We've been at this for weeks now. Shadow and Rebel have been out there interviewing everyone who's had dealings with him, following up on crimes that appear to be linked to him, while we're here waiting for the next package."

His frustration level was rising with every passing minute. Brianna was his primary concern, of course, but part of him wanted to be out in the field, searching for anything that would help them put this threat to rest for good. He paced back and forth, antsy from his own inactivity, and fighting guilt over wanting to leave Brianna to help Shadow and Rebel.

Noah's new—and secure—cell phone rang and Shadow's name flashed across the screen. "Talk to me, man. What have you found?"

"Rebel and I have been comparing notes on our new friend. Seems Ali Babek Turan has had several aliases over the last few years. He worked at a major software company as an intern while he was in college. His instructors, classmates, and former employers all say he was a computer genius. He walked into the program already knowing almost as much as his instructors.

"He's been involved mostly in cybercrimes, but there are some suspicious deaths, now that we're giving them a second look. Poisoning seems to be his preferred method, although there have been a couple of deaths that were much more...intimate."

"What do you mean 'intimate'?" Reaper asked.

"You know how they say that usually when someone kills another by shooting them, the crime is colder and less personal? Emotionally detached, all that shit," Shadow began.

"Yeah. Got it. Go on," Reaper replied.

"A couple of deaths were in very close quarters with a knife. Could have been a large hunting or fighting knife, but the wounds aren't completely consistent. He's not like most killers that pick one method over another," Shadow explained.

"Are you on your way back?"

"Yeah. We'll be there in a few hours."

"Okay. You can tell me about his cybercrimes when you get here," Reaper replied.

"Roger that, Reaper. See ya soon," Shadow said before they hung up.

Brianna approached him and wrapped her arms around him from behind. "I know you're going crazy being stuck in here with us."

He turned and wrapped his arms around her. "I'd never go crazy from being with you. What's driving me crazy is not being the one out there stopping this guy."

"You will," Brianna assured him. "Was that Shadow or Rebel?"

"Shadow. They're headed back here now, but it'll be a few hours before they arrive. Shadow said they found a few things, but I said to fill me in when they get back so I don't have to repeat everything for those guys." Noah jerked his head in the direction of the CIA agents.

"Why don't we take Liz and get out of here? We need to go see your dad again," Brianna suggested. "He didn't look well last week when we were there. He's doing his best to hide it, but I can tell."

"Yeah, so can I," Noah replied grimly. "Ask Liz if she wants to go, and let's get out of here."

Brianna walked into the kitchen where Liz was trying to entice Rob into playing a game of cards with her.

"What's the matter, sonny? Scared Granny will beat you like you stole something?" Liz taunted him.

Rob's eyes darted around the room as he searched frantically for someone or something to save him from Liz. When he locked eyes with Brianna, he all but begged her to step in on his behalf.

When Brianna's face lit up with her smile, he would've sworn she was an angel sent from Heaven above.

"Liz, Noah and I are going to see Steve again. Do you want to join us this time? You still haven't met his parents." Brianna continued her casual stroll into the kitchen and pretended to be oblivious to the deck of cards that Liz was flicking in Rob's face.

"I think I will," Liz replied. "I missed out last time because I thought I had Joe talked into a game of Twister, but then he got an urgent call. Damn thing lasted the whole time you were gone."

"That's too bad." Brianna feigned empathy. "Maybe you can help cheer Steve up."

"What's wrong with him? Is he on those little blue pills, too? I hear that needing those really messes with a man's mind." Liz shook her head. "Is that true, Rob?"

"Uh, I, uh… I need to go help Joe," Rob stuttered and quickly took the opportunity to leave the room.

Brianna doubled over in laughter and tears streamed down her face. "Liz, I can't tell you how much I've missed you. I love having you here with us."

"Sweet girl, I love being here with you and Noah. I think I'll stay in Miami once this is over. Don't worry. I'll get my own place. But I love being here with you and my boys," she replied.

Brianna didn't ask for clarification since she already knew that when Liz said "boys," she meant the men of Steele Security. Only Liz could get away with calling them "my boys" and not be corrected.

"So, what's going on with your father-in-law?" Liz asked.

"He has cancer," Brianna replied solemnly. "He doesn't seem to be responding to treatment as well as we hoped."

"You never told me that!" Liz exclaimed. "Let's go see him. Bring your iPad with you, Brianna. We need to FaceTime with my son while we're there."

With that, Liz rushed off to freshen up before she met Noah's parents for the first time, leaving Brianna feeling bewildered once again. From the moment they met, Liz had viewed Brianna as her own daughter. She sensed that Brianna was lonely, but she was also willingly closed off from forming close relationships. Liz continued to work on her every chance she had, and it finally paid off. Once she won Brianna over, she realized that Brianna had become the steady force in her life since her own children were seldom around.

She only hoped she had a chance to help Brianna and Noah, return the favor they'd given her when they'd so eagerly brought her into their home. Liz quickly changed clothes and rushed back downstairs to leave with Noah and Brianna. When they got in the car, Noah turned to speak to Liz.

"Don't forget to stay lying down in the backseat until we pull into my parents' garage. We don't want to risk you being seen by Ali until the CIA is ready to tell him."

"Oh yeah," Liz replied as she made herself comfortable on the spacious bench seat. "Do you know what they're waiting for?"

Over the past few weeks, Roman, Blake, Alex, and Brad had installed every imaginable security upgrade, including infrared cameras to pick up heat signatures even behind hiding places, glass-break detectors for the windows, and fog screens that billowed out smoke to disorient intruders or emit a gas that completely disabled intruders for up to twenty-four hours. Bullet-resistant doors with biometric sensors were installed throughout the house and handheld thermal imagers were brought in to conduct frequent sweeps for hidden surveillance devices.

After the upgrades had been completed, the only wild card Noah had left to contend with was Liz. Ali didn't know she'd survived, though Noah wasn't convinced that she even mattered to Ali at this point. If her death had been imperative, Ali would've employed another method and he wouldn't have left her before he was certain his plans had been carried out successfully.

"My guess is they want to use his failed attempt to taunt him, make him mad so he does something stupid. That's how a lot of men get caught. Their ego is their undoing," Noah replied.

"How about that! This tough old broad will be the criminal mastermind's undoing," Liz cheerfully boasted.

"Wouldn't that be something?" Brianna agreed. "I hope it's soon because his gifts are already on my nerves."

Before long, Noah pulled into his parents' garage and waited until the door closed securely behind him before exiting the vehicle. After the team finished the security upgrades to his house, Noah had sent them to his parents' house to update theirs as well. Constant surveillance helped ease his mind for the safety of his family, but until Ali was caught or killed, he'd always be on guard.

"Did you bring your iPad?" Liz asked Brianna.

"Got it right here." Brianna patted her oversized bag.

"Good girl. Let's see what we can do for Steve and Sara," Liz replied cryptically.

"Mom? Dad? Anyone home?" Noah called as he walked in.

"In the den," Sara called. "Come on in."

When he walked into the den, Noah had to fight to quickly rein in his shock and concern. Steve had lost even more weight since they'd last visited and his skin color had become more ashen. Noah swallowed hard, pushing down the lump of despair that had formed in his throat, and prepared to introduce Liz.

"Mom, Dad, this is Liz Stanton. We told you about her last week. She was Brianna's neighbor in Boulder, and she's staying with us for a while. Liz, this is my mom, Sara, and my dad, Steve," Noah said.

"Welcome, Liz. We're glad to finally meet you in person," Sara said when she stood to greet her.

"Nice to meet you, Liz," Steve said weakly. "Forgive me for not getting up. I'm a little under the weather today."

"It's so good to meet you both. You have a wonderful son and daughter-in-law," Liz replied. "If you don't mind my forwardness, I know a little about your medical condition, Steve. That's actually why I'm here today. I hope to be able to help you with it."

"What do you mean, Liz?" Brianna asked.

"Let's see that iPad of yours," Liz replied.

Brianna retrieved it from her bag and handed it to Liz. After a few clicks, the familiar ring of the FaceTime app filled the air.

"Hello?" a male voice answered. "Mom? Is that you?"

"You sound shocked, Daryl," Liz laughed.

"I am. I had no idea you knew how to use FaceTime."

"Of course I do. But that's not why I'm calling. Are you on your iPad, son?"

"Yes, I'm in the office today and I use it for almost everything."

"Good. I have a patient for you to consult with. Right now," Liz demanded.

Daryl recognized her tone of voice and knew this wasn't a request. This was an expectation. Since she rarely asked anything of him, he also knew that it was very important to her and he couldn't deny her—even if he was running behind on his patient appointments.

"Sure, Mom. Let's see what you've got." Daryl smiled.

"Good boy. This is Steve Steele. He has cancer. We need you to fix him," Liz replied matter-of-factly.

"No pressure there, Mom," Daryl replied sarcastically.

Steve laughed good-naturedly as Liz passed the iPad to him. "This is my son, Dr. Daryl Stanton. He thinks I pressure him."

"No pressure at all. I assume you're a doctor?"

"Yes, I'm an oncologist. Can you turn on as many lights as possible so I can get a good look at you? And tell me about your medical history." Daryl settled in behind his desk to begin making his notes and conduct his virtual assessment.

Over the next forty-five minutes, Steve and Sara answered

every question, and gave detailed information about his symptoms, surgeries, and treatments. Daryl covered every aspect of Steve's medical history prior to the cancer. "If you don't mind, I'd like to contact your oncologist and talk to him. I'm not sure what my mom has told you, if anything, but I'm part of a clinical trial for a new chemotherapy drug that you may be a candidate to join. There are a few things I need to verify first, so I need to caution you against looking at this as a sure thing. We are seeing positive results from it, though. If you qualify for it, we can start it there in Miami, coordinating with your oncologist, but you'll eventually need to come to Texas for the second phase of treatment."

"I don't mind at all, Doc," Steve replied, his voice full of hope again despite his attempts not to get ahead of himself. "I'll give you all of his contact information, and you can start on it as soon as possible."

"And there's nothing preventing you from moving to Texas for the second phase of treatment? It will last for several months," Daryl clarified.

"Not if it means I have a chance to beat this. I'll move to Texas for the next several years for that remote possibility," Steve replied. "Noah, Brianna, and our grandbaby will just have to put that corporate jet to use more frequently."

"I'll have my office manager send you a few forms to sign, and we'll start gathering your medical records. We'll have to submit them to the clinical trial board to get approval to add you, but I'll do what I can to help you," Daryl promised. "But there are no guarantees of anything. I'm emphasizing that because it's human nature to grasp at anything that even hints at making us well again."

"We understand what you're saying, Dr. Stanton. We appreciate your candor, but you don't have to worry. If Steve doesn't get approved, we won't hold it against you," Sara replied.

Steve gave Daryl his doctors' names, phone numbers, and

addresses, and they ended the call with Daryl's assurance he'd be in touch as soon as possible. Steve sat staring at the black iPad screen for several seconds afterward, overcome with emotion that someone who'd just met him would go to such great lengths to help him.

"Thank you so much, Liz," Steve started. "I can't tell you how much hope this gives me."

"Dad, remember he said—" Noah began.

"Not that kind of hope, son," Steve replied with a warm smile. "Hope in people again. Hope that my family will be well cared for regardless of where I am."

Looking at Liz, Steve continued. "You didn't know me at all. Never even met me before. But you walked in here with a plan specifically designed to help me, out of the goodness of your heart. Thank you for that."

"These kids love you," Liz replied and gestured toward Noah and Brianna. "If they love you, you must be good people. They mean the world to me, and they want you to get better. If getting you in touch with my son, the doctor, can help with that, then it's the very least I can do."

Misty eyes looked everywhere around the room, except where they could possibly find other misty eyes. Noah could no longer take the emotional stress and seriousness of the room.

"That's it. Group hug! We're having a pansy-ass group hug right now. Everyone. Just get this shit out of our systems and then we can move past all this heavy stuff," he bellowed. "And then we'll never speak of it again."

Laughter filled the room, sniffles ceased, and misty eyes returned to normal.

9

CHAPTER NINE

NOVEMBER

"That little bastard," Bull spit out, venom lacing his words. He shook his head in disgust as he huffed loudly. "I really want to kick his ass."

"Get in line. I called dibs on it first," Chaise replied dryly.

She flipped the sun visor down and attempted to fix her hair for the fifth time. Just as she finished, her window rolled down of its own accord for the sixth time. The air gusted into Bull's truck, whipped her hair in every direction, and she screamed in frustration. "He's really pissing me off."

"I've locked the windows, but he's evidently overriding the sensor." Bull shook his head.

All four passenger windows and the back sliding window had randomly opened and closed during their entire ride to their dinner reservation.

"Can he see us?" Chaise asked tentatively.

"I really don't know, babe," Bull replied. "But just in case, here's my one-finger salute, asshole."

The touchscreen navigation screen lit up and the automated voice filled the cab of the truck. "In five hundred feet, turn right."

Bull and Chaise looked at the screen in disbelief before they turned to look at each other. "What the hell? I didn't turn the GPS on. I know how to get to the restaurant."

"I said turn right!" The GPS voice yelled through the speakers. "Are you stupid?"

Chaise started touching all the buttons she could find to turn off the GPS, but nothing seemed to work. It continued to hurl hateful and sarcastic insults at Bull about his driving, his inability to ask for directions, and how late he would be for their dinner reservation. The more the voice spoke, the madder Bull became.

"If you can hear me, you son of a bitch, I think you're a complete pussy. Hiding behind a computer screen and taunting people doesn't make you a badass at all. Come meet me like a man and show me what you've got, face-to-face," Bull challenged.

The computer-generated voice in his GPS replied. "You will meet me again soon enough, Colton. Perhaps Chaise will be happy to be in the company of a real man then."

"Why don't you show me how you're a real man, Turan? Right now," Bull replied.

There was no response from the GPS voice, so he turned the engine off, and they walked into the restaurant.

"Hello. Welcome to The Crimson Table. How can I help you?" the hostess asked.

"We have a seven o'clock reservation for two," Bull replied.

"Wonderful. What name is it under?"

"Lanier," he replied.

She checked her computer scheduling system and verified the

last name again. "I'm sorry, Mr. Lanier, but we don't seem to have a reservation for you."

Bull stared at the woman and tried to control his temper when he replied. "We've had this reservation for two weeks. We've talked to the catering chef and the restaurant manager about the menu for our rehearsal dinner. Our reservation tonight is specifically to sample our customized menu."

"One moment and I will check with them," the hostess replied.

She quickly walked away, and Bull turned to face Chaise. "You don't think he…"

"If he did," Chaise cut in, "I'll completely lose my shit. He'd better stay in hiding, that's all I'm saying."

The hostess returned and her face showed her reluctance to share what she'd learned. "I spoke to both the manager and the catering chef," she started. "They each said that you contacted them by email and canceled your reservation."

"No, I didn't. Why would I do that?" Bull countered.

"They both said they distinctly remembered the email because…" She paused. "Because it said that your fiancée had left you for a real man, and you knew when you'd been beaten."

Bull cut his eyes to Chaise. "I'm going to kill him, Chaise."

"Not if I see him first," she replied.

Chaise turned to the confused hostess and explained. "We're being cyberstalked by a crazy man. He's obviously behind the emails the manager and chef received because neither us of sent them. We're still very much together, and we'd still like to have a rehearsal dinner for our wedding."

"I can make a new reservation, but there's no way we can do it tonight. I'm really very sorry," the hostess replied.

"I'm not making a new reservation just for him to mess with us again," Bull replied. "Let's go somewhere else, Chaise."

"You know what? You're exactly right, Colton. Let's go. I'd think that any reputable place would've called to verify an email cancelation of a rehearsal dinner menu selection," Chaise replied. "We'll take our business elsewhere."

When they reached the truck, Chaise had an even better idea. "I know what to do. I'm calling Brianna."

After several minutes on the phone with her sister-in-law, she had everything worked out. "Great news. Brianna's dad can have one of his top chefs handle our menu and the entire rehearsal dinner. We don't have to find another place. Let's just go eat somewhere easy to get in."

"I'm glad you're the brains of this team." Bull smiled at her.

"Yeah, you got real lucky there," Chaise laughed.

Her laughter stopped the second her window rolled down again. "You bastard!" she yelled. She turned to Bull and gave him a sly smile. "Screw him. Roll them all down, Bull. Let's just ride with the windows down tonight."

"Another great idea," Bull said as he rolled the other windows down and opened the back sliding window.

After they settled in to enjoy the warm Miami air, all of the windows rolled up and locked in place. They both slowly turned their heads to look at each other. Chaise pulled a pen and paper out of her purse and quickly scratched out a note to Bull.

Hurry and get us home. He has too much control over the truck.

Bull nodded, his face immediately registering the seriousness of the situation. Turan controlled the truck's computer, GPS, and windows, and Bull didn't know what he may lose control of next. He changed lanes to prepare to take the next exit off the interstate. He made a split-second decision to park his truck and call a taxi to take them home. By the time Turan found the car they were in, they'd already be safely home. As the truck slowed down, he breathed a sigh of relief.

Suddenly, the truck accelerated by itself and the steering wheel locked in place. "Chaise, tighten your seat belt," Bull yelled.

Without waiting for her to react, Bull reached over, grabbed her seat belt, and hitched it up so that the safety mechanism pulled her tightly against the seat. When the tires left the pavement, the tachometer revved into the red zone as the speed continued to increase. Bull tried in vain to turn the wheel, stomp on the brakes, pull the emergency brake, and even throw the truck into park. When they hit the steep grade of the embankment, the truck's angle was inherently dangerous.

"As soon as it stops, get away from the truck," Bull commanded.

"What?" Chaise gasped, scared out of her mind.

The high speed was aggravated by the grade and angle of the truck, causing the tires on the higher side to leave the ground completely. In a split second, the top–heavy truck cab tipped over. The sound of crunching metal, breaking glass, and exploding airbags was deafening as the truck rolled over several times before coming to a stop near the bottom of the ramp.

Dazed and confused, Chaise slowly opened her eyes and was momentarily unsure where she was. Everything looked upside down and only added to her confusion. Bull's last words to her were the first coherent thought she had.

The truck. The wreck. Get away.

When she turned her head to look for Bull, her heart felt like it stopped and her already ragged breath seized in her chest. "Bull!" she yelled, forcing the air from her lungs. He was gone— she was in the truck alone. "Oh my God." The panic rose in her chest. "Bull!"

She clawed at her seat belt buckle as she tried to free herself from its tight hold. The buckle refused to release her and felt as if it continued to tighten even more as she pulled at it. Two large, warm hands covered hers and stilled her movements.

"Relax, baby," Bull's calm voice soothed. "Let me get you out."

Bull slid the knife out of the sheath strapped to his ankle. He made a couple of slices across the seat belt and helped ease her out of the seat. "Are you hurt anywhere?"

"No, I don't think so. Just terrified." Her voice quivered when she spoke, and Bull gathered her into his arms.

"I know, babe." He slowly and methodically rubbed over her back to calm her but also to check for injuries her brain hadn't yet registered in her frightened state. "Are you sure you're not hurt?"

"I'm sure. Maybe a couple of bruises and burns from the tight seat belt and the airbags, but nothing to worry about," she replied.

Within seconds, Bull's cell phone began ringing. He pulled it out of his pants pocket and saw Reaper's name on the screen. "We're okay," he said as a greeting. "My truck is totaled, but we're not injured."

"Thank God," Noah exclaimed. "I'm so glad we added the emergency alert system for our personal vehicles. We're on our way to get you."

"No, don't risk it," Bull warned. "Turan had control of my truck. Locked up the steering, took control over everything. He could've hacked into yours, too."

"I'll call Rebel to come get you," Noah replied.

A few minutes later, Rebel arrived on the scene in his older model Jeep. He found Bull and Chaise giving detailed information about the wreck to the police. The cop was giving Bull a doubtful look as he explained how Turan had taken control of his truck, that was until the CIA and FBI agents elbowed their way in to take over the scene.

"This is Special Agent Landry with the FBI Denver office," Bill said by way of introduction. "He and his partner, Agent Daniels, will be working with us on this case in a joint CIA-FBI task force."

"You must have more information then," Rebel stated.

"There's been more chatter, both domestically and internationally. We're not taking any chances. Landry and Daniels both worked the case initially in Denver, so they're temporarily relocating to Miami," Bill explained.

"The local FBI office isn't happy about this, but we're not giving up our original case," Landry said.

Bull and Chaise retold their story from the beginning of the night, stressing they were sure Turan was also behind the mix-up at the restaurant. "He ensured you'd both be at his mercy inside the truck when he canceled your dinner reservation," Daniels agreed after Bull finished recounting their night.

"And what else does he have rigged?" Bull asked rhetorically.

"Exactly," Joe agreed. "We're towing your truck to one of our facilities to have it analyzed. Your team needs to be prepared for him to take control of anything with a computer chip that's open to a Wi-Fi signal."

"That's why I'm in my old Jeep. Everything's manual on it," Rebel replied.

"He's sending us back to the Stone Age," Chaise grumbled.

The CIA agents, FBI agents, Rebel, and Bull all snapped their heads to Chaise, then to each other. Bull stepped in front of her, pulled her face to his, and lovingly kissed her. "You're a genius, babe."

"Why? What'd I do?" Chaise asked.

"Are they okay?" Brianna asked when Noah hung up the phone.

"Yeah, they're fine," he replied before he rolled over to kiss her. "Rebel just dropped them off at Bull's. Chaise said she's just a little sore from the seat belt and airbags, and she's tired from a long night. She'll probably be even sorer tomorrow. It's amazing that neither of them has any major injuries."

"He could've killed them," Brianna stated. "Do you think he meant to?"

"No, I don't, because he's capable of killing them if that's what he wanted to do. I think he's still toying with us right now, but he's ramping up the stakes. The problem is, we won't know he's decided to take it to the next level until the moment it happens."

"We'll just have to catch him before he's had enough of messing with us," Brianna asserted.

"I'm all ears if you have a plan to draw him out."

"It seems like he wants to keep hiding behind his computer screen, like a bully. That's strange, though, because he didn't mind trying to kill Liz to her face. He's killed others, too, using different means. So everything has to be on his terms, according to his plans," Brianna spoke as if she were thinking aloud.

"Keep going. What are you on to?"

"When he killed people in the past, was it one-on-one, like when he tried with Liz?"

"I don't know, but I can find out. You think he's too afraid to take on more than one at a time?"

"Yes, exactly like a bully," she replied. "He'll make our lives hell while we're together and do everything he can to separate us. Once he gets us alone, he'll pounce. Of course, this is just a theory until we get more detailed information on how he murdered the others."

"We? You're getting that look in your eye again, Bri," Noah warned. "No more investigative reporting or snooping for you."

She smiled mischievously at him, but she softened her voice when she responded with feigned innocence. "Would I do that?"

"Yes, you would," he chuckled. "And don't think for one second that you're fooling me with that sweet, little girl voice."

"Wouldn't dream of it."

"Of what? Snooping or fooling me?"

"I'm not sure I understand the question," she replied.

Noah moved as quickly as lightning to cover her body with his, hovering just above her slightly protruding belly. "Brianna Leigh Steele, don't test me. I can make you disappear until this case is over, and I will do it if I have to," he spoke slowly and emphasized each word.

"It's so easy to get you riled up. Now, while you're in position, it's time for you to perform for your wife." She smiled seductively.

"For future reference, all you have to do is breathe and I'm primed to perform for my wife."

"Good to know," she replied as she raised her head from the pillow to kiss his lips. "I'm breathing."

"I feel you," he replied.

"I feel *you*," she purred.

∽

Early the next morning, Brad reported to Noah's house to share what he'd found. When Noah opened the door, Brad couldn't contain his smile. In the war on the man who had made everyone's life a living hell and made the entire team feel somewhat ineffective, he finally had a solid lead.

"Come on in, Brad. You're here early," Noah said as he ushered Brad inside.

"Yeah, this is something you and the guys will want to see for yourselves," Brad replied.

Brad got his laptop set up in Noah's home office while they waited for the other men to arrive. He opened several programs, one after the other, to show a specific layout of websites. Noah took his seat just as Bull, Rebel, and Shadow filed into his office.

Brad looked around. "No CIA or FBI today?"

"No," Shadow said as he closed the door and removed a device from his pocket. He placed it on the desk and nodded at the rest of the group. "Room is secure."

"We don't trust the CIA?" Brad asked, his brow furrowed and his eyes cutting from one man to the next.

"Never trust a spy, kid." Shadow smiled.

"Weren't you in the CIA?"

"Yep."

"But you left, right?"

"You never really leave the CIA, Brad," Shadow replied flatly. "Let's hear what you've got."

"Our man Turan really is a computer genius. I've had the program backtracking his location for the last few weeks. He built a very complex international network of signals and connections so he could stay hidden. He's good. He's very good.

"But I'm better," Brad rightfully boasted. "I've traced him back here to Miami where he's holed up, waiting to make his final move."

"You know his exact location?" Shadow asked.

"Yes, I do," Brad confirmed. "I verified it with satellite photography. He doesn't leave the house hardly at all, but he has opened the door for food delivery."

"Show us where he is," Noah said.

Brad pulled up the street-level map and also gave them satellite pictures of all sides of the house. "Are you going to go pick him up now?"

"No," Shadow interjected.

"No?" Brad asked.

"No, not yet. All we know right now is that he's being a pain in the ass to us. This can't be his only plan. And if we pick him up now, we may not find out in time. We need to let him think he's still winning, still playing us, while we continue to run our endgame on him," Shadow explained.

"You sure about this, Shadow?" Rebel asked. "This could

severely backfire on us. If we don't haul him in when we have the chance, and something big happens, our asses will be on the line."

"If we haul him in too soon, and something big happens, our asses are still on the line," Bull stated.

"I'd rather catch him with both hands in the cookie jar. I don't want him sitting in jail with a smug look on his face because we missed his master plan. He's not the type to just give it up on his own," Noah surmised.

"So, we're going to have a little fun with the computer genius who's having way too much fun with us?" Rebel asked.

"What do you say, Brad?" Noah asked.

"I say, hell yeah. Let's have some fun with him, aggravate him until he fucks up," Brad replied.

"I think we may be a bad influence on him." Shadow grinned. "It's about damn time."

"It's been too long since we were an unrecognized, government-sanctioned unit," Noah stated. "This feels like we're back home again." The five men began to plan their counterattack on Ali Babek Turan. They decided it was time to turn the tables on him, use his own game against him, but with a few twists of their own.

10

CHAPTER TEN

"I received an interesting call from a doctor in Texas," Steve's oncologist said as he entered the room. "Dr. Daryl Stanton. Name ring a bell?"

"It sounds a little familiar." Steve smiled. "Were you two talking about me behind my back?"

"Absolutely," Dr. Patel replied jovially. "We talked about you for quite a while. I emailed him some pictures of you—fairly compromising pictures, at that."

Steve and Sara chuckled while Dr. Patel took a seat and opened the chart to read from his notes. "I believe he said he explained some of the clinical trial information to you, correct?"

"Yes. He stressed that there was no guarantee that I'd be accepted. I also understand that it doesn't mean I'll be instantly cured either," Steve answered.

"The trials have shown very promising results from the test group. Dr. Stanton called back this morning and informed me that you've been accepted into the trial." He smiled.

Steve and Sara both gawked at Dr. Patel for several seconds

before either was able to speak. Sara finally forced the words out. "You're serious? He was accepted?"

Dr. Patel nodded. "Yes, this is very good news. Should I tell him you accept?"

"Yes," Steve exclaimed. "Yes, I accept!"

"You'll start phase one of it here with me, but we've set up a process so he can also monitor your status. I understand his initial assessment was done via FaceTime, so we'll continue that in the office. Once you finish the first phase, you'll have to relocate to Texas to start phase two, the more intensive phase," Dr. Patel explained.

"What am I looking at, Doc?" Steve asked, suddenly serious.

"The first phase is the administration of a single chemotherapy drug that's still under trial status with the FDA. Essentially, the preliminary results have shown that the new drug better prepares the body to accept and positively respond to the specific mixture of the two chemotherapy drugs in phase two.

"As with any chemotherapy treatment, every experience is individual. You can expect many of the standard side effects—weight loss, diminished appetite, nausea, vomiting, hair loss. But it's very likely those side effects will be more severe in phase two as the toxicity builds up in your body. The number of rounds you have to do depends on how well your cancer responds to the drugs," he concluded.

"When do we start?" Steve asked, unfazed by the daunting days ahead of him.

"I'll contact Dr. Stanton today and let him know you've agreed. We have some paperwork for you to complete, and then he'll ship the medication to me. We'll start phase one as soon as we receive the medication," Dr. Patel replied. "It should take about a week at the most, but we'll call you when it arrives. Since you've just finished a complete cycle of the current chemotherapy drug, we'll wait and start the trial drug next."

"That's great news, Dr. Patel. Thank you," Steve said as he stood to leave.

After stopping at the receptionist's area to complete more clinical trial paperwork, Steve took Sara's hand in his and they walked out together. Roman was waiting outside to drive them home. They climbed into the back of the SUV and Steve pulled Sara close to his side.

"I have an idea," he murmured in her ear.

"Oh yeah? What's that?" she whispered back.

"We need to get away together for the next week. Before the new trial drug arrives. Before our lives are centered around this cancer and my treatments again. Just the two of us—and our security detail. What do you say?"

"I say let's do it. Where do you have in mind?" Sara asked.

"Roman, do you have a girlfriend?" Steve asked.

"I'm seeing someone," he answered vaguely.

"Have you ever been to the Smoky Mountains in Tennessee?" Steve probed.

"No, can't say I have," Roman replied.

"Call your girlfriend. We're going on a trip to the mountains for the next week," Steve announced.

"Don't worry about our son. We'll take care of him," Sara added.

Roman shifted uncomfortably in his seat but didn't argue.

Steve retrieved his phone from his pocket and soon had a mountain cabin hideaway reserved for the week. He then dialed Noah's number and smiled at Sara. "Hi, son," he said when Noah answered. "Are you home? Okay, your mom and I are coming by right now. See you in a few minutes."

"You didn't give him much time to say anything in reply," Sara laughed.

"It's best not to," Steve chuckled. "Keeps him guessing."

Roman laughed and shook his head as he drove, but even he had to admit it was a good idea to get Steve and Sara away from the area while Turan was still on the loose. If that meant that he had to spend a week in the mountains, Roman decided he'd gladly take one for the team.

When they were securely inside Noah's garage, Roman opened the door and began to mentally prepare his argument for why his latest love interest should join him and the Steeles for their impromptu vacation. Before Roman joined them inside the house, he sent his girlfriend of the month, Tawnee, a quick text to persuade her to join him for a week away. After he pressed send, he slid his phone into his pocket and walked into the house to rejoin the Steele clan.

While Roman was busy on his phone, Steve and Sara found Noah inside the house and approached him together to present their idea jointly.

"Hey, Dad," Noah greeted him. "Hi, Mom. What's happened?"

Chaise heard them enter and joined her family in the foyer. She hugged her parents and stepped back. "What's going on, you two?"

Sara wrapped her arms around Steve's waist. "Your father has been accepted into the clinical trials with Dr. Stanton. Dr. Patel said the initial results have been very promising. Since your dad just finished a round of chemo, Dr. Patel said he'd wait until the new drug gets here to start the next round. So we have a week free of all treatments, and we want to take advantage of it."

Steve picked up where Sara left off. "I've rented a cabin in the Smoky Mountains, and we want to leave right away. Can you spare Roman to go with us and your pilot to fly us up there tonight?"

Noah's eyes darted between the two of them as he processed all the information that had just been thrown at him and Chaise. "First, the clinical trial is great news. I'm so relieved you got in. You definitely need a week off, and going to the mountains is a brilliant idea. Until we stop Turan, the farther away from here you are, the better.

"That is great news," Chaise exclaimed. "I'm so glad Dr. Stanton was able to get your approval so quickly."

"We are, too, sweetheart," Steve replied. "So very thankful."

"Roman, are you okay with going away for a week on such short notice?" Noah asked.

"I'm good, boss. I just need to make a quick phone call, throw some clothes in a bag, and I'll be ready to go," he replied.

"I'll call and have the plane ready to go as soon as possible," Noah replied. "I'm really glad to hear this news, Dad."

"We are, too, son," Steve replied. "Thank you both for everything you've done for us. We love you both, so much. We only wish your brother could be here, too."

"I love you, too, Daddy," Chaise replied. "I wish he were here, too. It's been so long since I've seen him."

Noah was surprised by the sudden outburst of affection from his father. He reasoned it could be just a natural side effect of the stress of the treatments, the news of the promising clinical trials, and sincere gratitude for helping them escape from it all. He hoped that was the cause behind it, but with his run of luck lately, he couldn't count on it.

"I love you both, too. But, Dad, you don't have to thank me. I'm happy to do whatever I can to help," Noah replied.

"Roman, you need a date for the week," Liz stated as she sashayed across the room toward him.

He flashed his sexy grin at Liz. "I actually just asked my girl about going with me. But, if she can't go…" He intentionally let his voice trail off, leaving Liz to infer whatever she wanted.

"You're trouble." Liz pointed her finger at him. "So, of course, I like you."

"Glad to hear that." He winked.

"Look at you, with your sexy little smile and your come-hither wink. Throw in your rugged, faded beard, that black hair, and those *drizzle-melted-milk-chocolate-all-over-my-body-and-lick-it-off* brown eyes…" Liz paused. "Dangerous combination. I'm not sure this 'girl' of yours will be safe. I should probably go and chaperone."

"I'm afraid we'd get in even more trouble if you went, Liz," Roman replied, his deep voice lowered to be more intimate. He'd watched how Liz interacted with the others, throwing them off-kilter because they didn't know how to take her. He knew how to flirt back, catch her off guard, and take control of the scene. "I'm sure my girl would be very jealous."

Liz put her hand on her side, cocked one hip higher than the other, and looked Roman square in the eye. "As well she should be."

With that, Liz turned and left the room, leaving the others in stitches as they tried to catch their breath from her comic relief.

"I have to give it to her. She knows exactly how to lighten the moment," Roman said when his fit of laughter subsided.

"I've missed her so much," Brianna said and wiped the tears from her face. "No matter how selfish it is of me, you can't take her with you this week. I need her here to help keep me sane."

"I don't know, Brianna." Roman shook his head. "I think it'd be best if she came with us. Steve may need her to call Dr. Stanton while we're away."

"I'll make sure to get his number for you before you leave," Brianna deadpanned. "You can call him from your own phone."

"You both can quit fighting over me now. My mind is made up. I'm staying here," Liz called from the other room. "I need to be here in case my boys catch Lee. They need to make sure he kisses my ass!"

Roman bit back his laugh when he met Brianna's shocked gaze. "You win."

"Obviously," she retorted, and they both laughed again.

"I have no idea how I lost control of my house," Noah said to his team, his dry sense of humor exaggerated in his tone. "One day, everything was fine. Everything ran like clockwork, with precision, down to the minute details. The next day, it just all went to shit."

"You probably just need some Pepto Bismol," Liz called. "It helps stop that problem really fast."

Snickers and coughs filled the room as Noah worked hard to resist replying. He turned back to his parents to find his mom with her hand over her mouth, covering her laughs, and his dad's broad grin lighting up his entire face. "I'll go call about the jet right now," Noah said before walking into his office.

"I'm going to my place to pack a bag and pick up Tawnee for our trip," Roman announced as he slipped his phone into his pocket. Noah stepped out of his office and lifted his eyebrow up in question at Roman.

"Is that your little tart?" Liz yelled from the den.

"That's her," Roman replied. "You want to go with me and meet her?"

"Nope. I sure don't," came Liz's clipped reply.

"Tawnee and I will take you to your house to pack your suitcase. She works for Noah, too, so she can help with security," Roman said to Steve and Sara, consciously avoiding making eye contact with Noah.

"You sly dog," Rebel laughed.

"We'll be right here. Thank you, Roman," Sara replied. "Sorry we're disrupting your life so much."

"No problem at all, ma'am. I'm looking forward to a week in the mountains," Roman assured her before he left.

Steve wrapped his arms around Sara and lightly kissed her lips. "I can't wait to have this time with you."

"I know this whole thing with Ali is added stress you don't need right now," Brianna said, her voice full of empathy. "Please remember that he's dangerous. You could be a target even if you're not right here with us."

"Brad finished the software upgrades on our fleet of vehicles so Ali can't control them any longer," Bull told them. "When he realizes that, it'll probably piss him off so much that he reacts irrationally. So far, he seems like he's a bit of a control freak."

"We'll be careful," Sara promised. "The cabin Steve reserved doesn't have Internet access and is very remote. It would be very hard for him to get to us from here."

"Just don't underestimate him," Brianna warned. "We don't know what all he's capable of or who he's in league with. There's always the possibility that he's not a lone wolf after all."

"I've lived in enough fear ever since the day I found out I had cancer," Steve replied. "We'll be safe and we won't put anyone's life in danger, but we're still going to live our lives."

Noah walked up between his parents and put his arms around their shoulders. "The jet is being fueled and prepped to go. A car will be waiting for you at a private airstrip outside of Knoxville. Let Roman do his job, Dad," Noah warned. "He and Tawnee know how to check the car and verify it's safe before you and Mom get in it. Enjoy your relaxing week in the mountains. I hope your cabin has a hot tub."

"It does, and we plan on putting it to good use." Steve elbowed him in the ribs.

"Really don't need that visual of my parents." Noah shook his head. "Could've gone all year without that."

"We'll take selfies and send them to you while we're away," Sara laughed.

"Send me some selfies of Roman in his mountain-man au naturel state," Liz yelled.

"Mom and Dad are safely tucked away in their mountain hideaway," Chaise told Noah. "It's been a long day for them, so they got takeout on their way to the cabin and they're staying in for the night."

"Good. They need the break from everything," Noah replied. "I wish we could get in touch with Silas."

"His handler still hasn't called back?" Chaise asked and Noah shook his head.

"Our brother is better at hiding than you are, Noah."

"It does seem like it, doesn't it?" One corner of his mouth lifted in amusement.

"Who's ready to play 'kick the Turan'?" Brad asked as he walked in.

"I am." Liz appeared out of nowhere. "What do you have in mind?"

"He just ordered pizza delivery. I think it's time to use his own tactics against him," Brad replied.

"What are we going to do? Increase his order to one hundred pizzas and breadsticks? Change his toppings to all pineapples and anchovies? Play ding-dong ditch at his front and back doors at the same time?" Liz asked excitedly.

"Actually, I thought we'd intercept the pizza delivery guy, attach a listening device on the inside flap of the pizza box, and monitor his conversations from here," Brad replied, suddenly unsure of his plan.

"Oh, well, if you want to go the *boring* route..." Liz dismissed him.

"Let's do it, Brad," Noah confirmed. "Shadow, you're up."

"On it." He smiled as he walked out.

"Bull, while he's distracted with the delivery, let's get one of our new devices on his vehicle. When he does leave, we need to know where he's going," Noah directed.

"My pleasure," he replied, retrieved the device from the office, and made his exit.

"Rebel, I had some luck in getting a few files from our missions since we've been drafted—I mean, reinstated. Why don't you take a load off and look through them, see if anything jars your memory?" Noah extended a large envelope toward Rebel.

"Sure thing, Reap," Rebel replied and took the thick package. "Anything that'll help take this shithead down."

"That's the highlight reel of our missions in the area we think he's originally from. Could be nothing in there that helps. I haven't had a chance to look through it myself, but I trust your eye anyway."

Rebel took the package into the dining room, cleared all of Brianna's decorations off the table, and started separating the documents and pictures by mission. He picked one, took a seat, and started going through every piece methodically. Many of the names and other identifying information had been redacted, but there was enough viable information left for him to fully recall the mission. When he reached the pictures, he carefully studied every face, remembered their words, dialects, and accents, and tried to make a connection to Turan.

Shadow waited outside the pizza restaurant for the deliveryman to return to his car. When he did, Shadow casually approached him, careful not to seem threatening or intimidating.

"Hey, buddy. How's it going?" Shadow asked like he was a long-lost friend.

"Good. How about yourself?"

"Can't complain." Shadow smiled warmly and glanced at his name tag. "I'm hoping you can help me out with something, Bobby."

"Sure, if I can. What do you need?"

"A buddy of mine is getting married this weekend, and a few of us have tried to get him to go out for a bachelor party tonight. He won't do it because his soon-to-be bride forbids that he have any fun at all," Shadow explained.

He leaned in close to Bobby, lowered his voice, and established eye contact to feign a friendly connection with the young man. "I have a feeling that pizza is for him, and that he's holed up inside in front of his computer again tonight."

"That sounds like the guy," Bobby confirmed. "He orders pizza several times a week. He has his whole living room set up with nothing but laptops, wires, control sticks. Guy's a serious gaming nerd."

Shadow shook his head exaggeratedly in mock contempt. "Not the games again!" he exclaimed. "Let me guess. The little Japanese creatures that don't really talk, just make strange sounds instead?"

"Every time I've seen his games, he's either playing a warfare game or a flight simulator game," Bobby replied.

"That's his life, man," Shadow replied. "Bobby, I just want to help get him out of the house so he can have some fun before his ball-and-chain makes *him* take *her* last name."

"Yeah, man, what can I do to help?" Bobby asked, fully engaged in the conspiracy.

"I need to get this microphone inside his pizza box. All I want to do is hide it where the cardboard folds. After he takes it inside, I'm going to yell at him to get the hell out of the house. He'll think I'm in the front yard. When he comes out to confront me, I'm going to sneak in the back door, lock the front door, and our friends are going to make him go out with us one last time," Shadow lied. "Can you help me out? This is my last shot at talking some sense into him before he makes the worst mistake of his life."

"Yeah, man, of course. Sounds like your friend has already surrendered his man-card. You definitely gotta help him get it back," Bobby replied as he opened the cardboard box.

"That's the damn truth, Bobby," Shadow replied. "Listen, if this works, we'll be at Club La Viva later tonight. You should stop by."

"I'm not old enough to get in yet," he replied.

"Aww, man, that's too bad," Shadow replied. "Thanks for your help, though. I really appreciate it."

Shadow gave Bobby a large tip and a manly handshake before he strolled back to his vehicle. He turned and looked at Bobby again. "Don't tell him what I'm planning now," he warned with a smile.

"Wouldn't dare," Bobby replied with a laugh. "Have fun for me, too, tonight."

"You know it." Shadow climbed into his car and waved at Bobby as he drove away. "Thanks, kid. You have no idea how much you just helped your country."

11

CHAPTER ELEVEN

Turan took the pizza box from the same kid who delivered it every time and absently handed him a tip to make him go away. A slow-moving cable van on the street in front of his rented house caught his eye. He chucked the pizza box on the counter and removed the first slice as he sat back down at his homemade network. His enemies had grown smarter since they'd locked him out of controlling their cars and phones. Noah's security system was virtually impenetrable, and Turan's frustration was growing daily.

The cable van gave him a new idea. The Steele Security family most definitely had cable. "Every greedy, entitled American family has cable television to waste their time, addle their brains, and avoid doing anything remotely constructive," Ali muttered as he clicked away on his laptop.

Once he'd gained access to the cable provider's website, he quickly found Noah's and Bull's accounts. Laughing maniacally, he changed their programming options so that every channel displayed the exact same one. While he worked on his grand scheme, every possible aggravation he could add to their lives was well worth the extra time and effort.

His laptop rang and he answered the Internet call. "Yes."

"Have you accomplished today's tasks?" the older male voice asked.

"Yes, I have. You don't have to call every day to ask that," Turan retorted.

"You know that I do," the voice replied. "Your focus on your assigned tasks has been lacking of late."

"I've accomplished my goals and more," Turan argued.

"Do you have the codes?"

"You know I can't go straight to those, or it'll trigger an internal alarm," he replied, exasperation lacing his voice as he'd explained this same fact too many times before. "I have to break it down one layer at a time."

"Are you still on schedule?"

"Of course," he replied indignantly.

"Until tomorrow then," the voice replied and promptly disconnected.

Turan released a litany of curse words in Farsi, flung his chair back from his desk, and jumped up to begin pacing the room to expel some of his pent-up frustration. "Fucking bastard," he yelled. "When this is over, I will make sure you get what's coming to you, too."

He grabbed a bottle of water from the refrigerator and drank half of it as he stalked back and forth, his agitation too high for him to sit still. Drawing his arm back, he hurled the bottle across the room and watched with a modicum of satisfaction as the remaining water splattered across the wall. "My talents aren't being used like they should be. I have much more potential than you give me credit for," he yelled at his computer.

"I'm tired of waiting. It's time I show more initiative. I'll never ask for forgiveness, but I won't wait for permission from anyone ever again. My rewards await me, and they're long overdue."

Turan took his seat and began typing furiously on his laptop. He talked to himself as he worked his way into the secure network his counterpart had questioned him about. "If you want to speed things up, we'll speed them up. But you won't like the consequences," he muttered.

"What is that stupid American saying?" He stopped typing, straightened his back, and stared blankly at the wall. A wicked smile covered his face when he recalled the phrase. "Oh, yes. There's more than one way to skin a cat."

His need to be in charge, to be in control of his destiny, and to exact his revenge on his own timetable began to consume him. A few keystrokes later, part one of his newly developed plan was underway.

"This should keep them busy for a while."

"Hear that?" Shadow asked the room.

"Sure did," Noah confirmed. "Brad, can you get a trace on where the call to Turan originated from?"

"Running it now. It's another labyrinth of networks, so it'll take a while to figure it out," Brad replied.

"The tracking device is in place on his car. He'll never find it, even if he looked right at it," Bull said. "If he leaves in that car, we'll know exactly where he goes."

"Can we remote into his computer?" Shadow asked.

"Not without him knowing. I've been combing through it, trying to find a back door, though." Brad replied. "I have to give him credit—he knows how to build electronic safeguards. He has a huge server solely dedicated to his computer network. Most medium-sized businesses don't even use a server that big."

"Why would he need one that big?" Noah asked.

"An individual wouldn't. That server has an enormous database that's housed on multiple hard drives. If one fails, the others will keep working without it," Brad explained. "He's either over-compensating for something, or he needs to access a lot of data within a split second."

A musical tone rang through the house, alerting the team that visitors had arrived at the Steele house. Noah glanced at the monitor and saw Bill, Joe, Landry, and Daniels waiting for admittance at the gate. He rolled his eyes and huffed loudly before letting them in. "Just when I thought we were getting somewhere, these clowns have to show back up."

"Remember when Chaise said he's trying to send us back into the Stone Age?" Bull asked. "Apparently our assigned agents and I had the same thought when she said that. He's a computer genius, a hardware master, a software nerd, but he also has a job to carry out and he wants revenge on us for some reason.

"Through all the harassment, he has shown us what he can do with a laptop and an Internet connection. What if his grand finale is to take away all the modern conveniences that we rely on? Phones, Internet, cars—everything we communicate with and our modes of travel. I don't mean just for the four of us, either. If he's a part of a bigger group, they could be working together to cripple multiple major cities at once." Bull leaned over, placed his hands flat on the table, and waited as his team considered his theory.

"Amazing that you've come to that conclusion," Bill stated dryly from the doorway. "Where did you get your intel?"

Bull drew up to his full height and turned to face him before he responded. "Gathering intel is my specialty. Do *you* have anything to share with *us*?"

Joe, Landry, and Daniels walked into the tension-filled room, their eyes shifting from one man to another as they read between the lines.

"Sorry to interrupt your meeting, fellows," Landry spoke first. "Daniels and I just got a judge to sign a warrant for a roving wiretap, and we have a team of guys discreetly gaining access to his computers."

"How are you doing that?" Brad asked.

"We have a few techy tricks up our sleeve that haven't been released to the public yet." Landry smiled.

"You called a friend at the NSA," Brad replied dryly.

"Well, there's that, too. Whatever it takes," Landry laughed. "We're also installing video and audio surveillance in his rental house."

"You know where he is?" Noah asked.

"Yeah…" Joe hesitated. "We know. We're watching his house."

"Oh, yeah?" Bull asked. "I guess you saw me there earlier then, huh?" The dumbfounded look the four agents gave him made Bull laugh out loud. "I'll take that as a no, then. Guess I'm not slipping as much as I thought was."

"We're not moving on him now," Noah stated. "We don't know what he's planning yet."

"We agree on that," Joe replied. "We've intercepted chatter that it's big, whatever it is. We can't wait much longer, though. If we can take him out and stop the attack in at least one area, we have to do it."

"How much time are we talking?" Noah asked.

"Impossible to say. We've located another potential person of interest, but it's more of a gut feeling than anything. If he starts making similar preparations, we'll have to move immediately," Joe answered.

"Speaking of," Brianna interjected. "We need to move immediately, Noah, if we're going to make our appointment time."

"Ready when you are, babe," Noah replied. He continued to

speak and directed his statement to the others. "We'll be back later."

When they reached the doctor's office, Noah drove through the parking lot several times to check every car, every potential hiding place, and scanned surrounding businesses for anything suspicious. Satisfied that Brianna was safe, he parked and quickly escorted her inside.

"You know, people stare at me like they're trying to figure out if I'm a celebrity or something," Brianna said after they signed in for her appointment.

"Why do you say that?"

"Because you act like you're my bodyguard, walking so close and hiding me from everyone," Brianna laughed. "I need to buy a pair of huge sunglasses to complete the look."

He reached over, took her left hand, and stroked her wedding band with his thumb. He dropped his voice an octave and spoke slowly, seductively. "You belong to me. You're mine to love, protect, and cherish. To have, anytime I want to have you."

Brianna lovingly stroked the stubble growing on his face, although he'd shaved only hours before. "I'm all yours, Noah. Nothing and no one can tear us apart. And you definitely can have me *anytime* you want me."

"Brianna Steele," the nurse called from the doorway. "Are you ready?"

"I'm definitely ready," she replied, but she kept her eyes glued to Noah's.

Noah stood, extended his hand, and helped Brianna to her feet. "Keep it up, babe. We'll both get arrested for lewd conduct in public."

"We'll have to keep the 'Busted' paper for our baby book," she quipped as she stood.

Noah swatted her ass playfully. "Get back there and show me my baby, woman."

"Whatever you say, my caveman."

After Karrie, the ultrasound technician, explained the protocol, she left Brianna to change into the paper gown. Noah approached her with an unmistakable look of desire. His fingers gripped the hem of her shirt. He slowly pulled it over her head before tossing it into the empty chair. He hooked his thumbs inside the waistband of her skirt and pushed it down over her hips. His fingers skimmed across the sensitive skin of her thighs until he fully knelt in front of her.

Her skirt fell in a pile at her feet as he felt his way back up her legs to repeat the same path to remove her panties. She stepped out of them and he tossed them into the chair with her shirt. As he rose, he intentionally brushed his face against the apex of her thighs.

"Mmm," he murmured against her. "Does that door lock?"

"No. Dammit," she complained, her voice thick with desire.

"That's too bad," he replied, purposely allowing his lips to brush against her as he spoke. "Maybe we won't get caught."

"You're killing me. You know I can't resist you," she purred and grasped his hair.

"I know, and I love it," he replied. He quickly stood, grabbed the paper gown, and grinned wickedly. "Better get this on you before she comes back."

Fire lit her eyes, but she reluctantly agreed because she knew he was right. The tech would be back any minute. "Fine," she spat out. "But you'll pay for this later."

"Oh, I'm counting on that," he laughed. "I can hardly wait."

The rap on the door kicked Brianna into high gear to get her gown on before the door opened. Noah's laughter echoed through the room, but he did manage to call out to the nurse through the door. "Just a minute, please."

Brianna narrowed her eyes at him in mock anger. "You can let her in now."

Noah opened the door and let Karrie in while wearing a suspiciously pleased smile on his face. She stopped in their tracks, did a double take, and continued into the room. "Ready to see that baby now?"

"Yes," Brianna replied excitedly. "I can't wait. Can I just take that machine home with me?"

Karrie laughed. "You'd be surprised how many times I'm asked that question. I'm afraid not. This one is fairly high-tech so we can see finer details."

"Are we taking bets on the sex of the baby?" she asked. "We couldn't get a good view in the previous ultrasound, right?"

"That's right," Brianna replied. "I say it's a girl, but she's being stubborn like her daddy."

"I say it doesn't matter to me what sex the baby is. All I care about is that we have a healthy baby and a healthy momma," Noah added.

"Awww, you're going to be such a good daddy," Karrie cooed at him.

Brianna rolled her eyes at both of them. Not because she didn't agree—she knew Noah would be the best daddy to their children. She'd seen too many women virtually fall at his feet when he flashed his killer smile at them. Picturing the strong, hulking man cradling a baby would definitely cause every woman's ovaries to burst into flames.

"Pregnant woman who hasn't peed in a very long time over here," Brianna reminded them.

"Well, let's press on your stomach and see that baby then," Karrie laughed.

When the lifelike image of their baby illuminated the screen, Brianna's eyes immediately filled with tears. Little hands floated up toward its face before little fingers fanned out to brush against its brow. The corners of the tiny mouth lifted slightly, teasing Mommy and Daddy, before a beautiful smile covered the baby's entire face.

Noah laced his fingers with Brianna's and leaned into her until their cheeks were pressed together. "That's you and me, Bri.

That's our love," he whispered, amazement and wonder filling his voice. "Look how beautiful our love is." He gingerly wiped the tears from her face and left soft kisses in their place.

"Everything looks really good." Karrie smiled. "All of the baby measurements are tracking right on target. Do you want to know the sex today?"

"Yes," they both replied simultaneously.

Karrie moved the wand around Brianna's stomach, spreading the gel to perfectly align the view on the screen. "Congratulations, Mom and Dad. You're having a baby girl."

"A girl?" Noah asked, even though he seemed dazed.

"We're having a girl?" Brianna repeated.

Karrie printed out individual pictures while the video continued to record. She knew from experience that once the shock wore off, the parents would naturally want to examine the image more closely for themselves. She turned with a warm smile and handed them each a picture of the defining moment.

"Noah," Brianna whispered. "We're having a baby girl."

Though he held firm to his tough-guy persona, the mist that covered his eyes was unmistakable. "I think it's really hitting me that we're going to be parents. We'll be responsible for another human life, a life that we created. Her every joy and pain, her fears and dreams… They'll all be ours to the millionth degree."

"My mom always said I'd never fully understand a parent's love until I had a child of my own," Brianna sniffled. "She was so right. It's a completely different kind of love."

Karrie continued to move the wand to give them as many views of their baby girl as she possibly could. "Okay, that's all for today," she said as she cleaned the wand. "Here's your recording of the ultrasound. I'm sure you both have plenty of people who want to get their hands on that video."

"Our parents, siblings, friends," Noah chuckled. "We'll be lucky if we get to watch it again before she's born."

"Better hide it for a while." Karrie grinned. "Family and

friends have ways of taking over babies. Will this be the first grandbaby?"

"Yes, on both sides. First niece, too. And between her daddy and all her uncles, she'll never be allowed to date." Brianna beamed.

Brianna stood to get dressed when Karrie left the room. Like magnets undeniably drawn together, she and Noah embraced in a moment of overwhelming emotion. His arms wrapped around her and held her securely against his body. She nestled into his body, closed her eyes, and inhaled the all-male scent that enveloped her. It was the scent that she associated with home, safety, and love, and it was unique to Noah.

"I know your job has always been dangerous," she said softly. "But please be extra careful. We need you, Noah… I can't do this without you."

His arms tightened around her. "I know exactly how you feel, Bri. One thing I know for sure is I wouldn't even make it a full day without you. And now, seeing our baby like that, it's intensified even more. I'm going to catch this asshole, I promise you."

"Let's go home, Noah. Our family will be excited to watch this video of our baby. Does Roman have the satellite phone with him?"

"Yeah, he has it. Why?"

"Let's Skype them in so your parents can watch it, too. Seeing these images of the baby may just give Steve an even stronger will to beat his cancer."

"Sounds perfect." He kissed her forehead and released her to finish dressing. "Is there anything you need from the store before we go home?"

"You already know that I want to go shopping for baby girl clothes," she laughed.

"Yeah, I know you well enough to know that," he agreed. "If you twist my arm, I'll let you talk me into buying her an outfit that says 'My Daddy Has My Heart' on it. I have a feeling I'll need that to fight Bull off."

"Bull will just mark through 'Daddy' and write 'Uncle Bull' in," she replied. "He claimed his place in our child's life as soon as he found out I was pregnant."

Before heading home, Noah drove to the shopping mall and picked out more items than Brianna did. As they walked through the department store on their way out, the display of flat-screen TVs that covered an entire wall showcased the various high-definition options. One by one, the images on every television changed to display a piece of a puzzle until the full image covered the entire wall.

The image was the 3-D still shot of Noah and Brianna's baby girl. A message appeared across the bottom of the screens that read:

Congratulations on your pink bundle of joy.
Hope you have a picture of her.
You'll need it.

12

CHAPTER TWELVE

"I figured it out," Rebel exclaimed. "I know why the bastard is so familiar now."

"By all means, tell us," Shadow replied.

"Remember the hostages we got out of the far northern region of Iran? He looks just like the guy who ran that compound, Hamid Madani," Rebel replied. "He shot at me as we were getting out and damn near took my head off. I returned fire and killed him."

"A family member out for revenge? A son or nephew with such a close resemblance, maybe?" Shadow suggested.

"We'll have the analysts do some digging on that name and see how it ties into Ali Babek Turan," Joe interrupted as he walked in. "Right now, we have more pressing concerns."

"What happened?" Bull asked.

"Multiple cyberattacks at once. He doesn't fit the regular mold of an extremist, and that makes me think he's going rogue," Joe replied. "Every personal cell phone on one floor of the Department of Homeland Security building in Washington, DC just started ringing at the exact same time. No two of the incoming numbers were the same."

"A couple of the employees answered their phones. It was a recording from their banks confirming $100,000 deposits into their checking accounts," Bill added.

"They all use the same bank?" Bull asked.

"No, that's the thing. It was the *same* recording from their *different* banks," Bill clarified.

"And the deposits were real?" Shadow asked.

"Yes, all of the money was transferred from the bank account of a US-owned oil refinery located in Oklahoma," Joe replied. "Since we already had the tap on his 'borrowed' Internet connection, we were able to trace it back to him pretty quickly."

"The money transfer is most likely a diversionary tactic, but he knows it can't be ignored. If I were a betting man, I'd say his real intentions are about to kick in," Bull said.

"I'd take that bet," Landry replied.

"Since you're all so ready to gamble, can I interest you in a game of poker?" Liz asked from the doorway. She waved a deck of cards at the men and flashed her sweetest smile. "I'll deal."

"That's very thoughtful of you to offer, Liz." Shadow winked at her. "Too bad we have a bad guy to catch before we can stop for playtime."

"There's always time to play, Shadow," Liz argued. "We're not promised the next breath. What if you step outside and get mowed down by a big truck? You'd die without having ever played a hand of poker with me."

"That would be tragic." Shadow nodded.

"It would be a travesty," she agreed. "There's only one solution. We should all play right now. You boys just go ahead and kick off your shoes, make yourself comfortable before we get started."

Bill and Joe exchanged glances and a shared idea seemed to

pass wordlessly between them. "You thinking what I'm thinking?" Bill asked.

"I'm sure of it," Joe replied before turning his gaze. "Liz, I think it's time we play our secret card and draw him out into the light. You game?"

"For catching that little bastard?" she asked. "I'm game."

"I'll get started on the breaking news reports," Bill replied. "I'll be back in touch later today."

"I'll get our analysts up to speed. We'll need extra manpower to catch the chatter and weed out the junk," Joe added before both men walked out the door.

"Looks like that leaves us, boys." Liz smiled and began to cut the card deck.

Moments later, the driveway alert sounded, and Shadow strolled to the window to look. "Reaper's back," he called out. Concern covered his face and he quickly added, "Something's wrong. He's flying up the driveway like a bat out of hell."

Shadow, Bull, and Rebel rushed to meet Reaper and Brianna inside the garage. Reaper slammed the door as he exited the car and rushed around to help Brianna out. Even in his aggravated state, they watched as their friend visibly calmed himself before he took her hand.

"What happened, boss?" Rebel asked.

"Get me the scissors, Rebel. I'm going to cut his balls off myself," Brianna replied.

Rebel's eyes darted between Brianna and Reaper, unsure of what he should do with that statement. "Whose balls are we cutting off, little lady?"

"Turan's. He's destined to live the rest of his days as a eunuch, courtesy of yours truly," Brianna replied.

"What'd he do now?" Bull asked. His lips drew into a thin line, his nostrils flared, and his brow furrowed. He had a good idea he wouldn't like Brianna's answer at all.

"Noah and I went shopping for baby stuff after our appointment. We were walking through the store to exit, and our baby's ultrasound picture was on a giant display of TVs. He added a personal note that said congratulations, hope you have a picture of your baby, you'll need it," she replied, anger dripping from her every word. "He used the very picture we just got from the ultrasound."

Bull's hands curled into fists at his sides. "I'll tear him limb from limb."

"Get in line, brother," Reaper replied.

"He's watching you," Shadow replied. "Probably from a traffic camera around your doctor or the mall. Did you have the picture out in the open at any time?"

"When we were walking out of the office," Brianna confirmed. "I was still staring at it."

"He's not going to get to you or the baby, Sunny," Bull promised. "Maybe you should take someone else with you when you go out."

"Bull, I won't take any chances, but I won't live my life as his prisoner either. The three years I already spent in that mode were more than too much."

"We'll just have to take him out sooner rather than later," Shadow replied. "I can handle it tonight if you want."

"I found the mission that I think tied us to him," Rebel said. "It was the hostage situation in northern Iran. He looks a lot like the group leader I killed. The analysts will start looking into a real name and known associations soon."

"Good job, Rebel. That brings us one step closer to figuring out who else he's tied to, who to watch, what their endgame is. And to closing this case for good," Reaper replied. "Hold that thought, Shadow. You may actually be on to something."

"He launched another cyberattack earlier." Bull repeated the conversation they'd had with Joe and Bill to bring Reaper up to speed.

"Turan's been busy today," Reaper replied. "More so than

usual. I don't like it. More reason why I think Shadow's on the right path."

"Have you heard from Mom and Dad?" Chaise asked. "Before you do anything, I just want to feel like they're safe."

"I talked to Roman on the satellite phone earlier," he confirmed. "They're fine. No landlines, no Internet, and no distractions. They're surprisingly all having a good time. Roman and Tawnee are being extra vigilant about security just in case, though."

"I'm glad to hear that. They need a break from all of this. It's too much stress on Dad in his condition," Chaise replied as she joined the conversation. "Maybe they should go on to Texas for his treatment and get away from all of this."

"That's a good idea, Chaise," Noah agreed. "We should probably talk to them about it when they get back from this trip tomorrow. I know I'd feel better if they were far away from Turan."

"Bull, it's time for us to go meet with the florist about our flowers for the wedding," Chaise said as she glanced at her watch. "We'd better hurry or we'll be late."

"Shit, I almost forgot all about that. I'm ready to go when you are." Bull leaned in and placed a kiss on her cheek. "My offer to run away and get married somewhere crazy still stands."

"Not a chance in hell, Bull," Chaise replied. "I want to see you in a tuxedo. This is the only way I can get you to wear one."

Bull shook his head because he knew Chaise would win him over, regardless of how or why he argued against it. "Let's go then, woman. Get the lead out."

"Yeah, yeah, let me grab my purse."

"Are we really moving on him tonight?" Bull asked Reaper.

"I think it's time we did something. We've listened to the CIA and the FBI. We've waited it out, kept tabs on his whereabouts, but he's still toying with us. The flurry of activity today doesn't fit the profile of someone is who cold, calculating, and patient. It says he's becoming sloppy, desperate, and too unpredictable," Reaper replied. "If we can pull him out of there, Brad and the CIA analysts can scour through his files, pretend to be him for a little while until we find out what their plans are."

"Worth a shot. We'll be back in a few hours. Don't go without me," Bull warned.

"Wouldn't dream of it," Reaper replied when Bull and Chaise started to walk off.

Shadow rubbed his hands together in anticipation. "Let's get our mission plan laid out while Bull's picking out pansies."

"Fuck off, man," Bull called over his shoulder.

"Fuckoff? Is that a type of pansy?" Shadow retorted.

Bull flipped Shadow his signature one-finger salute over his shoulder and didn't bother to turn around for a reaction. The men laughed good-naturedly and moved their discussion inside Noah's office. Rebel grabbed the street-level map, and they began to plan their incursion on Turan's stronghold.

Liz yelled excitedly from the den. "I'm on the television. I'm a star!"

Everyone joined her to watch the breaking news alert.

The national news anchorwoman was the poster child for perfect hair, makeup, and a commanding presence. As she spoke, she owned her audience with her urgency and passion. "Ladies and gentlemen, we interrupt the regularly scheduled programming to bring you this breaking news. Government officials, speaking on the condition of anonymity, have confirmed that an elderly woman from Colorado has survived an attempt on her life. Her attacker is a member of a known terrorist group with ties to extremists in Iran. If you've seen this man" —the picture of Turan filled the screen— "please call the authorities immediately. Do not attempt to apprehend him yourself. He is considered armed and dangerous.

"I have an exclusive interview tonight with this incredibly brave lady who barely survived after he intentionally poisoned her. Tune in as she describes the close call, her thoughts on living next door to a real life sleeper-cell terrorist, and what message she'd like to send to Ali Babek Turan now. We are working to bring you more details on anyone Turan may be working with and where. Stay tuned for more."

"Can you believe that? I'm going to be interviewed on the national news tonight. Everyone will know who I am after this." Liz beamed.

"We'd better get you ready for your fifteen minutes of fame, Liz." Brianna smiled. "Come on upstairs with me while your boys finish working."

"Make me look sexy," Liz replied. "I can't go on national television looking like a slob."

"Of course not," Brianna agreed. As she passed Noah, she murmured under her breath to him, "You owe me."

"It's so worth it," he replied with a smile.

"Guess Bill and Joe are making good on their promises," Rebel said. "This kind of exposure will push Turan over the edge. Everything's been on his terms so far, but his playing field just changed."

"Maybe tonight is perfect timing, then," Reaper replied. "When the other members of his group see this, it will not end well for him. Besides blowing their covers and all the time they've invested in their mission, he just dishonored all of them."

When his burner phone rang, rather than the VOIP on his laptop, Turan knew without a doubt that it would be bad.

"Hello," he answered.

"Look at the news," the voice said.

"What channel?"

"It doesn't matter. It's the same on all of them."

Turan quickly pulled up the national news website and saw his reflection staring back at him. He clicked "play" on the video and watched as the news anchor described his ties to terrorism, the crimes being attributed to him, and the exclusive interview with the elderly survivor of his latest known attack.

"They have your picture," the voice spoke slowly. "They have your known aliases. They can trace you back to us. You've put our entire agenda in jeopardy with your selfish personal gains."

"I am my own man, and I don't need your permission," he stated flatly. "This news changes nothing."

"It changes everything…for you," he replied and promptly disconnected the call.

"No, it doesn't—" Turan began to argue before he realized no one was on the line.

Over the next hour, he went to every news website he could find. He read countless articles about the miraculous survival and recovery of an elderly lady who'd been poisoned by a known terrorist. He learned that he'd been on the FBI Watchlist, but he fell off their scope for a short time.

The poisoning of an American citizen on American soil by a terrorist on a government watch list was big news. It threatened the safety and security of a nation, and that nation's citizens were angry about it. They were quickly turning on him in social media posts, in replies to news articles, and in groups that encouraged local militia to take up arms and find him.

"The modern version of a lynch mob," he mused. "Let's see how well some of you work in the dark. Right after you watch Liz's interview tonight, you'll begin to understand what terror really is."

Using one of his more powerful machines, he worked his way into the local power grid controls. With a few keystrokes, he programmed a change in the electric company computers that was scheduled to go into effect at midnight.

"Soon, the lights will go out and the line crews won't be able to find anything wrong at the substation. Everything will appear to function correctly," he sneered.

A breaking news bulletin flashed across the screen of his laptop and the video automatically started playing. "Local News 3 has learned that the survivor of the terrorist attack has moved here to Miami to recuperate with friends. Stay tuned as we carry the national coverage on her interview, the harrowing details of her attack, and how she managed to survive a death sentence. Coming up next on Local News 3."

"Liz is in Miami?" Turan narrowed his eyes at the screen. "Is she really here, or are you just trying to draw me out of hiding?"

When the special news coverage started, the well-known news anchor started the program with her usual ploy to create suspense and eagerness for the latest update. Turan rolled his eyes at her penchant for drama.

"Tonight, I have the distinct honor and pleasure of interviewing someone incredible. An older lady who, for all intents and purposes, should be dead right now after being savagely poisoned by her neighbor. It turns out that her former neighbor is a wanted terrorist and is tied to several other murders. Mrs. Elizabeth Stanton may very well be the only person who has survived an attack from this brutal man.

"Mrs. Stanton joins us from a secure, remote location for her safety. This madman is still at large and is considered armed and dangerous. If you see him, do not attempt to apprehend or even approach him on your own. Call the authorities immediately and report his whereabouts. Someone out there has seen him, and you may very well be the key to ending this nightmare that our nation is currently in."

Turan laughed at her assessment of him. *A madman. Armed and dangerous. Call for help, run for cover, hide and weep.*

"And now, I'd like you to meet Mrs. Elizabeth Stanton. Welcome, Liz."

"Thank you, Julia. It's good to be here with you," Liz replied with a smile.

"Liz, let's go back to the time just before your neighbor so viciously tried to kill you. What was he like?"

"He was boring, Julia," Liz stated bluntly. "He was like a wet blanket, putting the fires out around him from pure suffocation of fun. His social skills were nonexistent and his hygiene was severely lacking. I tried to befriend him, help him out of his shell, but obviously not everyone wants to be helped."

"Are you saying he didn't know how to talk to people? He was a loner?"

"Yes, he was definitely a loner. He never had anyone visit him at his townhouse. He went to work five days a week, came home alone, and stayed inside the whole time. He's a young man; he should've been out having fun, meeting people, forming relationships. But he sat at home all alone instead."

"Talk to me about the day of the attack. What events led up to it?" Julia asked.

"He surprised me by coming over to see me all of a sudden. I'd always asked him, and sometimes he'd come in for tea—he always loved my tea—but I could tell he didn't really want to be there. But the day he tried to kill me—and failed," she stressed, "he actually did want to be there.

"He helped me unload mulch from the trunk of my car and then helped me spread it in all of my beautiful flower beds. Now I know that he was just trying to make sure there was nothing out of place in my yard. My neighbors would've known that I wouldn't leave bags of mulch on my lawn, killing the grass.

"Anyway, when I invited him in for tea and croissants, he quickly agreed to it. But first, he went to his house and brought back this awful, bitter-tasting honey that he'd been bragging on. I didn't have the heart to tell him at the time that, even though honey isn't supposed to ever go bad, his must have been the exception. It had a very bitter taste, and we all know that *real* honey is sweet."

The more she talked, the more Turan's hands curled into tight fists. Every word out of her mouth was an insult, a dishonor, and an outrage. It was clear that they weren't lying—Liz really did survive. The next words caught his attention.

"Liz, it is very serious business to have active terrorists on American soil. Here, in our country, threatening our citizens. How much of a threat do you believe Ali Babek Turan really is?"

"Julia, I can only go by what I've personally experienced. He is a bumbling, inept, thug-wannabe. Really, if he can't kill a little, old, weak lady like myself, how much of a threat can he be to a real man? Of course, it's scary to think that his friends could be better at this terrorist business than he is. Maybe he's a trainee or something. I'd feel sorry for him, you know, if he hadn't tried to kill me."

"Liz, you must have a heart of gold and the patience of a saint. If I were in your shoes, I can say I wouldn't stop until he'd been punished to the fullest extent of the law," Julia replied, her admiration of Liz clear.

"Oh, Julia, don't get me wrong. If I see him coming, he'll definitely feel the wrath of Liz Stanton. The odds of that actually happening are small, though, because that would require him to leave the safety of his four walls. He'd have to actually face another person who knows what kind of sniveling weasel he really is," Liz clarified. "He'd be too scared to face me now. I can't imagine what a disappointment he must be to his family."

"I hope you're right, Liz." Julia started her response, but Turan wasn't listening. His mind was still reeling from Liz's last statements about him. Did she know that his father never approved of him? That he never met his expectations and his father died before he could prove that he was capable of being brave? Did she know that he was always a disappointment to his father, a regret in his eyes?

13

CHAPTER THIRTEEN

"I'm really sorry, baby," Bull tried to soothe Chaise. "I know how disappointed you are."

"How is he staying a step ahead of us? I just don't get it. We have super-techy guys working this case, too."

"Nothing against Brad, but this Turan guy is a genius when it comes to programming, and apparently at hacking, too," he explained. "We know where he is, we've just been—"

"Waiting." She finished his sentence for him. "I understand not wanting to show your hand, but at some point, enough has to be enough, Colton. The man tried to kill Liz, we know he killed other people. There's enough evidence to hold him."

"Actually, we wouldn't even need that evidence with the laws on terrorism," he admitted.

"That really doesn't help right now," she replied through gritted teeth. "We know he's a terrorist. Go. Get. Him."

"We're going to his house tonight," Bull replied. "Late. We'll get him."

"Okay, as much as I want you to get him, I'm a little worried about pushing you to go to his house now. What if something happens to you?"

"Won't happen, babe. I'm too stubborn to get hurt. I'm too mean to be killed. And I'm too good at my job to be caught." He grinned at her.

"There's the cocky, confident Bull I love." She smiled back. "Please be careful tonight."

"I will, babe. I really am sorry about the flowers," he said again. "I'll kick his ass for you when I get to him if you want."

"Yes, please do. He deserves it. There's no way to get my flowers now. They'd have to be planted, grown, and harvested since he canceled my order and the ones I need were given to someone else. They were going to be perfect, too." Chaise scowled.

"We can choose another type of flower," Bull offered.

"I'll think about it. I'm just really so disappointed and disgusted right now, I can't even think straight."

"Well, it's a good thing I know what'll make you feel better, help you forget that disappointment, and have you singing from the rooftops."

"Colton, take me away," she agreed. "Shouting your name from the rooftops may be exactly what I need."

"Hell yeah." He pressed the gas pedal harder. "I'm taking you up on that—no take-backs."

"No take-backs," she agreed. "I'm all yours. I need the energy release and the whole body relaxation I get when you're finished working me over."

"You know it turns me on when you talk like that."

"I do know," she confirmed. "I'm counting on it, my lover."

"That's my girl."

When they walked inside the house, Bull leaned his back against the closed door, set the alarm system, and let his eyes rake over Chaise's body.

"You just going to stand there looking at me?" she asked coyly

"No." Bull shook his head. "I'm going to do a lot more than look at you. First, I'm going to strip every article of clothing from that gorgeous body of yours. Then I'm going to massage every inch of your body, loosen up those tight muscles, and work some of your stress out. When you're relaxed and limber, I'm going to make you mine in every known position, and maybe a few we make up on our own."

Chaise's shock was evident on her face—and in her physical reaction—as she let go of her purse at the same time her bottom jaw dropped open. Her chest rose and fell in rapid succession as her breathing became shallow. Her face flushed as desire burned through her veins like liquid fire. "You're the only one who knows how to make me forget everything else that's going on in the world."

Bull nodded slowly. "Tonight, there is nothing else, and no one else. Only you and me."

"Yes," she said breathily. "You're all I need."

He pushed off the door and walked directly to Chaise, his eyes never leaving hers as he advanced on her. "Come with me."

Bull led her into their bedroom and stopped her at the foot of the bed. As he unbuttoned her shirt, his fingers lightly brushed against her and sent chills rippling across her skin. As he pushed her skirt over her hips and down her legs, he left openmouthed kisses in his wake. He lazily traced her sensitive flesh through her silky panties with his finger. "It feels hot in here," he said as his hand reached between her legs. "Is it wet, too?"

"You can touch it and see for yourself," she offered.

"It's mine, isn't it?" he asked rhetorically. "I'll do a lot more than touch it. But I want you to tell me. So, is it wet?"

"Yes, it's very wet," she panted.

"I bet we can make it wetter," he ventured. "We haven't even started yet."

He slowly removed her panties and stood to remove her bra just as painfully slowly. His every touch branded Chaise, made her want him more, and made the wait even more excruciating. She knew if she tried to make him hurry, he would purposely make her wait even longer. His plans for her had been made known, and all she had to do was relax and let heaven come to her. Exhaling slowly, she allowed her muscles to relax and let all the stress begin to fade to black.

Bull moved her to the bed and motioned for her to lie on her stomach. When she was in place, his strong hands began massaging her neck and shoulders. Soothing scents filled the air when he removed the oil from the nightstand and poured it into his hands and rubbed them together. The friction warmed the oil enough that Chaise felt the heat seep through her skin when he began rubbing her shoulders again.

He moved down her back, running his finger along the hollow of her spine to the top of her ass. "I love this." He covered both of her cheeks with his hands and sensually squeezed. "I could feast on this all day."

While he kneaded the backs of her thighs with his strong hands, he imagined their lives together after everything settled down. He hadn't had much downtime between cases, Noah and Brianna's wedding, and planning his own wedding. The moments like this had become his refuge, his solace in the world of madness. He never imagined his life would take this turn and give him someone he couldn't imagine living without. There wasn't anything about her that he didn't love, even the things she did that drove him nuts.

"Just looking at you makes me crazy," he muttered. "You're so beautiful. And sexy. You make it impossible not to want you wherever we are. Sometimes I have to remind myself that I don't want any other man to see you naked just so I don't strip you bare when we're out somewhere."

She sighed heavily and melted even more into the bed. "If we could get away with it, would you want to have sex in a public place?"

"I think it could be fun," he replied. "But I don't think we could be quiet enough."

"You're probably right," she giggled. "It's hard to be discreet with you."

The growing bulge that strained against his zipper became painful, especially when he thought about the sounds she made and the way she looked when they made love. "This is what you do to me," he said as he slid his erection across her ass, grinding his hips against her as he moved.

She moaned appreciatively and pulled her legs up until her knees were underneath her to better accept him. When he made a second pass, his movements mimicked the act of taking her from behind. Her fingers curled into the comforter and gripped it in a vise-lock. "Colton," she begged.

The sound of his zipper and the shuffling of denim were all she needed to hear to know that he'd also reached his limit of waiting. With his clothes shed, she felt him move behind her on the bed as his legs framed hers. With one sudden thrust, he entered her soft, wet channel and dug his fingertips into her hip bones.

"Baby, you feel so good," he said. He repeatedly pulled back and pushed forward, drawing her moans and screams to a pinnacle. He felt her inner muscles squeeze him as if they were trying to hold him in place. "You're close," he boasted, felt the rush of warmth from her release, and then joined her in his own.

He rolled her over and she curled into him with her arm across his chest. "That was incredible. Every bit of it," she exhaled.

Bull kissed the top of her head. "You're always incredible, my love."

"Are you still going tonight?" she asked tentatively.

"Yeah, it'll be late, but I'd feel better if you wait at Reaper's while I'm gone."

"Okay. Brianna and Liz will keep me company until you get back," she agreed. "Just don't stay out past your curfew. You know I don't like to wait."

He chuckled, knowing she was joking with him. "Yes, ma'am. I'd hate to keep you waiting and get in trouble when I get home."

"You'll be in more trouble if you don't kick his ass for all the trouble he's caused us with our wedding. I want to go with you just to be the one to make him pay for it," she replied.

"If I could take you with me, just for that reason, I definitely would. You're scary when you get mad."

She playfully swatted his chest. "You'd better remember that yourself."

Bull lovingly stroked her back with his fingertips, back and forth until she was lulled into a restful sleep. He remained awake and mentally recounted the preplanned sequence of the night's events. Turan's car hadn't moved in a week, but like clockwork every night, he had food delivered to his house. Joe and Bill were being kept updated on the intercepted messages as the analysts dissected any information that was remotely close to their case. Nothing indicated that tonight would be any different than last night. No intelligence pointed to a sudden change of plans.

The plan was that the four-man team would approach the residence from different directions, each covering a specific side of the house. House blueprints, undercover pictures, and the information obtained from the wiretap were all memorized. Every step had been planned well ahead of time to avoid as many problems as possible. *Best laid plans*, was on repeat in Bull's mind.

He'd never had jittery nerves before an operation before now. Skirmishes in a foreign desert or reconnaissance work in an opulent mansion, the job had always felt like second nature to him. Get in, get what was needed, and get out. Move silently, take no prisoners, and take no shit. Stay cool, keep calm, and follow the plan—that was always how the operation went. Chaise moved in her sleep and drew his attention away from his thoughts. The change in his demeanor suddenly made sense to him.

"It's because now I have something to lose," he murmured aloud. "Something I know I never want to be without. Someone I want to make it back home to."

He let her sleep in his arms for as long as he could before he had to meet the others. He gently shook her shoulder to wake her. "Chaise, baby, we have to leave in a few minutes."

"I haven't slept that well since this whole thing started," she said sleepily. "Please be extra careful tonight. I expect you to come home to me, safe and sound and in one piece."

"Try to get rid of me," he chuckled. "Even a restraining order won't keep me from you."

Chaise and Bull got dressed and left so he could drop her off at Noah's and get to his rendezvous point well ahead of time. She held his hand with both of hers during the entire drive, gently stroked her fingers along his, and glanced nervously at him a few times.

"Here we are," Bull announced as they pulled into Noah's driveway. "Stay here with Brianna and Liz until we get back. There are security men in the yard and along the perimeter. You'll be safe."

"You need to be safe, Colton. Call or text me as soon as you can to let me know you're okay."

He smiled. He'd never had to check in with anyone before now. "I will, babe. It'll be fine—you'll see."

After a long kiss— *"until later, not goodbye"* —Chaise got out of the truck. Brianna met her at the door.

"Come on in." Brianna smiled. "We'll have a slumber party —you, Liz, and me."

"I'm not playing poker with her," Chaise stated.

"Chaise! We're playing Twister! I have everything ready," Liz yelled from the den.

"Sadly, I'm in no condition to play Twister." Brianna patted her stomach. "So, it'll be you, Liz, and the poor, unsuspecting security guy twisting," Brianna replied.

Bull waved to them both and pulled out of the drive. When he hit the road, his cell started ringing. "Hey, Reap, what's up?"

"Just making sure you remembered we have a date tonight."

"Have I ever stood you up before?" Bull asked.

"There's always a first time for everything," Reaper joked.

"Not for that," Bull replied. "Brothers don't stand each other up."

"Let's take this shithead out tonight and be done with him."

"That's what I'm talking about," Bull replied.

He pulled onto the side street that gave him the best vantage point of Turan's yard. The house was completely dark except for a small glow in the living room. The team's cell phones were turned off and their secure wireless communicators were on.

"The car hasn't moved, but either the house is empty or our boy is sound asleep. There's no movement, small glow in the front of the house, but nothing moving around on this side," Bull reported.

"Same here," Shadow replied. "That glow is from a laptop, but he's not in the living room."

"I'm below his bedroom window," Rebel whispered. "I hear snoring. Let's get this guy."

"Copy that," Reaper replied. "Everyone move into your position. We're doing this by the book."

Bull glanced down at his watch just as he moved into his position at the back door. Two minutes until midnight. In two minutes, everything could change. This case could be closed, the bad guy could be apprehended or killed, and they could be going home to their families. Or, in two minutes, life as they knew it could all change. In the blink of an eye, everything could go wrong because they rushed into a trap set by an extremist bent on killing as many people as possible.

Bull pulled his gun close to his chest. It was locked and loaded, ready to fire. The single-word command from Reaper came across the airwaves. "Go."

Without hesitation, Bull placed a strategically swift kick to the back door and sent it flying open. He immediately stepped to the side for cover and extended his arm to aim. Quickly stepping into the room, he thoroughly searched the room before moving on to the next one. Just as he rounded the corner, he saw a door in the hallway move slightly. "Got movement," he whispered into his comm. "Door in the hallway. Going in."

"On your six," Reaper replied as Bull stepped through the door.

"Stairs, looks like a basement," Bull advised.

Light briefly illuminated the basement before it disappeared.

"He's on the move," Bull said and flew down the stairs. "There's a door down here."

Reaper was close on Bull's heels. "It's a crawl space door. He must be going for the car. Shadow, Rebel, get outside now!"

Reaper and Bull followed into the crawl space while Rebel and Shadow ran outside.

"Flashlight moving," Shadow called. "I'm on it."

"I'll cover the car and the house," Rebel replied.

Reaper and Bull emerged from the other end of the crawl space and out of the half door that Turan had exited. A bulky giant ran past them in the dark with the signature prowess of Shadow. His strides lengthened and his speed increased, then he lunged through the air and landed on a much smaller form. The scuffle only lasted a second or two before Shadow sat completely on top of him, had his arms twisted behind his back, and hand-cuffs locked around his wrists.

"And that's a wrap," Shadow said into his comm. "Shadow, one. Pansy-ass terrorist, zero."

The other men laughed into their comms, sharing in the revelry of the moment. As Shadow stood Turan up to walk him back into the light with the other men, the power to all the houses and businesses shut off for as far as they could see. Turan smiled from ear to ear. His face was covered in sand and dirt from his scuffle with Shadow, his clothes were dirty, and his hair was matted. But the pride on his face was evident and the fact he refrained from speaking about his accomplishment demonstrated his resolve.

This one wouldn't give up his secrets easily.

"Brianna. Chaise. Liz," Noah whispered to Bull. "Rebel, call the others and tell them it's safe to get out of their cars now. They can take custody of this asshole now."

Turan glared at Rebel as he called Joe and relayed Reaper's message. Within thirty seconds, Joe and Bill walked up. "You knew we were watching?"

Reaper looked at them like they'd just asked the dumbest question ever. "Of course, I knew. You can't tail a subject for shit," he chuckled. "Take this guy to your office and interrogate him. Call us if you need any tips on effective interrogation techniques."

"We got him," Joe replied. "Come on Ali Baba. Time to pay the piper."

"Let's get home. I don't like this at all. Something's up," Reaper said when Turan was out of earshot. "Get Brad over here to go through everything he has on these computers. We need to know what he's already done and what he's about to do."

"On it, boss," Shadow replied as Reaper put his phone to his ear.

"Brianna" The urgency in Reaper's voice was palpable. "Are you okay?"

"I'm fine, Noah. The power went out, but the generators are on and we're okay. Are you okay?"

"Yeah, babe. We got him, but it feels a little too easy. Call it a gut instinct. I'm on my way home. Keep the doors locked and keep the guns close. If anyone but me tries to get in the gate, shoot first and ask questions later," he ordered.

"Hurry home, Noah. But be careful," she replied. "I love you."

"Love you, too, babe. I'll be there within twenty minutes."

14

CHAPTER FOURTEEN

"Ladies, don't panic." Liz extended her hands out in front of her, spread her fingers, and exaggeratedly pumped them up and down. "We'll be fine. There's no reason to be scared."

"We're fine, Liz," Chaise replied calmly. "Anyway, the generators kicked on when the power went out, so the security system is still operating."

"We also have a couple of security guys outside. Plus, we're both armed." Brianna motioned between Chaise and herself.

"I won't let anything happen to either of you." Liz continued her attempts to soothe them.

"We feel so much better with you on guard," Brianna laughed.

"Are my boys all okay?" Liz asked.

"Yes, they're all fine," Chaise answered. "Colton just called and they're on the way home now."

"I'd better get the Twister mat ready for our game now," Liz replied. "Shadow and Rebel are mine tonight."

"Here, let me help you," Chaise offered. "I actually want to see this."

"Feel free to take notes, girly. You might need them later for Bull," Liz replied with a wink. "I've got the moves."

Liz and Chaise spread out the dotted mat on the floor and giggled like schoolgirls as they chatted about the mental pictures of Rebel and Shadow twisted into strange positions. They heard the squealing tires before the driveway alarm rang to alert them. Brianna rushed to the window just in time to see the tail end of Noah's truck flying into the garage. The door from the garage burst open when Noah and Bull both rushed inside, weapons drawn and aimed at the floor.

Noah stopped when his eyes met Brianna's. "You're okay?"

"We're fine, babe. Thanks for rushing home so fast, though." She smiled. "Where's Ali?"

"Joe and Bill took him in for questioning. I expect to hear from them soon," Noah replied.

Chaise walked into Bull's waiting arms. "I'm so glad you're okay," she told him.

"I'm fine, baby. We were never in any danger at all," Bull replied. "The whole thing was a piece of cake."

"Something's definitely wrong with that picture," Brianna said. "I can't believe the house wasn't booby-trapped, he didn't put up a huge fight, or really even try to wipe his hard drives."

"You know too much about this kind of thing," Chaise replied dryly to Brianna. "It scares me sometimes."

Brianna laughed. "Yeah, well, my time as a reporter, on top of my years with Noah, has taught me a few things. I've asked to officially join the team, but they won't let me."

"It was definitely too easy," Bull replied. "I'd like to know what's going on right now in that interrogation."

"Shadow and Rebel should be here soon. Let's see if Shadow can get any information from his CIA buddies," Noah suggested.

"Have you gotten used to this yet?" Chaise asked Brianna.

"Used to what? Noah putting his life in danger and waiting up to see if he'll make it home safely?" Brianna asked. "No, I'll never get used to it. He knows that. All I can do is trust that he's the best at what he does."

"Can I get a GPS tracker on you?" Chaise asked Bull. "One that sends me constant updates to let me know you're okay"

"I'll see what I can do," he chuckled.

"You and Noah could each wear one of those adventure cameras on your heads. Then Brianna and I can watch your missions together and rush in to save you if you get in trouble." Chaise grinned mischievously.

"You can use those cameras in the bedroom, too," Liz added. "Spice up your love life and all. Can I borrow it?"

"Sure, as soon as we start wearing cameras on our missions, we'll let you borrow it," Bull replied.

"Be sure to look at Shadow. A lot. From behind," Liz answered.

"Who's looking at my behind?" Shadow asked from the doorway, his sly smile covering his face.

"Bull will watch it with the adventure camera he'll wear on his head," Liz replied.

Shadow's smile faltered as his eyes bounced around the room, met the others' amused gazes, and decided it was best to not pursue the topic. "Good to know," he laughed. "Reap, Bull— need to talk to you both outside. Rebel's already out here."

"You got it," Noah replied and stepped toward Shadow.

"Be right back, babe." Bull kissed Chaise.

They met Rebel in the driveway and huddled up for the update. "Bad news, boys," Shadow started.

"What?" Noah asked, instantly on alert. "I knew it was too easy."

"Yeah, Turan has already been released," Shadow relayed. "As soon as Joe and Bill got him into the interrogation room, Bill received a call from the higher-ups. They had to release him because he has diplomatic immunity. His uncle, Bachar, is the ambassador from Turkey. Turan is also considered a diplomat since he works for his uncle."

"But he's a terrorist," Bull countered. "How can he be protected under our laws if he's a terrorist?"

"We don't have enough hard evidence to prove he is. We can't expel him back to Turkey without evidence. Legally, we're not even supposed to have the wiretap on him, and we can't use that evidence since it wasn't obtained legally."

"That's why he was smiling smugly at us," Rebel said. "He wanted us to catch him so we'd find out he's untouchable."

Reaper inhaled deeply and gave each of his brothers a hard gaze. "You all know what this means. If you want out, I understand, but this changes nothing for me. The government disavows any knowledge of my actions anyway, so I don't view this any differently. He's threatening my family and my country, and a law that protects terrorism isn't valid in my eyes."

"I'm in," Bull replied instantly.

"Me, too," Rebel answered.

"You know I have no problem with breaking silly laws like that," Shadow replied. "Landry and Daniels have been pulled from the case. Joe and Bill will still be around but, *officially*, not as much as before."

"We should expect retaliation soon," Reaper warned. "He won't be satisfied with just being let go. He'll want to cause more trouble for us."

"Exactly. He's been waiting for us to show up at his house, waiting for us to make a move on him, just so he could blatantly make his next play," Rebel replied. "He wants to rub it in our faces."

"What if we let him?" Shadow asked. "He can make his next move, get it out in the open, and we'll use his momentum against him. With every blatant attack, the news can keep carrying coverage of how he's at large. The pressure from inside is bound to reach his uncle and the rest of his cell."

"That's taking a big risk, though. Look around—we already don't have power. Have either of you heard any updates on that?" Bull asked.

"I talked to Joe," Rebel said. "They know he's behind it, and the crews are at the substation looking for the problem. Joe said Turan laughed openly, like he knew they wouldn't find anything."

"Call Brad, get him to help dig through Turan's online activities. Maybe he can identify something the crews would miss," Reaper replied.

"He's been free for almost an hour now," Shadow said. "I don't see him waiting long for the next move. We need to make some decisions—fast."

"Let's go inside and have some coffee. The emergency generators I had installed will be put to good use. It's late, or actually, early, and it doesn't look like we'll get to sleep anytime soon," Reaper said.

They walked inside and relayed the news to Brianna, Chaise, and Liz. "You should go to bed, babe. Looks like we'll be pulling an all-nighter," Noah said. "Chaise, you can pick one of the spare bedrooms and make yourself at home."

"I'm leaving the Twister mat where it is," Liz said. She pointed her finger at Shadow as she issued her demand. "Don't play without me."

"Don't worry. It wouldn't be any fun without you." Shadow winked.

Inside Reaper's home office with a full pot of coffee, the four men went over every possible scenario they could prepare for in advance. The wild card was the same as it had always been—Turan didn't fit the profile of the typical jihadist. He didn't strictly follow the cell's rules to remain invisible until the very last second, until the time his enemy had no time to react.

Contingency plans were in place for direct attacks on their

households, but plans for their extended family were harder to account for. Bull's parents, John and Beth, were traveling the country and enjoying his retirement. Steve and Sara were away but due to be back in a matter of hours. Silas, Noah's brother, still hadn't been located.

"Noah," Brianna called sleepily from behind him.

"Yeah, baby?" He turned toward her, his demeanor instantly changing from trained killer to protective husband.

"Just got a call on your cell from the guys in the office. Steve and Sara's house was just broken in to and ransacked," she said grimly. "A couple of your guys are on the scene with the police. The power is still out over there, too, but they knew you'd want to know."

"Could be a trap to draw us away from here," Bull replied. "If he's been watching the house, he knows the security detail was pulled when Steve and Sara left town. I say let the men handle it until morning. We'll go over there together, pack up Steve and Sara's stuff, and send them to Texas early."

"I agree, Reap," Shadow replied. "It has to be part of his play."

The cell in Brianna's hand began to ring again. She glanced down at the screen and a concerned look covered her face. "It's the office again," she said. "Hello?"

She was silent over the next several seconds as the person on the other end relayed more information to her. "That was Brad. Good news or bad news first?"

"Bad," Noah replied.

"Turan's house just burned to the ground. We've lost all virtual connections to him and the information we were getting from the wiretap," Brianna replied.

"And the good?"

"Brad was able to retrace his keystrokes in to the power substation software just in time. He said it'll take him a couple of hours to rewrite the code, but he'll have power restored pretty soon."

"Did he say anything else about the fire?" Rebel asked.

"Obvious accelerant used—like blatantly used everywhere. It was a total loss. The crews are still on the scene making sure it's completely out before they leave," she replied.

"Reap, he couldn't have got to your parents' house and torched his house that close together. Not when they're still on the scene at Steve and Sara's house outside of Miami and the firefighters are still on the scene at his house here," Bull said.

"It'd be nice to know if we're dealing with more than one cell member in one location, or if his own cell torched his house to take him out," Reaper replied as he stood. He moved around the table to Brianna, kissed her goodnight, and took the phone from her hand. "Get some sleep, baby. I'll take phone duty for the rest of the morning."

"You know where to find me if you need any help." She smiled sleepily and stroked his cheek.

"No way am I leaving her tonight to go check out either scene," Reaper said when Brianna was out of earshot. "He's hit my parents' house and possibly torched his own place. I'm not giving him any opportunity to get to my family."

"Agreed. We should all stay here tonight and take shifts," Rebel replied. "He could've planned the fire timing with an extra-long wick or something slow burning, just to throw us off. I think he's trying to split us up."

"You know, Brianna said the same thing a little while back. She thinks he's like a bully who's afraid to take us on as a group, so he'll try to get us alone and stab us in the back," Reaper replied. "I have to agree. He shut the power down for a reason, but I doubt he accounted for the generators keeping my security system intact."

"The sun will be up in a couple of hours. Get some sleep and I'll keep watch until daylight. I doubt he makes a move with all of us here, but I'm not willing to risk anyone's life on that," Rebel said.

"You sure? I don't mind staying up," Shadow replied.

Rebel shook his head. "No need to, man. I got this."

"We have guys outside, Rebel. Like you said, it'll be daylight in a few hours. They can handle it until then. We should all get some rest. I have a feeling it's going to take all of us to convince my parents to get out of town after they see their house in a few hours," Reaper replied.

"All right," Rebel agreed. "I just feel responsible for all of this."

"Don't. His father, or whatever relation they were, was responsible for taking those hostages. He also made the choice to fire on us," Reaper replied. "None of this is on you."

Rebel nodded slowly, not fully convinced but at least considering his friend's assessment. "All right. Let's all get some shut-eye then."

Turan stood outside of his rental home and stared at the charred remains in disbelief. A few firefighters still combed through the remnants of his possessions, using their picks and axes to check for smoldering fires under the larger pieces of debris. Everything he owned was in that pitiful excuse for a home. Every possession and piece of technical equipment besides the cell phone in his pocket had been inside, but now it was all burned beyond recognition by the fire and covered in water and fire retardant residue.

"I hate all of you. Bastards. You'll all pay for this," he cursed under his breath. "I'll never stop."

Turan dug his keys out of his pocket and climbed back into

his car. He backed out of the driveway, put the car in drive, and aimlessly wandered around the city until the sun appeared on the horizon. The lights across the city began to flicker on, people began to stir, and he realized his grand scheme to throw Miami into a complete blackout had been thwarted. Parked in a public parking lot, desperation and defeat got the best of him. He retrieved his cell phone and dialed the number from memory. He held his breath and put the phone against his ear. Dread filled him with each ring that passed.

"I told you never to call this number," the man answered.

"I didn't have any other choice," Turan replied. "I need your help."

Silence met him, and he pictured the other man pinching the bridge of his nose in irritation and aggravation. "What do you need?"

"Money. Laptops. Somewhere to stay," Turan replied.

"You lost everything I gave you?" he asked, anger filling his tone.

"There was a fire. Everything is ruined. It was a total loss."

"You weren't there when the fire started?"

"No," Turan replied hesitantly. "I had to go out for a while. The house was burned to the ground when I got back."

"Your instructions were to remain inside and stay away from others until you were told otherwise," the man replied. "If you'd been there like you were supposed to be, maybe you could've prevented or put the fire out before you lost everything. Do you have any idea what this does to our plans?"

"I know. I've let you down, disappointed you again. I'm very sorry," Turan rambled.

"Give me a couple of hours. I'll be in touch."

With that, the line disconnected, and Turan stared at his phone for several minutes. "These Americans have cost me too much. I've been too lenient, too lax in my approach. I've underestimated them for the last time," he vowed. "They've played me for a fool for far too long. I'll show them. I'll make them pay. And the only form of payment I'll accept is their blood."

Nearly four hours later, Turan sat on the beach alone and watched the waves crashing into the shore when his cell phone rang. He answered it before the second ring finished.

"Yes."

"Your apartment is waiting for you," the man spoke slowly. "Do not screw this one up. It is your last chance."

"Understood."

Turan memorized the address and thanked the man for his assistance. "Will I see you before the appointed day?"

"It is possible," the man replied. "But you really need to focus on your assigned tasks instead of worrying about that. I expect everything to be completed and ready to implement by tomorrow."

"It will be," Turan promised.

"We're counting on you," the man replied before he hung up.

Turan drove straight to the address he'd been given and climbed the stairs to his third-floor apartment. It was in even worse condition than the small rental house had been. Somehow, he'd taken yet another step down the ladder rather than up. That solemn thought seemed to accurately sum up his entire life.

New laptops, multiple display screens, and other peripherals had been placed on the desk in the bedroom. A new, prepro-grammed burner cell phone lay on the bed and indicated a new text message waited.

Don't screw up again.

"If only it were that easy," Turan sighed and began to set up the new equipment.

Hours later when he had everything up and running again, he clicked on the local news website. A surveillance video on the news site's home page was on continuous replay. His name was splayed across the top of the page in a large, bold font. The video footage showed a man breaking in to the home of Steve and Sara

Steele. When the frame froze, he stared into his own eyes through the security camera recording. His ties to his uncle, Ambassador Bachar, and his diplomatic immunity were being dissected and scrutinized by the public.

He turned on the television in the furnished apartment and quickly found the national news channel. He immediately knew that the commentary from the aggressive news anchor would seal his fate.

"Ali Babek Turan has been identified as the terrorist who attempted to murder his neighbor by poisoning. We've learned that he was taken in for questioning about that crime, and many others that appear to be related to him, but the authorities were forced to release him because of diplomatic immunity. We have obtained a video of Turan actively breaking in to and entering this home, and sources at the scene tell us that he vandalized it to the tune of tens of thousands of dollars.

"Knowing all of this, I'm appalled that our government officials haven't stepped up and insisted upon his deportation back to his country, at the very least, or to press charges and have him arrested under his country's laws. It's time for the people of this great nation to stand together and demand that our rights to life, liberty, and the pursuit of happiness be taken seriously. He is a threat to all of us and does not deserve to have immunity from the consequences of his actions.

"Ambassador Bachar, it is time for you to step up and do what is right, sir. Using your political advantage to protect a murderer must stop."

Turan dropped down into the ugly, lumpy chair and stared at the video in disbelief.

15

CHAPTER FIFTEEN

"I am so relaxed. Nothing can take this feeling away from me," Steve boasted on the ride home from the private airstrip.

"We need to do this more often," Sara agreed. "The crisp mountain air and getting away from everything that's so stressful in our lives was just what the doctor ordered."

Roman couldn't bring himself to tell them about his conference call with Noah while they were still on the plane. Their relaxing week at the mountain lodge, hidden away from the rest of the world, was about to come to a screeching halt. The damage done to their home was substantial and would take a small army of contractors and workers to renovate it. Noah was already up and hard at work, calling construction crews in and having new plans drawn up to try to make it into a positive experience for his parents. But he knew better than to count on that.

When Roman pulled into their driveway, Steve took one look at his home and froze midsentence. Sara looked at him expectantly, waiting for him to finish his thought, before her eyes followed the path of his stare. She gasped loudly before she grabbed the door handle and jumped out of the truck.

"What the hell?" she asked aloud. "What happened here?"

"Mom, calm down," Noah spoke in low tones. "He's mad at me; he's trying to get to me however he can. If that's through you and Dad, then he'll do that. We talked about this."

"I know," she stammered. "I know we did. I guess I just didn't expect…that he'd really do it."

"On a positive note, you can remodel now." Noah smiled. "It's not a total loss. Just a really big mess."

"Did he do this?" Steve demanded, suddenly standing next to Noah. "Was this that little bastard who tried to kill Liz?"

"Yes, Dad," Noah confirmed. "It's a bit more complicated than we realized. He has diplomatic immunity, so it makes it harder for us to touch him."

"Bottom line, son. Cut to the chase," Steve ordered.

Noah looked his father square in the eye. "Okay. It'd be in your best interest to move to Texas now, do your treatments out there, and let us finish up business here. He's a slippery bastard, and he has the law on his side. His uncle is an ambassador to our country, and he's on his uncle's payroll. His house burned to the ground last night, so we lost our connection to him. It's not safe for you or Mom to be here."

Steve was shocked at Noah's candor at first, but he turned his softened gaze on Sara. "There was a time I would've been hardheaded and insisted we stay here. Guard the fort. Never be backed down by another man," Steve said softly. "But right now, all I can think about is getting you as far away from here as I can. If anything happened to you, that would be it for me."

"What if he does something worse to our home while we're away?" Sara asked as she glanced at their house.

"This building—" Steve gestured toward the house "—isn't home. It's just a structure full of furniture, clothes, and trinkets.

Home is wherever you are, babe. That's all I need. I don't care about all the extra *stuff* anymore."

"You're right, Steve." Sara smiled warmly. "As long as I'm with you, I don't care about the house or anything else in it."

"We'll go to Texas, Noah," Steve replied. "If that's what you think we should do, I'm willing to follow your lead this time."

"Good. You're making the right decision," Noah replied. "I talked to Evan, Brianna's dad, this morning, and he insists that you stay at his hotel in Houston. His staff will help take care of you, and it's an ultra-swanky hotel. You'll love it, Mom."

"We can't impose on him like that," Sara replied.

"You can and you will," Brianna replied as she walked up behind her. "You're family. We'll accept nothing less."

"But we'll be there for months, what with Steve's treatment and then the clinical trials," Sara protested.

"That doesn't change anything." Brianna smiled. "Let Dad and Mom do this for you. They honestly want to help, and it's not an imposition at all."

"You're sure?" Steve asked.

"Positive," Brianna replied. "Just pick out which renovation plan you like best, and Noah and I will oversee the construction while you're away."

Steve and Sara took turns hugging Brianna and Noah. "You've both been such a big help to us. I don't know how we'll live in Texas for the next several months without you."

"We'll be there to see you after the baby's born," Noah promised. "You have to spoil her like good grandparents would."

"Her?" Steve asked.

"Her." Noah beamed. "We just found out while you were in the mountains. We're having a baby girl."

"I'm going to be a grandfather," Steve announced, as if he'd just realized it for the first time. "I'm going to get better. I'm going to kick cancer's ass. I'm going to spoil my granddaughter!"

~

"Thanksgiving wasn't the same without Mom and Dad here," Chaise commented. "It was the first one that Noah and I could've been together with them again. It's so wrong that our first Thanksgiving as one big family has been ruined by a cyber-stalking, pansy-ass terrorist."

"I agree. Them not being here didn't feel right to me, either," Brianna agreed. "It wasn't the same without my parents and sisters here, either."

"I can't believe your parents went on a cruise for Thanksgiving," Chaise laughed.

"I know!" Brianna exclaimed. "They said they have to get their vacations in now because they won't leave once the baby gets here."

"Any word on Turan?" Chaise asked. "Where is he? What's he doing? Why has he been so quiet for the last couple of weeks?"

"I don't know, but it's definitely not like him. He was so smug when the guys caught him, like he knew he was untouchable. Then when that security tape was leaked to the press—" Brianna furrowed her brow, deep in thought "—everything changed."

"Joe and Bill had to be behind that," Chaise replied. "Colton said they denied it, but it's not like they'd tell the truth anyway."

"That is definitely a good possibility," Brianna agreed.

"What? What are you thinking? I know that look."

"It's not all adding up for me," Brianna began. "Something's off...something's not right."

"What do you mean?"

"The security tape—how would they have gotten it? It's on Noah's servers at the office," Brianna replied. "Noah said he didn't give it to them."

Chaise shrugged. "The CIA has their own computer guys

who know how to get to whatever they want. They probably hacked in to the servers and stole it."

"You're probably right," Brianna agreed. "Still, there's something on it I want to watch again."

She opened her laptop and pulled up the video. When it reached the frame that clearly showed Turan's face, she paused it and moved it a single frame at a time. "Right there," she exclaimed. "Did you see that?"

"What? See what?" Chaise asked as she leaned toward the screen.

"Watch when the frame changes," Brianna said. Slowly moving the video frame by frame, she stopped when she reached the exact microsecond she needed. "Right here, there's a different image. It looks like this one of Turan has been placed on top of the original."

"I don't see it."

"Watch again."

"I still don't see it. I see Turan with his back to the camera. Then he turns around, like something caught his attention, and he keeps walking into the house," Chaise replied.

Brianna played it again and again, unsure of what she thought she originally watched. "Maybe I'm looking for something that's not there to be found," she sighed. "Now I'm doubting it myself."

"We all need a break. This case has been going on for way too long. The guys have been working nonstop and they're becoming crabby," Chaise laughed.

"It would be nice if Noah and I could get away one last time before the baby gets here," Brianna replied. "But I know they won't stop until they get their man. And he'd never leave them at a time like this."

Chaise sat back and thought about Brianna's comments. The bond between these men was unshakable. Knowing that any one of them would help her and protect her regardless of the situation had given Chaise a real sense of family. She wanted that same bond and closeness to carry over into the family she and Bull would have one day. "The way it's been going, Colton and I will never get married. Turan has gone out of his way to destroy my plans."

"Maybe you should just do a destination wedding and let them handle all the details. Just pick out what you want and let the consultant do all the work for you," Brianna suggested.

"That's a great idea. I think I'll steal that from you." Chaise smiled.

"Woman," Bull called. "It's time to go home."

"Whatever you say, caveman," Chaise laughed.

"You love it when I'm a caveman," Bull retorted.

"Can't deny that," she replied.

In his truck on the way home, she turned to Bull and told him about her conversation with Brianna. "What do you think about a destination wedding?"

"Sounds good to me. Can we do it tomorrow?" he asked.

"No, we cannot do it tomorrow," she chastised him playfully. "Or the next day, before you even ask."

"Damn. You're too quick." He winked. "Whatever you want, babe. As long as you're the bride and I'm the groom, I don't care if I'm in shorts and a T-shirt or a monkey suit."

"Monkey suit?"

"Yes, an actual monkey suit, complete with a tail. Not a tuxedo. I have to draw the line there."

"I'm genuinely concerned about the amount of time you're spending with Liz," Chaise quipped.

"I can't disagree with that," Bull replied thoughtfully. "I'm afraid she is starting to rub off on me. Want to play strip poker tonight?"

"No, I don't," Chaise said adamantly. "I've already planned a night of Twister."

"If you insist," Bull replied, and they both had a good laugh.

"It feels so good to laugh again. Everything has been so serious lately, thanks to Turan," Chaise said. "Any new developments with him?"

"He's apparently in hiding now. Joe said his uncle has disowned him because he publicly shamed him. It doesn't look good for an ambassador, the one person who represents the country internationally, to have a thug on his staff," Bull shrugged. "He'll have to show his face sooner or later. I'm betting on sooner."

"Do you think he'll try something else?"

"I do. I'm positive of it. He was shamed and apparently disowned, so he'll be looking for retribution."

"Is it wrong that I wish he'd just hurry up so we can get this over with?" Chaise asked.

"If you're wrong, then I'm wrong, too," Bull chuckled. "I'm ready to put this case to bed myself."

"Did you say you're ready to take Chaise to bed?"

"Yes. Yes, I did. That's exactly what I said."

"I thought that's what I heard." She grinned. "Colton, what if this case isn't finished before we get married? Will we have to postpone the wedding?"

"Not a chance," he replied. "We can still get married. I won't be able to go on a honeymoon outside the country, but that's about the only limitation I'd have."

"So I can go ahead and plan the destination wedding?"

"Yep—for as soon as possible." Bull grinned. "Before you change your mind and hightail it out of here."

"You can't get rid of me that easily, Colton Lanier. You're stuck with me."

"Stuck like crazy glue." He winked.

"I'm excited." She smiled broadly. "I feel like we're finally moving forward, and I haven't even called them yet."

"Who?"

"Our destination wedding place," Chaise said cryptically. "I want it to be a surprise."

"That means you'll have to take me there." Bull cut his eyes at her.

"That's right. That means I'll be in charge of Bull," Chaise giggled.

"I'm under no illusions about being the one in charge in this relationship," Bull laughed. "But if you want our wedding location to be a surprise, I'll go along with it. Just inside this country."

"It is." Chaise grinned mischievously. "Now I have to look at moving the date up because I'm too excited to wait. And I won't be able to keep it a secret long enough."

"Good. My plan is working then."

"Yes, you evil mastermind. Your dastardly plan of ensnaring me and forcing me to marry you in the destination wedding of my choosing has worked out perfectly. I never suspected a thing."

"I'll have to use this tactic on you again in the near future," Bull quipped. "I'll have you eating out of my hand before long."

"Yeah. Eating wedding cake out of your hand."

The following day, Chaise made several phone calls to begin the plans for her dream wedding. She had never felt so excited about planning for the wedding and couldn't wait to enlist Brianna's help. Even though she wanted to keep the location a secret, she knew she'd have to tell Brianna where it would be held and Brianna would, in turn, enlist Noah's help to get Bull there.

Noah was Colton's best man and Brianna was her matron of honor, so naturally they both had to be in attendance. Rebel and Shadow were equally as important to both Chaise and Bull, so there was no question that the whole Steele Security family had to agree to the travel. Since they'd added Liz to the group, she couldn't imagine the ceremony being complete without her there, too.

"The only people who can't be there are Mom and Dad," she said sadly. "I can't believe my parents will miss my wedding, and my daddy won't be giving me away." Steve began the new treatments the week after he moved to Texas, so there was no way he could travel so soon. Even if he were still close by, she realized he might not have the strength to walk her down the aisle after taking the strong chemotherapy drugs.

By the time she finished verifying all the details of her idea, she was convinced it was the perfect solution. "Time to get Brianna on board." She smiled. "Then Noah won't have a choice but to say yes."

An hour later, she called Brianna and gave her the details of her grand idea. "So, what do you think?"

"I think…" Brianna paused. "It's brilliant. I can't wait. This will be an epic wedding, and I'm so jealous I didn't think of it first. Now Noah and I have to get married again so I can do it, too."

Chaise burst out laughing. "Do you really mean that? You like my idea?"

"Seriously. I love it. I think Bull will, too. I absolutely cannot wait to see this wedding."

"Can you help me convince Noah that we don't have to wait until the case is over?"

"He won't take much convincing, Chaise. He loves you and he loves Bull. He wants you both to be happy," Brianna replied.

"I know he does. But I also know he's very focused on this case and may need some convincing that he's allowed to step outside of Miami for a little while."

"Leave that to me. I've got your back," Brianna laughed. "Speak of the devil. He's just getting home now."

"Oh my gosh, go work your magic on him and let me know what he says later," Chaise said hurriedly.

"Okay," Brianna laughed. "I'll talk to you later. I'm so excited!"

"What are you excited about?" Noah asked as he walked into

the kitchen. "Excited because I'm home and you missed me today?"

"That's a given," Brianna cooed. "I miss you every day when you leave me. And I'm always excited when you come home."

"Who was that?" Noah asked after he made her dizzy with a thorough kiss.

"Your sister," she replied. "She's made a decision about the wedding. It's a destination wedding and she's moving the date up. We'll have to go out of town for a few days."

Noah pulled his face back to look Brianna in the eye. "With this case still open?"

"Yes, Noah. Turan has turned our lives upside down enough. We all need some normalcy, some semblance of security. This will be good for everyone, including you. We need the break, and you and I need some time alone before the baby gets here," Brianna explained.

"I love the sound of that last part." Noah flashed his sexy smile. "Where are we going?"

"If I tell you, you can't tell anyone else. Especially Bull," Brianna warned. "Chaise wants this to be a surprise for him."

Noah slowly lifted one eyebrow in amusement. "This should be good. I can't wait to hear the details. Tell me all your secrets, princess."

For the following half hour, Brianna explained every detail of the destination wedding, how they'd get Bull there without actually telling him where they were going, and about the premier package Chaise had picked out.

"I'm telling you, it's brilliant. I told her you and I have to get remarried now because I wish I'd thought of it first," Brianna laughed.

"I will marry you as often as you want and anywhere in the world you want," Noah replied before he kissed her. "You don't even have to hide the location from me."

"So, you'll do this for Chaise and Bull—without a fight?" Brianna confirmed.

"You knew you had me from the second I walked in the door," Noah replied, pinning her with his bedroom eyes.

"Of course I knew," she said as she wrapped her arms around him. "It's still good to hear it, though."

"Where you go, I go. Doesn't matter where, when, or for how long. Everything that's important to me fits right here in my arms. I can live without all the rest of it."

"You are both my strength and my weakness. I'm the luckiest woman in the world, without a doubt."

16

CHAPTER SIXTEEN

"You're quiet," Shadow stated. "What's going on up there?"

"It's like the calm before the storm," Rebel replied. "He's out there, waiting to pounce, and we lost him."

"Clever of him to ditch the car the way he did, huh?" Shadow replied.

"Yeah, that was great. Thought I had him with the GPS tracking, but he gave it to a homeless man who must've driven over every square inch of this city before he ran out of gas," Rebel laughed sardonically. "He was probably watching me chase that old coot from one corner to the other."

"He'll show back up. Don't worry. Roaches have ways of finding their way out of the dark and into the light."

"But what damage will he have caused first?" Rebel asked rhetorically.

"Brad has been watching for sudden spikes in broadband usage. He has to come back on the grid eventually. He's a computer geek. He's probably going through withdrawals right now."

"Could it really be that simple?" Rebel asked aloud. He jerked his cell phone out of his pocket and quickly dialed the number. "Brad, are you monitoring the deep web for Turan? He's so techy and so cocky, he's probably trolling for something illegal right now. Try high-grade weapons—ones that are really hard to get your hands on, like chemical warfare shit."

Rebel and Brad continued to talk about the difficult logistics of flushing someone out of the deep web when it was designed and used specifically for anonymity. They banked on Turan's lack of conformity to standard terrorist profiles as being his ultimate downfall. Rebel knew from experience the extent of his arsenal couldn't be limited to poisoning, stabbing, and turning the power off. He must be planning something big, something that would catch everyone completely off guard.

Rebel then had a better idea.

"Put out a hit on me," Rebel directed Brad.

"Wh-what?" Brad stammered.

"Order a hit on me. He'll bite," Rebel replied. "Give enough information about me for him to identify. Play up to him losing his father, use a similar story. Close enough to relate to him but different enough that doesn't raise any red flags."

"If you say so, Rebel. This will bring all kinds of freaks out of the woodwork, though," Brad replied.

"I'm just fishing for one freak. We'll know it when he finds it."

A week later, Rebel received a call from Brad. "Our freak-bait seems to have worked for our fishing expedition."

"What'd we catch?" Rebel asked.

"One Ali Babek Turan, who is willing and eager to relieve you of your head," Brad replied. "And he's only charging me one bitcoin to do it."

"Don't sound so excited. He doesn't get the payment until he has my head in his hands," Rebel deadpanned. "You'll get to keep all of your bitcoins."

"Good. Do you know how hard it is to generate them?"

"How do you know it's him?" Rebel asked, intentionally ignoring Brad's question.

"I have a very powerful program that can trace dark web exchanges. It's definitely him," Brad replied. "If he's known by any other name, none of our government databases has it listed."

"Good job. We're finally going to nail this prick. When is it going down?"

"He just accepted the contract, and the money is being held in escrow until he delivers on the hit. I've sent him your address and said it had to be done within a week from today. So be ready for him at any time, Rebel," Brad pleaded. "Reaper will have my head for this."

"Nah. I'll fill him in. Thanks for hiring a hit man to kill me, Brad," Rebel said as he hung up.

Rebel strode into the office with a smug smile on his face.

"What have you done?" Reaper asked.

"Who says I've done anything?" Rebel replied with a question.

"You do. Your smile gives you away every time. That's your shit-eating grin that says *You'll never guess what shit I just pulled.*' We know you very well," Bull replied.

"Let's hear it," Reaper said.

"I got Brad to hire a hit man to kill me."

"What's the punch line?" Bull asked.

"The hit man is Turan," Rebel replied. "He's coming after me."

Reaper leaned back in his chair and narrowed his eyes at Rebel. "What if it's not him?"

"Then we'll catch whoever it is that tries to kill me." Rebel shrugged. "Either way, we'll take another bad guy off the street."

Rebel took his seat and briefed them on his entire conversation with Brad. The next seven days would be even more trying than the last couple of months had been combined. Every member of the team would have to be on their top game, adrenaline flowing, their minds set, and their bodies ready to react in a split second. When they'd stayed in that hyped-up state for extended periods of time in the past, it had always taken a big toll on their bodies and their minds.

"What if he shows up with an RPG and blows your house up?" Shadow asked, the twinkle of mischief shining in his eyes.

Rebel barked out a laugh. "Turan's not big enough to hold an RPG. The recoil alone would knock him on his ass."

"RPGs don't have recoil," Bull replied, his brow furrowed in confusion.

"Exactly," Rebel laughed.

"Okay, if we're really going to do this, we'll have a lot of backup," Reaper replied. "That's not negotiable."

"That's fine. Just don't let anyone spook him. This has been the never-ending mission, and we all need to get on with our lives," Rebel answered. "Especially me."

Reaper caught the last couple of words that Rebel muttered to himself. When their eyes met, Rebel nodded once to tell his friend that he was fine. The benefit of having his captain as one of his best friends was that they knew enough about each other to not have to verbalize everything. Rebel knew that, regardless of the situation, his brothers would have his back.

"It's a good day to catch a terrorist," Bull replied with a smile.

"Gather 'round," Reaper announced. "Let's lock this down. Everyone has to be on their best game until we catch him."

Over the following several hours, they established their plan to capture Turan in the act and use all of the evidence they'd gathered on him to help expel him from the country. They argued amongst themselves about the benefits of using him to flush out the other members of his cell, but they ultimately decided that it was best to get rid of one known terrorist than wait idly for more to show up. If his fate brought the others to their doorstep, they'd deal with it at that time.

"Let's go over tonight's assignments one last time," Reaper

announced. "Rebel, you'll be inside your apartment, watching TV and relaxing. Bull, you and Roman will cover the back. If he's literally after Rebel's head, he'll try to get in as quietly as possible and come up behind him. That's the most likely point of access into Rebel's apartment, so we're counting on you.

"Shadow, take Alex and cover the east side. There are a couple of windows, one of which Rebel will be visible through.

"I'll take a couple of guys and cover the front. Blake will have one man with him on the west side. Brad will have access to satellite imagery and will be on comms with us. If anything or anyone moves, we'll know it. Let's not mess this up."

"My head and I would appreciate it," Rebel replied. "But if he happens to slither into my place, I'll have a few surprises waiting for him myself."

"Don't do anything out of the ordinary this week, Rebel. Let's not spook him," Shadow replied. "He's most likely been watching you over the past week since the offer was posted. Checking your patterns, getting to know when you come and go, seeing if you're preparing for him. If you do anything drastically different this week, he'll know it's a setup and we'll never get this chance again."

"Copy that," Rebel replied.

"Do you even own a TV?" Bull asked.

"Yes, I have a TV, Bull," Rebel replied with a shake of his head.

"You're just not the *relax and watch TV* kind of guy." Bull shrugged.

"And you are?"

"Touché."

"How would you know how a hit man thinks, Shadow?" Bull asked. "You said that like you've been through this before."

"Ask me no questions, I'll tell you no lies." Shadow grinned. "That's actually a lie in itself."

"You wound me," Bull replied, mimicking a stab to the chest. "I thought we told each other everything."

"I could tell you, but then I'd have to kill you."

"You've been waiting years to use that line on me, haven't you?"

"You know me too well, Bull."

"I'll be over later, and we can braid each other's hair."

"I'll be waiting with bells on," Shadow joked. "Ladies, I will see you later tonight. There are some new toys I need to prep. I've wanted to try them on a perp for a while now." Shadow waggled his eyebrows. His gaze swung to Rebel. "You've got a good head on your shoulders. You really need to keep it there."

"I agree. Hold him off at the line of scrimmage when he comes for me and we won't have to consider my taxidermy options," Rebel replied with a straight face.

"Interesting. A stuffed and mounted Rebel perched above my mantle. I could make it work with my décor," Shadow answered on his way out the door.

"You know that means he wants you to be careful tonight, right?" Reaper chuckled.

"Yeah. He's not at all ashamed to show his feminine side," Rebel retorted. "I'm headed home to act normal and pretend I'm not up to anything. Apparently, I have to be more careful with that than I realized since my smile gives me away."

"Smile at Turan if you see him tonight," Bull suggested. "It'll scare the shit out of him."

"We'll cover your back, Rebel," Reaper said. "And your neck."

"Thanks, 'preciate it." He nodded. "This is going to work. Trust me."

"I don't doubt you, man," Reaper replied.

"I'm headed to the gym now. Have to keep up my ruggedly handsome good looks," he laughed and waved goodbye.

~

"This is a nice neighborhood," Turan said to himself as he walked around the block. "How different would my life be if I'd been born here in the US?"

The past couple of weeks had been increasingly difficult on him. When he first saw the video of the house vandalism, he immediately thought the men of Steele Security were behind it. *What a pitiful attempt to discredit me*, he thought smugly at the time. *Anyone with a shred of experience in videography can tell that's fake.*

But no one said it was a fake. Everyone believed that he was the one in that video. When his uncle, Ambassador Bachar, confirmed it and publicly disowned him, he knew without a doubt that his enemies weren't behind it. His own people had turned on him, offered him up as the sacrificial lamb, and left him to fend for himself.

"That was when I knew I had to move," he said aloud as he walked. "They put me up in that apartment, and they could get back inside it with no trouble. I'd be killed before I finished my own plans. I pawned all but one of the laptops and all of the peripherals, bought a junker car, and I've been living out of it ever since."

He'd gotten lucky when he replied to an ad for a dog walker. The pay wasn't great, but one dog quickly led to another, and soon he'd earned enough money to survive from day to day. They were all neighbors in the same apartment complex, making it easy to drop one off and take the next one out. He'd found being with the dogs was infinitely better than being around their humans.

"No one can be trusted, Duke," he continued speaking to the Great Dane. "That's why I'm here with you."

His eyes slowly shifted as he glanced around the complex. The second big break came when he visited a well-known hacker site in the hidden part of the Internet. The place where people only visited if they were looking for something they didn't want displayed in their search history. It was a virtual hangout that didn't track the presence of the users with cookies and ISP addresses. A place where people like him were free to post and respond to requests without the judging eyes of others watching.

The request from a comrade in similar straits caught his eye. At first, it seemed a little too good to be true and he was more than leery of it. Like any good soldier, he'd been doing his own reconnaissance work and watching his prey without anyone knowing. He'd been watching every day for almost a week and, so far, he was satisfied that he could safely take the job. He decided that accepting money for it would be an insult to his honor. One bitcoin wasn't much in the grand scheme of things, but it felt like a fitting exchange. In his mind, it was one penny for one life.

"Tomorrow, I will tell my comrade that I'll take the job," he avowed.

His target would be home anytime now if he stuck to his normal routine. "His real name has been hidden from me, Duke," he continued speaking to the dog. "But I will make him reveal it before I relieve him of his head. My knife is sharpened and ready. Sure, I could use a bullet and end this quickly, but I must look into his eyes as he dies. He must look into mine, and he must *know* I'm the one who has won."

The deep rumble of the 1969 Ford Mustang Boss 429 could be heard well before the car was seen. That was his cue that the one called Rebel was home. Loud, proud, and arrogant, his muscle car announced to the world that he'd arrived. The throaty engine turned heads all over the complex, especially from the single women who fawned over the muscle-man owner. Turan hid behind the ornamental trees in the landscaping bed and watched Rebel slide out of his car, grab his gym bag, and casually stroll to his ground-floor apartment.

Inevitably, one or two women always emerged at the precise moment Rebel arrived home and at least one needed help with something that she couldn't handle on her own.

"Can you open this jar for me? You're so strong," Turan mocked in an unusually high-pitched voice. "I'll just die if I can't eat this specific pickle right now."

Envy consumed him inside from watching the scene play out in front of his eyes. He imitated Duke's owner when she called out for Rebel's help next. "Oh, please, Mr. Muscle Head, my car won't start because I disconnected the battery cable when you weren't looking. Pay attention to me."

Duke cut his eyes up at him and quickly looked away. He laughed at his initial thought. "You're embarrassed to be seen with me? You should be embarrassed because of your owner. Look at her. She's pathetic."

Duke seemed to roll his little dog eyes, at least in Turan's mind. "Don't roll your eyes at me. I know what you're thinking. I am not jealous that she rushes outside for two seconds with him but won't even look at me."

Duke grumbled and began to walk, pulling Turan with him. They walked around the opposite end of the complex with Turan suddenly feeling superior when he realized that Rebel wasn't even aware of his presence. *He isn't as smart and cunning as he thinks he is,* Turan thought.

When Rebel finally tore himself away from his adoring fans, Turan took Duke home and purposely tried to flirt with his owner. "Hello, Greta. That color is very flattering on you."

"Thank you so much for walking him. He gets so bored inside." She dismissed him. "Same time tomorrow?"

"Sure," he replied. "I'll see you tomorrow, then."

"Good night," she called absently over her shoulder before she closed her door.

He walked to his car parked behind the apartment buildings and climbed in. He closed his eyes and let sleep overtake him.

The next day, he sat outside a local café and used the free Wi-Fi to get back into the deep web. After he found his contact, he agreed to take the contract on Rebel.

Turan's suspicions were still high, even after verifying the validity of the man who hired him. He continued to walk the dogs in the complex and used the time monitoring Rebel's habits to his advantage. The day he decided to make his move, he napped in his car until darkness completely enveloped the area. There was no point in even trying to access Rebel's apartment until long after sundown with the numerous people coming and going. He laid his seat back and rested his eyes, his imagination on overdrive as he planned his exact route in his mind.

When the parking lot became quiet, Turan ensured the dome light was off before he eased out of his car. He softly closed his car door, careful to not make any loud noises that would draw attention to him. "This is one time that I actually *want* to be invisible," he muttered.

The spacious ground-floor apartments each had a back door and a small patio area. The upper-level apartments had decks, but each level was staggered so that everyone had ample access to the Florida sunshine. He moved stealthily behind the buildings until he stood on Rebel's terrace and peered into his kitchen window. Rebel walked to the pantry, retrieved a bag of popcorn, and threw it in the microwave. Then he pulled a bottle of beer out of the refrigerator and popped the top.

He moved around in the small kitchen with ease as he cleaned up after himself. Within minutes, everything had been put in its place and the counters were tidied. Rebel grabbed the popcorn and walked back toward the living room. Turan's eyes never left Rebel's form as he walked away. His smile covered his face when he felt that sense of pride return to him. Rebel didn't know he was even there.

I was staring him down and he never even knew, Turan thought.

His original plan to kill Rebel sooner rather than later

morphed into a competition in Turan's mind. A competition that Rebel didn't even know he was in. Turan decided he'd test Rebel daily to see how far he could push the limits, how far his superiority would take him. He stepped closer to the back door and gripped the knob in his palm. He slowly turned it, testing it, and found it was locked, but the door opened when he pushed it. Even to his keen eyes, it appeared to be solidly closed.

A faulty lock, Rebel? So careless, he thought smugly.

He stepped into the kitchen and strained his ears to listen over the sound of the TV for any sign that Rebel was aware of his presence. After sixty long seconds of nothingness, he carefully placed one foot in front of the other until he reached the doorway to the living area. He'd looked in the front windows while walking the dogs over the past week, so he already knew that Rebel's back would be toward him.

Rebel laughed out loud at the comedian standing center stage. He held a ventriloquist's dummy dressed up as a terrorist and another doll that looked like an angry old man. The comedian and the two dummies exchanged insults, each in their own voice, and interacted as if a conversation were actually taking place. Turan became distracted by the comedian's show until Rebel's laughter jarred him out of his trance.

He slowly backed away from the entryway and made his way back to the door leading to the patio. Before he left Rebel's kitchen, he memorized everything about the room. His masculine touches around the room brought life to it, made it feel lived-in. He pictured a room full of friends and loved ones gathered around Rebel, laughing and having a good time. The same as when he got home from work, Rebel was the center of attention in his own place. Everyone clamored for his attention and time.

His eyes floated to the kitchen window he'd been watching through earlier. His reflection stared back at him, reminded him that he was an outsider, alone, and not welcome. In his own eyes, he could picture himself outside, looking in, and wishing he could change places with Rebel. His hands began to tremble, and his heart began to race. Before he did something stupid like getting caught breaking into Rebel's apartment, he quickly stepped through the door and silently closed it behind him. He retraced his steps until he reached his dilapidated car and crawled back into it.

"At least the Miami winters are mild," he sighed and cracked his windows for air. Settling into the seat for the night, he welcomed the reprieve when sleep overtook him.

17

CHAPTER SEVENTEEN

"Say again. He's *what*?" Bull whispered into the comm. "I'm sure I heard you wrong."

"He's watching TV with Rebel," Reaper replied again. "I've said it three times now."

"Does he have a weapon? A bomb strapped to his chest?"

"Negative. He looks like he wants to laugh," Reaper replied.

"He's not shitting you, man. I can see him, too," Shadow said. "Funniest shit I've ever seen."

"He's over your right shoulder, Rebel. In the doorway to the kitchen. Laugh if you copy," Reaper instructed.

Rebel laughed louder than usual, exaggerating it to confirm his reply. His hand slipped down between the couch cushions and gripped the handle of his trusty Bowie knife. If Turan decided to make a crazy play, he'd have one hell of a fight on his hands.

"He's backing away, coming back toward you, Bull," Reaper called.

"Copy. I got eyes on him," Bull replied. "He's out now."

"Let him go if he wants to leave. We need to catch him in the act to seal his fate," Reaper replied.

174

"It'd be so easy, though. One shot, he'd fall," Bull replied. "And he wouldn't get back up."

"Maybe he'll try to kill me tomorrow night," Rebel replied.

"I'm following him. Seeing where he's hiding out," Shadow advised. "Stay put."

"Don't let him see you," Reaper replied.

"Do you even know who I am?" Shadow answered incredulously.

Amusement erupted over the airwaves in the form of muffled laughter and snorts. "What do you see?" Reaper asked, his mood lighter.

"He has a new ride. And it's an older, shittier car than the one he gave the homeless man," Shadow replied. "Parked behind the complex in a vacant parking lot. He just laid the seat back and is going to sleep."

"Rebel, you have three guys on duty all night—two outside and one inside. That's an order," Reaper said resolutely.

"Yes, sir," Rebel replied. His voice held respect for his CO, but the twinge of disgust wasn't completely hidden.

"I'm not taking any chances, Rebel. He could very well come back in the middle of the night with explosives and take out half the building," Reaper reminded him.

"You're right. As usual," Rebel conceded. "Go home and get your beauty rest, girls. For some reason, I think he'll want it to be much more up close and personal than an IED would be."

"Fix that lock on your back door just the same," Reaper directed. "You know how to reach me if you need me."

They silently retreated to their vehicles and met back at Reaper's house to debrief and consider changes to the lineup for the following night.

"I think our boy is more screwed up than we realized," Shadow spoke first.

"How so?" Bull asked.

"Watching TV with Rebel? Sleeping in that dilapidated car?

He's an outcast who's tried to fit in everywhere, but he doesn't really belong anywhere," Shadow answered with a shake of his head.

"Feeling sorry for the guy who's planning to kill Rebel? And already tried to kill Liz?" Reaper asked. "You want to adopt him?"

"Don't go talking all crazy on me," Shadow replied. "I'm just saying, again, that he doesn't fit the profile of any murderer I know."

"You've been friends with a lot of murderers over the years, have you?" Bull asked.

"You'd be surprised," Shadow replied.

"I have to admit, when he was watching TV with Rebel, he looked…" Reaper's voice tapered off as he searched for the right word.

"Lost," Shadow interjected.

Reaper nodded in agreement.

"He's a kid, man," Shadow said with aggravation. "He should be living it up in college, partying in the fraternity house, enjoying his life. Not putting himself in a predicament where we're forced to take his life before he's even lived it."

"He's older than we were when we joined the Army," Reaper reminded him. "He's grown. Old enough to know what he's doing and be responsible for it."

"Don't get me wrong. If he makes a move for Rebel, I'll take him down in a split second. Just saying he should've made different choices for his life," Shadow clarified.

"I hear ya, man," Reaper answered. "Let's cover tomorrow night's assignments while we're here."

The three men talked about the different vantage points, the blind spots, and the vacant parking lot. "We need someone covering his car so we know what he's carrying before he even reaches Rebel's place," Reaper said. "If he happens to show up with C-4 strapped to his chest, I'd rather know as soon as possible."

"Agreed. Let's put Blake covering the parking lot. There are no windows on that side of the building anyway," Bull suggested. "One man can cover it."

After a few more changes, Bull took Chaise back to their home and Shadow left for his. Noah settled into the couch and Brianna snuggled up into his side. "Feels good to have you home again," she said and hugged him tightly. "I'm so glad you're okay."

"It was a strange night, but nothing dangerous happened," Noah replied before he kissed her. "It's good to be home with you."

"Strange how? What happened?"

"Turan went into Rebel's apartment through the back door, like we knew he would. But then he just stood behind Rebel and watched TV with him. Then he left. He didn't try anything at all. Just …watched TV."

"He what?" Brianna sat up and looked at Noah.

"You sound like Bull now. He asked that three times," Noah laughed. "I'm not kidding. He watched TV with Rebel and then he just left."

"I heard what Shadow said about him being an outcast and how he doesn't fit in anywhere," she replied. "He's not a kid who went on a joyride in his parents' car, Noah. He tried to kill Liz. He left her for dead. He's tied to other crimes, too. You have a wonderful heart, but when it comes down to it, it'll be you or him. He will always choose to kill you. When that time comes, you can't hesitate…because our baby and I will always choose *you* over him."

"I promise, babe, I won't hesitate." Noah rubbed her belly lovingly. "There's no choice if it comes down to that. I will always choose you and our baby."

"Speaking of, we really need to start picking out a few names. Then we can narrow it down from there."

"Do you have anything in mind?"

"Noah Steele," she chastised him. "Don't think you're fooling me. I know that means you haven't even considered a name yet, and you're leaving all the work up to me."

Noah laughed, knowing he'd been busted. "Fine, fine. I've just been a little busy lately and haven't had time to look through that gigantic book of possible baby names."

"I know you have." She ran her fingers lovingly through his hair. "You always work too hard."

"Have I left you alone too much?" he asked, concern covering his face.

"I'll always take more time with you, Noah," she replied. "But, there's no reason to worry. You're home with me every night, and I fully realize I'm so very lucky for it."

"You are very lucky," Noah agreed. "And if you take me upstairs, I can be persuaded to let you get lucky several more times tonight."

"That's an irresistible offer. I think I'll take you upstairs and start *persuading* you right now."

Noah jumped up and swept Brianna up in his arms. He took the stairs two at a time and raced down the hall toward the bedroom. Brianna squealed and laughed in delight, caught up in the moment with him. When his mouth covered hers, she felt her entire body melt into his. She held his face in her hands briefly and then wrapped her arms around his neck. He tilted her head to the side and deepened the kiss, eliciting a needful whimper from her.

He kicked the door shut as they entered, and he put her down next to the bed. His hands slid down her silky nightgown, making her temperature rise with desire. He bunched the fabric up in his fingers and pulled it over her head. "You're the most beautiful woman in the world," he whispered.

"You make me believe that," she whispered back. "In the way you look at me. In the way you love me.

"I wouldn't have it any other way."

She helped him out of his work clothes, pulling his black T-shirt off and running her fingers, lips, and tongue across his expansive chest. Once she had him out of his BDUs, she gently pushed on his chest, and he willingly fell back on the bed. She took her place beside him and wrapped her hand around him, surrounding him with her small fingers as she began to stroke him. Leaning over, she took him deep into her mouth and his hands tightly gripped her hair.

"Mmm, baby," he praised. "Damn, you feel so good."

She continued working him, her hand and mouth moving in tandem, until he made her stop. "Bri, babe, I want to be inside you. *Now.*"

"If you insist." She grinned slyly.

She climbed over him and straddled his hips. She guided him to her core, dropped her head back when he entered her, and relished in the sensation as he stretched and filled her with his girth. She rocked her hips front to back, took him fully inside her, and dug her nails into his skin as her body adjusted to accept him. They soon found their rhythm, moving in tandem to love's intimate song and dancing to the rapid beat of their joined heart.

His fingers gripped her hips. He pushed and pulled her, lifted and lowered her, all while he continuously drove into her. She felt the pull low in her pelvis, her muscles contracting and gripping him like a velvet vise, and then her orgasm ripped through her body. She cried out his name and felt the warmth of his release immediately after hers subsided. With her body limp and satisfied, she dreamily slid back to his side, laid her head on his shoulder, and draped her arm across his chest. When her leg slid over on top of his, she was somehow touching him from head to toe.

"You okay, baby?" he asked.

"Perfect," she replied. "I may not let you out of bed tomorrow."

"Don't tease me like that," he chuckled. "You know I'd quit my job if you asked me to."

She opened her eyes and tilted her head up to fully look at him. "You love your job."

"I love you more. My job isn't my life. You are."

"Would you really quit? For me?"

"Absolutely." He stroked her arm back and forth, leaving chill bumps with his every pass. "Do you not believe me?"

"I've actually never even thought of that, Noah," she admitted. "It's so much a part of you, it would be like asking you to stop being you."

"Don't misunderstand. I enjoy having my business, doing my job, and working with the guys. Having everything means nothing without you, though. The more I see in my job, the more that fact is seared in my mind."

"If you're unhappy in your job at any time, you're not bound to it. You can do something different if you want. The only thing you can't get out of alive is this marriage." She smiled sweetly. "They'd never find your girlfriend's body."

Noah laughed at her reply. "That sounds pretty badass. It's kind of turning me on again."

"Why am I not surprised?"

"You shouldn't be," he agreed. "But you should know by now that you're the other half of my soul. I've said it in every way I know how."

"My husband. The father of my baby. The love of my life. My provider, my protector, my best friend. My lover, owner of my heart, rocker of my world. There is no part of my life that doesn't revolve around you."

Noah pulled Brianna into his arms, held her tightly to him, and they slipped off to sleep. When Noah woke the next morning, they were in the same position. Their arms and legs were still wrapped around the other. The safe, secure, and content expression on Brianna's face as she slept filled him with pride.

"What are you grinning about so early in the morning?" she asked groggily.

"You make me happy."

She managed to partially open one eye. "You make me happy, too, babe. And right now you're making me nervous. What have you done?"

"Me? Nothing," he replied. "Well, I may have rented the top floor of the hotel for Bull and Chaise's wedding present."

"Do you think they want us to stay with them for their honeymoon?" she asked dryly.

"I rented it for *them*," Noah spoke slowly. "So no one would bother them. Our rooms are at a different hotel."

"That's so sweet of you, Noah," she cooed. "I married the best man."

He leaned in and gave her a long, sweet kiss. "Time for work. I love you."

"I love you, too."

~

"On the move," Roman whispered into the comm. "Carrying a fighting knife on his belt."

"Got him," Blake replied. "Moving toward the back of the building."

"Rebel, if he goes inside, I want you to get up and move toward the kitchen. Let's see what he does. Alex, be ready to help stop him."

"Copy," Alex whispered.

"He's pulling his knife out. Looks to be between eight and nine inches long. He means business," Blake advised.

Turan tiptoed through the darkness, lurking in the shadows and scurrying across the occasional beam of light. When he'd almost reached Rebel's building, his bravado quickly grew and his guard dropped. The feeling of invincibility enveloped him and made him stand tall on his way to extinguish his enemy's light, once and for all. He stepped into the path that was illuminated by the lights in the parking lot and didn't attempt to hide.

He didn't see the arm that quickly extended out of the shadow of the building. He didn't see the light glint off the shiny silver prongs. By the time his brain registered that something had touched him, it was much too late to react. The silver prongs dug into his skin. The arm that held the silver-pronged devil was strong and steadfast. The lightning that arced from the prongs lit up the dark night, and his screams of pain echoed off the brick walls of the numerous apartment buildings.

"Aaaah! Aaaah!" Turan screamed uncontrollably before his knees buckled and he dropped to the ground. The intense stinging that coursed through his nerves stopped for a second, only to quickly start again. Followed by his spontaneous screams and more uncontrollable body jerks.

"Take that, you little bastard," she yelled gleefully. Then she zapped him again.

"You want some more? I'll give you more." She followed with another zap. "There. Have all you want."

She moved over to his other side. "This side is jealous," she proclaimed. Then zapped him with the stun gun again.

When he screamed and convulsed, she laughed until tears rolled down her face. She danced around him as if she were chanting and performing a ritual and he was her sacrifice.

"This thing is too much damn fun," Liz exclaimed. "Watch this."

Zap. Zap-zap-zap. Zap.

She doubled over with laughter and wiped the tears from her

face. "This is the best invention ever. Think I can make him pee his pants?"

She bent over and extended her arm toward his crotch, but Shadow stopped her just in time. "I think he's had enough, Liz," he chuckled. "How about you let me take that now?"

"What if he jumps up and comes after me? I have to be able to protect myself."

"If he gets up, I'll shoot him," Shadow promised. "But, for some reason, I don't think he'll be getting up on his own anytime soon."

Turan moaned and cursed her with garbled words.

"Did he just call me a white-haired she-devil?" Liz pointed at him in disbelief. "Give me that stun gun."

She reached for the stun gun, but Shadow blocked her arm. "You're quick," he said when she made a play for it with her other hand. He held it up above his head, far out of her reach.

"Shadow…" She put her hand on her hip. "I have ways of making you drop your arm, you know. That won't stop me for long."

Shadow quickly lowered his arm and drew the stun gun in close to his chest. "You're scary, Liz."

"What the hell is happening back here?" Reaper asked as he jogged up to join the others.

"Our backup got a little overzealous," Shadow reported. "Situation is under control now."

Reaper's eyes shifted to Liz and narrowed. "What are you doing here?"

"Helping you boys out. You're welcome," she replied.

Rebel walked out of his back door and tried to hide his huge smile. "Are we having a party back here? My invitation must've gotten lost in the mail."

"Lee Ali-baba Babek Turan Clover was our entertainment. Sorry you missed how he serenaded me," Liz answered. "Make

Shadow give me my stun gun back, and I'll make Ali sing just for you. He sings like a girl, though."

Shadow quickly turned his back and took a few steps away from the crowd. His shoulders shook violently as he tried to regain his composure.

"He was dancing a little jig, too," Liz told Rebel. "He doesn't have the moves like I do, though." She shook her hips and danced to a song only she could hear. "He looked more like a fish out of water, flopping around on the ground."

Shadow then lost any semblance of control and horse-laughed over Liz's description of Turan being repeatedly shocked by her stun gun. "Okay, you deserve it back now. But only use it if he tries to come after you."

"Okay," Liz agreed.

Shadow turned his head to look at Reaper, who was still not sure how his team had lost control of the scene, when he heard another zap and another girly scream. He whirled around with his mouth open and looked at Liz disbelievingly.

Liz gave him a sheepish look in return. "It slipped." She shrugged. "My fingers just aren't what they used to be. What are you going to do?"

18

CHAPTER EIGHTEEN

"Wait." Brianna held out her hands in the universal sign for stop. "Back up. *Liz* was there? How? Why? What?"

"Now you know exactly how I felt," Noah harrumphed. "Imagine the scene. All my professional soldiers are in place. We have every step of his path covered. He's approaching Rebel's back yard, he has a large knife on him, and we're all ready to pounce. Then Liz takes him down with a *stun gun*," Noah stressed the anticlimactic scene.

"I've already said you're welcome," Liz said as she strolled into the room. "You don't have to keep painting me as the hero."

"How did you get there?" Brianna asked. "You were supposed to be here with Chaise and me."

"Yes. Do tell Brianna how you got there," Noah urged.

"*How* isn't important. I'm just thankful that my timing was impeccable," Liz replied.

"Liz, how did you get there?" Brianna stood and arched her eyebrow at Liz.

"I may have borrowed a car," she replied.

"She stole my guy's car after she hit him with the stun gun out in the yard," Noah elaborated.

"Liz!" Brianna exclaimed.

"That'll teach him to trust strangers." She shrugged. "He didn't know me from Adam. I could've been a deranged lunatic."

"Well, clearly, we dodged that bullet," Noah replied sardonically.

"I don't know how this place even managed to run before I came here." Liz shook her head. "No worries, I'm here now."

Noah shook his head and exchanged glances with Brianna. "So, obviously you got him this time, right?" Brianna asked.

"Yes, we got him this time. Every initial in the government was represented at the scene when we called it in to Joe and Bill. They took him to a high-security federal holding center to await deportation back to Turkey," Noah replied.

"Does that mean he's also undergoing interrogation tactics to get information about the other cell members while he waits?"

"I'd say that's a 100 percent accurate assumption." Noah smiled.

"I can make him talk," Liz replied. "I can make him sing like a girl, too."

"How long will he be in holding?" Brianna asked.

"As long as they want to hold him. It could be anywhere from a couple of weeks to a couple of months. It really depends on how talkative and forthcoming he's being."

"I don't know which is worse—knowing he's still here or knowing he'll probably be freed once he gets back to his country," Brianna replied.

"Personally, I'd prefer that he stayed locked up here. At least we'd still have access to him if something else happens," Noah said.

"I'm packed. When are we leaving?" Liz abruptly changed the subject.

"First thing in the morning." Brianna smiled. "I'm so excited for Bull and Chaise. The timing worked out perfectly on the case and the last-minute cancellation they had."

"I may have had something to do with the 'last-minute cancellation' part," Noah confessed.

"What did you do?"

"I called them this morning and explained the situation with Dad. They actually didn't have an open spot, but they added one for our special circumstances." Noah shrugged nonchalantly.

"You are the best brother, the best husband, and the best man." Brianna beamed. "Why didn't you just tell them that?"

"I don't want to meddle in their business. I honestly think they should just get it done now before something else happens to delay it."

"Yeah, I think Bull would come unglued if one more thing happened," Brianna laughed.

"He still doesn't know where we're going. I love that we're all in the know and he's not," Noah laughed.

"I can't imagine Bull doing that for anyone but Chaise," Brianna said. "The Bull I met in the desert wouldn't have trusted anyone like that. It's good to see him happy."

"Are there any craps tables there?" Liz asked.

"No, Liz." Brianna shook her head. "There aren't."

"Crap."

"Let's go, Bull. We're going to be late," Chaise called from the den.

"On my way, babe. Keep your panties on. Or don't. That's fine, too," Bull answered as he walked down the hallway.

As he rounded the corner into the den, he came face to face

with Noah, Rebel, Shadow, Brianna, Liz, and Chaise. "Whoa. What's everyone doing here?"

"It's time, Bull," Noah stated flatly.

"Time for what?"

"It's time for your ass-whooping for dating my sister," Noah replied.

"Okay. I can take it," Bull replied. "I'm not giving her up, though."

Noah smiled. "It's time for your wedding, brother. But tonight, we're having your bachelor party."

"Are you all packed, babe?" Chaise asked.

"Yep. Ready to go. Where are we going again?" Bull asked.

"Nice try." Chaise smirked. "Time to get in the car."

"Okay." Bull nodded and started toward the garage where his truck was parked.

"Not that car," Chaise said. "The one that's out front."

Bull narrowed his eyes at her and walked to the front door. His long, low whistle confirmed that she'd chosen the right transportation.

"Did you pick that out?" he asked.

"Yes, I knew you'd love it."

"I do." He kissed her. "I love you more."

"I love you, too. Let's get on the road," Chaise replied.

Bull carried their bags out to the long, black stretch Hummer limousine that seemed to take up most of the length of his driveway. The driver took the bags from him and placed them in the back with the others.

"Am I the last one to know about this?" Bull asked.

"Yep." Noah grinned and climbed inside. Rebel and Shadow laughed and climbed in behind Noah.

When Bull stuck his head inside, he was shocked by the roomy interior. The long, plush leather seats lined one entire side and wrapped around the back. Strip lights illuminated the smoke-colored mirrors on the ceiling. The minibar was lit and brimming with choices. Shadow was at the elaborate stereo system, flipping through stations and changing the settings to add more bass to the music.

"This Hummer has everything," Bull said enthusiastically. "Move over, Reaper. You're in the way."

"Make yourselves comfortable," the chauffeur spoke over the intercom. "Everything in the vehicle is stocked just for you, so feel free to help yourselves to anything you find. We'll arrive at our destination in approximately four hours. My name is Miles. Just press the button if you need anything at all."

"Four hours?" Bull mouthed.

"That's right," Chaise replied. "Now, relax and enjoy the ride."

He pulled her into his arms. "As long as I'm with you, I don't care where we go," he whispered against her skin.

"That's good, since you're about to be stuck with me for a very long time," she laughed.

"Only forever. That's not nearly enough time with you."

"You're such a sweet-talker."

"That's enough of the lovey-dovey shit," Shadow announced. "I won't be subjected to that kind of cruel and unusual punishment for the next four hours. It's bad enough that I have to endure it for the next few days."

"I think Shadow is jealous," Bull replied. "Never thought I'd see the day."

"You haven't seen the day," Shadow replied. "We're nowhere near that day."

"Is there a Mrs. Shadow in the near future? We really should meet her first, give our approval, that kind of thing," Bull continued. "Make sure she fits in our family."

"There's no future Mrs. Shadow," he replied bluntly. "There's no maybe Mrs. Shadow, or a weekend one, or any other kind of

Mrs. I'm not catching your bouquet—no offense, Chaise—or your garter. I'm not next in line. For-get-it," he stressed each syllable.

Bull's wide smile covered his face and his eyes danced with laughter. "So who is she? How'd you meet her?"

Shadow stared at Bull, expressionless. "I'm not telling you anything."

"That's just mean, Shadow," Bull laughed. "I can help you out. Give you some advice when you need it."

"No."

"Chaise can help your girl, too," Bull volunteered. "She probably could use some help managing you."

"No one manages me," Shadow replied with a furrowed brow.

"That actually explains a lot." Bull smiled triumphantly.

"You shithead," Shadow laughed.

The group of friends and family enjoyed their luxurious limo ride in the best way they knew how—by relentlessly teasing, razzing, and picking on each other the entire time. The four-hour ride flew by and, before they knew it, the driver had turned into the entryway for their destination.

"Where are we anyway?" Bull asked and turned in his seat to look out the windows.

"Surprise!" Chaise exclaimed.

"I feel like a kid," Bull laughed. "Are we seriously getting married here?"

"Yes, we are. Their sign says it all. '*Walt Disney World–Where Dreams Come True*,' because this is where my dreams will come true," Chaise explained.

Bull punched the button for the chauffeur. "Miles, can you stop the car right here? Chaise and I would like to take our picture in front of the sign."

"Yes, sir," Miles replied.

Noah stepped out to take their picture in front of the sign that stretched across three lanes of traffic. As he captured the surreal moment on his phone, he flashed back to the time when his younger sister was still little. The regret over the years he missed in her life was palpable. Brianna immediately noticed the change in him when he got back in the limo.

"What is it?" she asked.

"You can smack me now. I deserve it," he admitted.

"What have you done?"

"I just realized, I mean, *really* realized, that I did the exact same thing to Chaise that I got mad at you for doing to me," he admitted. "But I was out of her life for much longer, and for much more selfish reasons."

"You're here now. You love and support her now. That's what matters," she assured him.

"You're here now. You love and support me. That's all that matters. Just wanted to be sure *you* know that."

"I do," she answered.

"We're here. Get out already," Shadow yelled as he jumped out of the limo.

"Have you ever been here before?" Noah asked.

"No. And you're wasting daylight. Check in, do your business, and let's go," Shadow demanded.

"Hang on a second," Noah replied and Shadow stopped in his tracks. "Chaise, Bull, before we check in, I should tell you that Brianna and I have a surprise for you."

"More than this?" Bull asked.

"In conjunction with this," Noah replied. "We reserved the entire top floor of the Four Seasons Resort for your wedding present. Thought you'd appreciate having some privacy for your honeymoon. We all have suites in this hotel tonight, but you'll move to the Four Seasons after the wedding."

Tears welled up in Chaise's eyes, and she threw her arms

around Noah's neck. He wrapped his arms around her waist and picked her up to hug her. "Thank you so much, Noah. We appreciate it more than words can say."

"You're welcome, baby sis, and congratulations to you both. Bull's getting one hell of a wife," Noah replied.

Bull stepped up to Brianna and enveloped her in a bear hug. "Thank you, my little sister. You and Reaper are the best family a man could ask for. Soon, I'll literally be your brother."

"Bull, whether you knew it or not, you've been my brother from the second I met you in the desert. I couldn't love you more even if you and I shared the same blood," Brianna replied as she hugged him back.

"This is all very touching and beautiful," Shadow interjected. "But need I remind you people—We. Are. At. Disney. World. Move it."

"He's so bossy," Brianna teased.

"Fine. Let's check in, drop our bags off in the rooms, and meet back down in the lobby in thirty minutes," Noah decided.

"Sounds good to me," Liz replied. "I'm ready to have some fun. Can I go to the bachelor party tonight?"

"No," several voices replied in unison.

"Liz, I need you to help me tonight," Chaise explained. "With my bachelorette party."

"You got it, sweet girl." Liz patted her cheek. "It'll be a night you never forget."

They checked in and had the luggage delivered to the rooms, then met in the lobby to make plans for the rest of the day.

"What do you want to do today, Chaise?" Bull asked.

"Actually, I need Brianna and Liz to come with me today to finish up some last-minute wedding shopping. Brianna's sisters will be here later this evening, but it'll be too late by then. Why don't you guys go have fun in the parks, enjoy your bachelor party, and I'll see you back in the room tonight?"

"Will I enjoy this last-minute shopping in our room tonight?" Bull asked seductively.

Chaise laughed. "You never know what I'll find, Colton."

"Sounds good. You ladies be careful and call me every five minutes or so to let me know you're still okay," Bull joked.

"I'm taking custody of Chaise today," Brianna replied. "Don't make me hide her phone so we can spend quality sister-time together."

Once they were separated from the men, Brianna turned to Chaise. "So, wedding dress, veil, bridesmaids' dresses, shoes. Pick out the cake and check on the flowers. What am I missing?"

"Matching shirts and Minnie Mouse ears for my bachelorette outing tonight," Chaise laughed. "This is all so exciting."

"I can't wait to see you in your dress," Brianna exclaimed. "You'll be the most gorgeous bride ever."

"Let's go, ladies," Liz urged. "Sounds like we have a lot to do."

"Brianna," a voice called from across the room. "Oh my gosh, look at you. You're glowing."

When she found the owner of the voice, her eyes grew big and her jaw dropped open. "Missy!"

Missy, Jessie, and Ashley rushed up to Brianna to hug her and rub her pregnant belly. "You look absolutely beautiful," Jessie gushed.

"Liz, these are my sisters." Brianna made quick introductions all around and turned back to her sisters. "What are you three doing here already? I thought you couldn't come until later tonight?"

"Change of plans. Chaise only gets married once, and we don't get to see our sister enough as it is," Missy replied. "So we came down early and we're here to help."

The ladies spent the rest of the day finalizing all the wedding plans and buying matching tank tops for their evening out.

Chaise's tank top was white with "Bride" printed across the front. Brianna and her sisters' tank tops were black with "Bridesmaids."

"Time for your bachelorette party. Though it may not be as fun as it could have been." She patted her stomach. "This kind of limits what I'm able to do."

"I don't need a drunken party, Bri. That's not really my thing anyway. Spending time laughing and being silly with you ladies is plenty enough for me," Chaise replied.

"Let's go then," Missy chimed in. "Everyone have their mouse ears on?"

"I've got mine," Liz replied. "And my tank top."

The ladies burst out into laughter when they saw the tank top Liz wore. "You're our 'Chaperone' tonight?" Chaise asked.

"That's right. I'm the only one trustworthy enough to be in charge of all you girls," Liz replied. "Let's get this show on the road."

"I may have planned our night out, just a little," Jessie admitted. "First stop is dinner reservations, to feed my niece. Then, we're going to the Cirque du Soleil show. The tickets are my treat."

"That's so thoughtful of you, but you didn't have to do that," Chaise replied.

"I just thought it would be easier on Brianna. She's almost seven months pregnant now, she can't drink, and I thought being on her feet for a long time would be too hard on her," Jessie shrugged. "This way, we can all enjoy it."

Brianna hugged her. "You always think of everyone else first. Thank you, Jessie."

As they walked through the park toward the restaurant, the sight of them in matching bridal party tank tops and mouse ears turned many heads. They laughed, talked, and enjoyed their time together. Chaise's thoughts frequently turned to Bull and what he was doing for his bachelor party. When they entered the restaurant, her questions were quickly answered.

"Bull?" Chaise asked and was unable to hold back her laughter.

He shook his head from side to side, his lips drew into a thin line, and he crossed his arms over his chest. "Bastards."

Bull stood in the reservations-only restaurant wearing a bright pink tutu over his shorts, a neon green feather boa around his neck, a top hat with "Groom" written on it, and a genuine ball and chain attached to his ankle.

"Did you lose a bet?" Chaise asked.

"No," he replied curtly. "Not exactly."

"You took a dare," Brianna guessed, and Bull quickly locked away. "Oh my God! You did!"

"That's even worse than losing a bet," Liz stated. "Although I do have to admit you look very handsome in hot pink and lime green."

"Bastards," he muttered under his breath.

"Would you ladies care to join us for dinner? We can ask for our tables to be put together," Noah suggested.

"I'd love that," Brianna replied.

"What else do you boys have planned for tonight?" Liz asked.

"We mysteriously had dinner reservations made for us and tickets to a show delivered to us," Rebel replied. "Know anything about that?"

"I think Jessie knows something about it," Liz replied with a laugh.

"I'm sorry." She smiled, showing she wasn't really sorry at all. "Missy, Ashley, and I just don't get to spend enough time with all of you. I didn't want to be separated for our one night of fun."

"It's all good with me," Noah replied. "We've never been conventional anyway. Why should our bachelor and bachelorette parties be?"

"Your tables are ready," the hostess said. "Follow me."

"Come on, babe." Bull smiled at Chaise. "You can sit by me."

When she wrapped her arm in Bull's, multiple cell phones

emerged at once to snap pictures of them together—Chaise in her "Bride" tank top and wearing ears on her head, and Bull in his "Groom" top hat, neon green feather boa, pink tutu, and carrying his ball and chain.

"Blackmail insurance for later," Shadow said and snapped a few more pictures.

19

CHAPTER NINETEEN

ull walked the streets of the Venice-themed area alone, wearing his white tuxedo, silver vest, and white and silver mingled tie. The day he'd previously never believed would come was actually happening. That very morning, he realized he'd never been happier in his life. The woman he'd never dared to hope for was about to become his wife. Their lifelong commitment had started well before that day, but there was a difference in the air of his wedding day.

"Colt?" a voice called to him.

His head jerked toward the voice and his eyes grew wide. "Mom? Dad?" He rushed to meet them halfway and pulled them into a warm embrace. "I thought you were traveling. What are you doing here?"

"I'd never miss my only son's wedding," his mother, Michelle, replied. "You know me better than that. Besides, it's Christmas week. What better present could you give me than a daughter-in-law?"

"I'm glad you're here, Mom."

"Looking good, son," John said. "Are you nervous?"

"Not at all," Bull replied. "I'm ready to get that ring on her finger before she comes to her senses."

"Chaise loves you, Colt," Michelle replied. "Anyone can see that."

"It's about time to take our places," John said as he looked at his watch.

"I'm ready," Bull replied.

He approached the plaza and noticed the hordes of people standing to the side, watching the small group congregate for the wedding. His parents walked down the white carpet that lined the aisle and took their seats. Brianna's parents, Evan and Diana, arrived next. Liz and Ashley approached and took their seats.

"Any second thoughts?" Noah asked from behind him.

"Not a one," Bull replied. "You have any second thoughts on being my best man?"

"Nope," Noah replied. "I'm honored to be your best man."

"I know Chaise wishes your dad were here to walk her down the aisle. I do too, truthfully."

"Yeah, we all do, including Mom and Dad. But we've got it covered," Noah replied.

Bull nodded. "Rebel okay with it?"

"You know Rebel," Noah replied and left it at that.

The music started, and that was his cue to take his place at the altar and wait for his bride's arrival. He turned to look Noah in the eye before they walked out together. "You're the best friend I could ever ask for. I promise to be the best brother-in-law you could ever ask for."

"You're already the best brother I could ask for, Bull," Noah replied sincerely.

Bull nodded once and turned to walk out of the cover of the buildings and onto the elevated plaza to declare his lifelong love in front of everyone. Family, friends, and strangers would be watching intently when he pledged himself to one woman for all of eternity. They'd listen to his vows and watch him kiss his bride. They'd all know the moment that he and Chaise became one.

And he was more than proud to let them witness this public display of affection.

He walked toward the minister to take his place. Noah, Rebel, and Shadow walked to the staging area where they'd meet the bridal party and escort them down the aisle. Noah's smile grew when he saw Brianna in her bridesmaid gown, an elegant, knee-length rendition of Belle's dress from *Beauty and the Beast*.

"You look very handsome," Brianna complimented him.

"Babe, you look gorgeous in that dress," Noah replied. "I'll be your beast later tonight."

"Ladies and gentlemen, can I get you to line up with your partner right here, please?" the wedding planner asked. "We're starting the bridesmaid procession now."

Jessie and Shadow lined up first, followed by Missy and Rebel, and finally Brianna and Noah. The ladies each held a ribbon-tied bunch of calla lilies that matched the color of their dress.

"Wait until you see your sister," Brianna whispered. "She's the most stunning bride I've ever seen."

"I'm sure she's gorgeous, but I guarantee you were still the most beautiful bride," Noah replied.

"Good reply," she giggled. "You're learning."

"I'm serious," he insisted. When they reached the end of the aisle, Noah leaned over and kissed his wife before they separated.

The bridal march started and everyone waited with bated breath to see Chaise. Especially Bull. He'd watched each of the bridesmaids approach, and he appreciated how they were all beautiful in their own way, but there was only one woman he had eyes for. He held his breath when Brianna took her place and waited for Chaise to make her grand appearance.

The clip-clop of horse's hooves hitting the pavement echoed around the plaza. Heads turned and people watched in amazement as the white pumpkin-shaped carriage stopped at the end of the aisle. A large, intimidating man stepped in front of the carriage door and assisted Chaise as she stepped out of it. Bull craned his neck, trying to see around the man to catch a glimpse of Chaise.

When she stepped into his direct line of sight, he lost his ability to breathe entirely. Her beauty stole his breath, and he couldn't tear his eyes from her. Her ball gown was strapless and formfitting at the top. The bottom was full and the sheer tulle that covered it was sprinkled with glistening sequins and glitter. Her long, dark hair was styled in an updo, revealing her long, graceful neck.

The smile on her face was solely for him.

The man who helped her out of the carriage turned to face Bull, and Chaise wrapped her arm around his. Bull's head jerked toward Noah, but his eyes didn't leave Chaise. "Reap?"

He heard Reaper chuckle. "That's Silas."

"Your brother?"

"The same."

"What are they holding?"

"My parents," Noah replied.

"What?"

When Chaise and Silas got closer, Bull realized what Noah meant. With their arms intertwined, they each held an iPad. Silas held the one that had Steve on FaceTime and Chaise held the one that had Sara. Her plan effectively brought her parents to her wedding. Her father virtually escorted her down the aisle and her mother was also able to be part of their big day.

Chaise handed her iPad off to Liz as she passed so that Sara could continue to watch the event. Everything was going perfectly with her plan. Her brother Silas stood for her father and gave her away in marriage. She'd had to convince him to give her away to a man he'd never met, never approved of, but who'd earned their brother's love and respect over the years.

When they neared the altar, Silas stopped just short of reaching Bull and thoroughly regarded him. The minister seemed to understand Silas's intent and cleared his throat. "Who gives this woman to be married to this man?"

Steve spoke up, his voice loud and sure. "Her mother, her brothers, and I do. We welcome Colton into our family."

Silas remained as motionless as a statue, staring at Bull and obviously considering his options. The few people in attendance, along with everyone who had stopped to watch the ceremony, laughed when Chaise blatantly elbowed Silas in the ribs and made him move. Even Silas, with his naturally unreadable face, smiled and lightly shook his head from side to side.

"You sure about this, baby girl?" Silas whispered, using his nickname for her. "I can still get you out of here."

"Not a chance, big brother," Chaise whispered back. "One more step."

Silas held Chaise's hand in his and took a deep breath before speaking. "You are a beautiful bride, baby girl. I'm so proud to be here with you today, standing in for Dad to help give you away. My wish for you is simple—for you to have all the love and happiness in the world."

Chaise watched with tears glistening in her eyes as Silas placed her hand in Bull's. Only because she knew him so well did she recognize the pain in his eyes. She gave him a small smile, lifted up on her toes, and kissed his cheek. "I love you, Silas."

Silas looked at Bull. "Take care of my baby sister."

"Every day of my life," Bull replied.

Silas gave a quick nod to his brother as an informal "hello" before he moved to take his seat. When he stepped away, the happy couple turned to face the minister. He was an older man with short, salt-and-pepper hair, kind eyes, and a peaceful demeanor. He smiled at Bull and Chaise and began his prepared speech.

"Dear family and friends, on behalf of Colton and Chaise, welcome to their wedding ceremony. We are here today to encourage, support, and celebrate the lifelong commitment these two will pledge before God. Their love is the reason we are here, and it is by that love that they promise to hold fast to one another, regardless of what circumstances life presents tomorrow.

"Colton and Chaise have not entered into this covenant lightly. After talking with them separately earlier today, I've learned that they're both very loyal, they both have a high degree of respect for the other, and they have the love and support of their family and friends. Those are all the ingredients for a very healthy start.

"Colton and Chaise, after forty-five years of marriage, I like to think I'm qualified to give marital advice." He paused for an impactful smile. The guests and onlookers laughed and nodded in agreement. "These five tenets, if you both abide by them, will help make a happy home. Winning an argument isn't worth losing your love. The strongest person is the one who can bend the most. No one is always right, especially you. Forgive and forget, you don't live in the past. Your spouse always comes first.

"Please face each other and hold hands," he instructed. "Colton and Chaise have each written their own vows and would now like to share them with you. Colton, you may begin."

Bull raised Chaise's hands to his mouth and kissed the back of each one. "Chaise, you changed my life for the better the first day I met you. Every day since then, you've shown me the meaning of unconditional love. You've filled my home with the best memories with your smile. You've filled my heart with pride because I call you mine.

"I promise to make you fall in love with me every day. My heart, mind, and body are yours and yours alone. As long as I live, I promise to love, honor, protect, and cherish you. The only tears I'll ever cause you will be tears of joy, happiness, and laughter. You'll never question your place in my life because it'll always be first."

Chaise carefully wiped the tears from her eyes and smiled lovingly at Bull. She knew how hard it must have been for him to say just those few words in front of the growing crowd that had gathered for their wedding. But, as he'd proven so many times before, he honored his commitment and came through for her.

"Chaise, you may begin your vows," the minister prompted.

"Colton, there are no words to describe how happy you make me. I've never felt more loved and protected than when I'm with you. You freely give me your strength, your love, and your trust, holding nothing back. You are my hero, my inspiration, and my love.

"I promise to be faithful and honest in our life together, always putting our love and happiness first. You will be my confidant, my best friend, and my lover through sickness and health, days of plenty and days of want, through good times and bad. I will stand beside you no matter what the day brings. With you by my side, I can face anything."

"Those are beautiful vows, Colton and Chaise. Your personalities both shine through your words," the minister said. "Now, you probably didn't know that your friends have a few words they'd like to say as well."

Bull and Chaise both froze and searched for the words to respond. Noah cleared his throat and began the litany of impromptu vows before either had a chance to react.

"Bull, as your best friend and your best man, I promise to stop threatening to kick your ass for dating my sister. If you leave our family now, I'll have to kill you."

"Bull, I promise to always take Chaise's side in an argument, because we all know you're usually wrong," Rebel added.

"Bull, I promise to use the pictures from your bachelor party as blackmail against you as often as possible," Shadow said.

The crowd erupted in laughter, cheers, and loud clapping after each man recited his vow. Bull and Chaise joined in the good-natured revelry as they laughed and accepted each vow with humility.

"If I'd known this was customary, I would've prepared vows for each of you, too. Let me see what I can do, though.

"Reaper, I promise that you'll leave this family before I willingly leave it. Rebel, I promise that Chaise really doesn't need any help to win an argument with me. And Shadow, I promise that you will suffer daily if those pictures get leaked."

After the renewed laughing, cheering, and clapping died down, the minister continued. "Despite the joking, or maybe I should say because of the joking, the love between all of you is obvious. Some of the best people I've had the privilege of calling family were no blood relation at all. But they support my wife and me, our marriage, our love, and our children. Colton and Chaise, you have that in the people here with you this evening. Never be ashamed to ask them for help when you need it.

"Colton, do you take Chaise to be your lawfully wedded wife, for all the days of your life until you die?" the minister asked.

"I do."

"Chaise, do you take Colton to be your lawfully wedded husband, for all the days of your life until you die?"

"I do."

"Colton, do you have Chaise's ring?" he asked.

Noah handled Bull the wedding band and Bull held it up.

"This small circle symbolizes never-ending love and commitment. It seals your vow that the promises you've made here today have no expiration date. Colton, place the ring on Chaise's finger, and repeat after me."

Bull slid the ring on her finger and lovingly stroked her hand with his thumb. His eyes never left hers as he repeated the words.

"This ring is a token from my heart. It symbolizes my desire for you to be mine, and for me to be yours, from this day forward, until we both shall die. Just as this ring is eternal, so is my love. With this ring, I thee wed."

"Chaise, do you have Colton's ring?"

Brianna gave Chaise Bull's wedding band. She slid the ring on his finger and repeated the same words back to Bull.

"By the power vested in me by the state of Florida, the world of Walt Disney, and the magic of Mickey, I now pronounce you husband and wife. You may now kiss the bride." The minister smiled.

"Finally!" Bull yelled. He wrapped his arms around Chaise, picked her up off the ground, and covered her mouth with his. The sound of multiple throats clearing behind him finally caught his attention and he reluctantly released her back to her spot.

"Wow—I'm not sure my legs will hold me up now," Chaise laughed.

"I'll always be here to carry you," Bull replied.

"It is my pleasure to now present Mr. and Mrs. Colton Lanier. They've asked that you join them for their reception just across the footbridge on the private terrace. Congratulations to the happy couple!"

Everyone moved to the private terrace while Bull, Chaise, and the bridal party had professional photos taken. The staff strategically placed the iPads at the reception so that Steve and Sara had an unobstructed view of the entire party. When Bull and Chaise finally joined the party, the band began playing to give them the first dance.

"I picked this song—just for you," Bull said as he pulled Chaise into his arms. They began to sway to "Amazed" by Lonestar, and he sang the lyrics to her in whispered tones. With every step, he felt her meld with him. She gripped him tightly and sighed with every verse he sang to her.

"Can I interest you in a honeymoon suite at the Four

Seasons? The entire top floor happens to be reserved just for two people. We can make as much noise as we want," she whispered her proposition to him when the song ended.

"It's time to go. Everyone go home now," Bull announced loudly.

"No, you don't, young man," Bull's mom chastised him. "We still have a lot of pictures to take tonight."

Bull grinned because he knew that was the response he'd receive from at least one of the ladies.

"And you haven't cut the cake yet. And Chaise hasn't danced with Noah, your dad, or my dad yet," Brianna added. "So zip it."

"Ah, tell the truth, Sunny. You just want to dance with me," Bull replied.

"I'll dance with you," Liz answered for Brianna. "Your dance card will be full all night."

"I get the first dance with Chaise," Silas's deep voice called from behind them. "Get in line, boys."

"Silas." Chaise smiled. "You really should officially meet my husband now. Colton, Silas. Silas, Colton."

"Bull," he replied. "Only Chaise and my mom call me Colton."

Silas shook his hand. "Chaise has told me a lot about you since I arrived this morning. It seems like I've known you for years now."

"We've been trying to reach you for a while now. How'd she find you?" Noah asked.

"Mom got a message to me," Silas answered. "I've been deep undercover and couldn't risk contacting anyone until the case was over."

"So you're out now?" Chaise asked. "For good?"

"For this case, baby girl," Silas replied. "It'll be a while before I take another undercover case, though."

The band moved on to the next song and Silas smiled at

Chaise. "I think they're playing our song. May I have this dance?"

"Of course," she replied. She turned to Bull and kissed his lips. "Now's a good time for you to dance with Brianna."

"Don't mind if I do." Bull smiled and took Brianna's hand. "Come on, little sister, dance with me."

The four walked onto the dance floor and started their dance. The sun had set, and the lights strung around the terrace illuminated the dance floor. The flash from several cameras cast more light on the two couples as they laughed and swayed to the music. When Noah couldn't stand it any longer, he cut in on Silas for his turn with Chaise. Silas, in turn, cut in on Bull to officially meet his sister-in-law.

"They miss you," Brianna told Silas. "They've spoken of you often. Especially since we found out about Steve's cancer."

"They're good kids" Silas replied. "It's best that I don't contact anyone when I'm undercover. Besides putting them in danger, I'm just not a nice person when I'm in character. But I'm back now, so I'll be around so much, they'll wish I was back undercover."

They danced, ate, drank, and enjoyed each other's company until the park closed for the night. Then they took their party to the reserved top floor of the swanky hotel. The floor consisted of a nine-bedroom suite, a four-bedroom suite, plus eight additional guest rooms outside the suites. Chaise walked from room to room, gawking at the amenities and the view the picturesque windows afforded.

"Noah, this is too much," she said. "You didn't have to do all this for us."

"I wanted you to have the fairy-tale wedding and the fairy-tale honeymoon you've always dreamed of. You deserve it, Chaise," he replied. "I remember you always said you'd get married at Disney when you were a little kid."

"I did," she laughed. "I never dreamed it would be like this, though."

"It is amazing."

"Thank you so much for everything you've done," she hugged him. "I love you, Noah."

"I love you, too. I only want you to be happy."

"I am. So very happy."

20

CHAPTER TWENTY

Turan paced in the cell he'd been held in for what felt like several days. But in reality, it was more likely that it had been only a couple of days. There were no windows anywhere, so it was impossible for him to accurately gauge time. In fact, he was almost positive that he was deep underground in a basement somewhere. The agents who'd delivered him there wouldn't answer any of his demands to know what would happen to him. His aggravation from being at their mercy was at an all-time high, and he needed to release his pent-up energy.

However, the four walls that contained him disagreed.

One of the CIA agents opened the thick steel door to his solitary confinement and slid the barred gate across the floor until it locked into place. "Now, let's have a talk," the agent said as he sat.

"What do you want, pig?"

"You've been very busy lately. Want to tell me what you've been doing?"

Turan laughed smugly. "I don't know what you're talking

about. I'm an innocent diplomatic worker. You've got the wrong man—again. Seems to be a pattern for you."

He smiled at Turan. "Your choirboy act doesn't fly with me, Turan. I can keep you here for as long as it takes for you to decide to talk. My job says I can do whatever it takes to get you to talk."

"I'm not scared of you, pig."

Turan would never admit to anything. He knew he was a genius with the computer. He could break into secure systems others could only dream of accessing. He'd already proven it, but no one knew yet. He'd built somewhat of a safeguard into the last private network he'd accessed. If anything happened to him, the program would launch itself after seven days of inactivity.

"Have it your way." His smile didn't reach his eyes. His eyes seemed to change between warm and cold with the flip of an internal switch.

The CIA agent rolled the bars back into the wall and stared at Turan with a look that was all too familiar—he had the cold eyes of a killer. Turan was caught in his own thoughts momentarily and missed the agent's discreet movements as he slid the brass knuckles onto his fingers. The loud thwack of the metal hitting bone rang in Turan's ears before he realized his cheekbone was on fire. Turan stumbled backward, lost his balance, and landed on the floor.

Heavy, steel-toed boots repeatedly pounded his ribs, stomach, and back. He curled into a fetal position, trying to protect his head with his arms, but the bruising boots were relentless. Warm blood flowed from his busted nose, the metallic taste of blood filled his mouth, and he realized he was becoming numb. His body was shutting down.

Hands reached under his arms and around his ankles, picked him up, and placed him on something that felt harder than his bed. He was dizzy from the beating and disoriented from the blows to his head, but he knew he was being moved. *A gurney, maybe?* Cool air flowed over his injuries and made him shiver. He tried to open his eyes to see where he was and what he faced, but they were just so heavy.

"Clean him up and put him back in his cell. We'll continue when he feels better," the agent snickered.

Time passed, but Turan only drifted in and out of consciousness. It could've been hours or it could've been days, he wasn't sure. When he had brief moments of lucidity, he thought he'd felt a pinprick, but then he was quickly out again. Through the fog and haze in his mind, he realized they must have drugged him to keep him quiet. He carefully lifted one eyelid to determine where he was being held.

He was alone in his cell again. He slowly sat up on the side of the cot and waited for the dizziness to pass. When he was sure he could stand, he walked to the sheet of reflective stainless steel that served as his mirror. His wounds had been cleaned and looked better than he'd thought they would. He estimated he'd been out about three days from the appearance of his injuries.

His tray suddenly slid through the small opening at the bottom of the door, and he rushed to the window.

"Hey!" he screamed. "How long are you keeping me here? Don't I get a phone call or something?"

"No, you don't," a voice replied.

It was the only voice he'd heard since he'd arrived there besides the CIA agent who continually harassed him. The few people he'd seen refused to speak to him for any reason. The one who brought his food simply opened a small door at the bottom of the door and slid his tray inside. The two people who picked up his trays every evening didn't acknowledge his existence.

"What's happening? When will I get to go home?" he asked.

"You're not going home," the man said as he approached the steel door. He stopped to look Turan in the eye through the window as he finished, "Ever."

Turan's eyes flew open wide, his jaw dropped, and he struggled to find the words to say. "Rashad." A name was all he could manage.

"You seem surprised," Rashad replied.

"I am. I don't understand what's happening," Turan replied.

"What's happening?" Rashad mused. "You've continually screwed up, not paid attention to what's going on around you, and followed your own agenda. You've put the needs of the brotherhood last on your insignificant quest for your own revenge. That's what's happening."

"Are you working for the Americans?" Turan asked in his attempt to catch up.

Rashad released a sarcastic laugh. "No."

"They work for you?"

"I gave you a chance, Turan. You were released. You could've arranged safe passage out of the country, or even just stopped your foolishness. But I had to accept that you wouldn't stop until you'd ruined all of us."

"So what happens now?"

"Now, *I* move forward with our original plans. For *you*, now is all there is," Rashad replied. "Goodbye, Turan."

Rashad turned and walked away while Turan called his name after him, increasing in volume and intensity with each breath. Rashad left the building and placed a call on his burner phone.

"In the next two weeks," he said and hung up.

No further explanation was needed. It bothered Rashad that he'd secretly feared he wouldn't be able to say the words. If his men knew he held a soft spot for Turan, they would question his leadership skills. If they questioned his leadership skills, he'd automatically lose his position and, with it, his life. His clipped commands at least gave the illusion of control and decisiveness.

He dragged his hands over his face and through his hair. Anger filled him at being put in this predicament in the first place. "Why should I feel guilty for the problems he causes?" Rashad asked aloud. "It's not my fault. I've *told* him."

He looked back at the plain building and made peace with his decision. "Goodbye, Turan. Until we meet again."

~

"I don't want to be the one to call him," Brad insisted.

"You have to call him. You have to explain what you found," Roman replied and secretly smirked inside. He was just glad he wasn't the one who was going to interrupt Reaper on his Christmas vacation for his sister's wedding.

"Damned if I do, damned if I don't," Brad said solemnly.

"Ah, come on. Reaper's not unreasonable. Trust me, he'll want to know about this. You'll be better off telling him now than waiting until later," Roman assured him.

"Here goes nothing," Brad replied and picked up the phone.

After a few rings, Reaper picked up and Brad readied himself for the conversation.

"Steele."

"Reaper, this is Brad. Hate to bother you on your vacation, but I found something I thought you'd want to know about."

"Let's have it."

"Roman brought Turan's laptop back for me to have a look at what he's been up to. He'd hacked in to the Air Force's drone control center and set it up to launch if he hadn't logged in to the system in the previous seven days. I've found a way to disable it, but I'm frankly alarmed that he was able to do that at all," Brad explained.

"What was the drone programmed to do when it launched?"

"It was to launch a fully armed MQ-9 Reaper drone to fire on Miami. Think it's a coincidence he chose the Reaper?"

"Not at all," he replied. "I'll contact Commander Adkins and give him a heads-up. I'm sure there will be several agencies interested in hearing what you've found. Good job, Brad."

"Thank you. Sorry to bother you."

"Don't be. It's all good. I'd rather know what's going on than not know," Reaper said. "And if I don't talk to you again this week, have a Merry Christmas."

"Thanks, Reap. You, too," Brad replied before they disconnected.

"What was that about?" Brianna asked Noah.

"Our friend Turan is one slippery bastard," Noah replied and then relayed the conversation to the group.

"I told you he needed more shocks," Liz said to Shadow. "You should've listened to me."

"I'm not sure how that would've helped this situation, Liz," Shadow replied.

"It would've made me feel better. That's how," she replied.

Silas stared at Shadow and Liz, trying to decide which one was crazier. Liz, for the things she said, or Shadow, for continuing to try to talk sense into her. "Is your guy alerting anyone?" Silas asked Noah.

"No. I'm going to call Commander Adkins and brief him now. He can run it up the chain," Noah replied. "I'll be right back."

When Noah left the room, Silas watched his retreating back intently. When Noah closed the door, Silas stood and walked around the room until he was positioned just outside of it. He heard as Noah asked for the commander and said he'd hold. Silas feigned interest in the artwork that hung outside the bedroom in the elaborate suite.

"Silas, how long has it been since you were able to be yourself for Christmas?" Shadow asked.

"Too many years to count," he replied vaguely.

"Yeah, I'll bet it's rough when the years start blurring into one," Shadow replied. "How long were you undercover for this last case?"

"About three years," he replied, purposefully keeping his answers short. The last thing he wanted right then was to encourage a long-winded conversation.

"Do you usually jump from one case immediately into the next?" Shadow persisted.

"We have a mandatory decompression time in between," Silas answered and noted he'd let his irritation slip through his cool façade.

"I bet you've had to drastically change your appearance before, huh?"

Silas turned and completely faced Shadow. "Yeah."

Noah walked out of the bedroom, slipped his phone into his pocket, and stopped when he saw the stare-down between his brother and one of the men he considered his brother. "What's going on?"

"Nothing." Shadow smiled in triumph but didn't move his gaze from Silas. "Just talking with your brother about undercover work."

"I'm sure you two have plenty of stories to share," Noah replied.

"How's that?" Silas asked.

"I'm former CIA," Shadow replied.

Silas looked disgusted and glared at Shadow. "Is that right?"

"Get everything squared away?" Shadow asked Noah.

"Yeah, turned it over to Commander Adkins. He's scheduling a meeting with the Joint Chiefs to brief the President," Noah replied.

"Good. Let them handle it. We're out of the mix now," Shadow replied and cut his eyes to Silas.

"Couldn't agree more," Noah replied.

Silas left Noah and Shadow and walked off to his room

alone. When he was out of earshot, Noah crossed his arms over his chest and quirked one eyebrow up at Shadow. "Let's have it."

"What?"

"Don't what me. You've never tried to get out of a mission before, never handed it off to someone else to finish. What's the deal?" Noah demanded.

"After all the years we've worked together, I never thought I'd have to ask you this," Shadow started. "But if it comes down to it and you have to choose, whose side would you pick? Mine—or your brother's?" Shadow asked.

"Why would I have to pick sides between you and my brother?"

"Trust me when I say I recognize the signs of a spy. Your brother isn't here only for Chaise's wedding. I don't know what his angle is, but you need to be prepared to make that choice when the time comes," Shadow replied.

Noah nodded. "Understood."

He walked to Brianna and took his seat next to her, but his mind was a million miles away. Faced with a problem he'd never even considered, he decided to do a little digging of his own. His first interrogation subject was Sara, his mother. He pulled out his phone and tapped a quick text to her. When his phone alerted him of the response, part of him didn't want to look.

Noah: Meant to ask earlier, how'd you finally get ahold of Silas?

Sara: I didn't. He called me.

Noah closed his eyes and contemplated his next move. Now that he'd confirmed the first lie, he knew he had to keep digging.

Noah: Didn't realize he called you that often.

Sara: He doesn't. This was out of the blue. Perfect timing. J

Noah stared at the text for longer than he should have. The others were busy watching TV, talking, or napping, but Brianna could read him like a book. He felt her fingers in his hair before she started to play with the top of his ear. He couldn't help but smile. *Of all the body parts she has to choose from, she picks my ears to play with,* he mused.

"Something's wrong," she stated. "I know you."

He handed his cell phone to her and let her read the message. Her natural inclination to ask probing questions would kick in as soon as she read it, and she'd know exactly where his mind was. She looked up, and when her eyes met his, he knew that she completely understood what he faced.

"What are you going to do?" she asked, understanding thick in her voice.

"The only thing I can do. I'm going to confront him."

"I'll go with you, if you want. For no other reason than to support you, but I'll be by your side," she replied.

"I love you," he answered. "But I don't want you there if it turns ugly."

"Now I'm going for sure."

"Bri." He looked down at her protruding belly. "If anything happened to you or the baby, I'd go to prison."

"Fine. Just know one thing—that excuse will only work for so long. If anything happens to you, I can't be held accountable for my actions."

He chuckled at her bravado. "I'd expect nothing less from you, babe." Before he got up, he leaned in and kissed her passionately. "Wait here. I'll be back."

Shadow watched Noah rise and leave the room. He felt eyes on him and turned to see Brianna pinning him with her stare. She raised her eyebrows and inclined her head toward the door Noah had just walked through. When he didn't move fast enough, she mouthed the word *"Go!"* and made a jerking motion with her thumb stuck out. Shadow bit his lip to keep from laughing out loud and silently rose from the couch.

He stepped into the hallway outside the suite and instantly

heard raised voices. He moved quietly toward the door and listened to the conversation.

"You lied to me, and I know it," Noah yelled.

"What does it matter how I got here? The point is I'm here," Silas dodged.

"No, that's not the point, and you know it."

"What are you asking me, Noah?"

"Are you working this case behind my back? Are you still undercover?"

"What makes you think that?"

"Stop answering my questions with a question. Be a man. Hell, be a *brother*. Answer me," Noah roared.

There was dead silence and Shadow readied himself to kick the door down. If he was correct in his assumption about Silas, there would be one hell of a fight but there was no way Silas would fight fair. Even with his brother. Shadow wouldn't take any chances with Noah's life.

"I think you'd better leave now," Silas replied. He was a little too calm and collected in Shadow's opinion.

"No, Silas. I think *you'd* better leave now. I'm afraid you've worn out your welcome," Noah replied.

"You really want to do that to Chaise during her honeymoon? And to Mom and Dad during Christmas, when they're already going through enough?" Silas replied.

Shadow knew Silas had used the only tactic that would get to Noah. He waited for the reply from Noah that was inevitable. Not that he blamed him, but he knew that Silas was only using their family as leverage over Noah. That was something that Noah would never do.

"Maybe you should've thought about that before you made us part of your undercover case without our knowledge. We work in dangerous conditions all the time, but we work as a team. One doesn't run off half-cocked and get us all killed. This is my family you're putting in danger. Two of them are your sister and your brother-in-law, not to mention your sister-in-law and your niece, but none of that seems to matter to you," Noah shouted. "Mom and Dad would be *ashamed* of you."

Shadow was pleasantly surprised at Noah's response. "You go, brother."

"Wait," Silas finally answered.

Shadow pictured Noah standing at the door with his hand on the knob, prepared to drop the bomb on the family and out Silas. Because they were family, Noah would give Silas one more chance to make things right. If Silas was smart and could read people at all, he'd take that chance.

"Have a seat," Silas continued. "Let's talk."

21

CHAPTER TWENTY-ONE

"Good morning," the nurse called as she entered the room. "How's my favorite patient today?"

"I bet you say that to all of your patients," Steve answered with a smile.

She stopped and dramatically dropped her bottom jaw. "I can't believe you'd say such a thing to me," she chastised him playfully. "And on New Year's Eve of all days." She *tsked* him and then giggled. "How are you feeling today, Steve?"

"I actually feel better today. I'm hopeful that the treatments are working. I can tell a difference in my energy level over the last few days."

"That's great. What about your diet? Are you eating well? Keeping your food down?" she probed.

"This week has been much better for that. I've eaten more and gotten to keep it down for the most part."

"The lab tech will be in this morning to draw blood. As soon as those results are ready, the doctor will be in to talk to you. Do you need anything while I'm here?" she asked.

"A sixteen-ounce T-bone steak, medium, loaded baked potato, salad with ranch dressing, and a large sweet tea," he joked.

She pretended to write it down on her hand. "Got it. You wait right here for me to bring it back to you."

This had been their daily game since Steve was admitted to the hospital a few days before Christmas. Sara and Steve still hadn't told their children that he'd had a reaction to the first dose of medication and had to be hospitalized. Dr. Stanton adjusted the amounts, and Steve better tolerated the treatment afterward. The lab work would tell them if the adjusted dosage was working. If not, they would have to start from square one again.

"Thank you, Heather," Steve replied. "You're the best nurse. You always make me smile. Can you work every day? Nurse Allison is the devil."

Heather tried to keep from laughing at Steve's comment. The harder she tried, the more impossible it became. "Okay, I'll give you that one. If you need anything, just hit the button. I'll be back to check on you in a bit."

"Will do." He smiled.

Steve couldn't bring himself to tell Silas, Noah, and Chaise about it during her honeymoon and their Christmas vacation. When he'd virtually walked Chaise down the aisle, he was sitting in the hospital room praying no one would notice the wall behind him. He'd sat on the side of his hospital bed wearing a suit jacket, shirt, and tie, and propped the iPad up on the tray table. He'd refused to eat anything that day in hopes that he wouldn't become ill again. He'd made it through the ceremony and partly through the reception before he'd disconnected and let exhaustion overtake him.

But on that particular day, he'd noticed a marked improvement in his energy and his appetite. He could finally joke about food without it turning his stomach. He could smell food without his skin turning a bright shade of green. At last, he dared to hope that the treatments were working, and he'd soon be free of the cancer that had taken up residence in his body.

Throughout the day, Heather checked on him several times and brought his next dose of chemotherapy. His breath still hitched in his chest every time they hung the bag of IV fluids that contained his life-giving, cancer-killing toxins. Sara returned from her day of pampering that Steve insisted she do for herself.

"How's my favorite husband?" Sara asked. It had become a joke by extension that started after Heather asked about her favorite patient. The playfulness of the simple question helped make them both feel better about the situation.

"I'll ask him when he comes out of the bathroom," Steve quipped.

"Oh, look who has a sense of humor today. You must be feeling pretty good," Sara said enthusiastically.

"Sara, I really do. I'm afraid to say it out loud, but I'm actually convinced my labs will come back with positive news," he replied.

"I agree. So let it be said, so let it be done," she replied.

"You look beautiful, babe," he said as she took her seat beside his bed. "I can't wait to get out of here."

"Thank you," she replied sweetly. "I can't wait for you to get out of here either. I miss sleeping with you."

"When this is over, you won't be getting any sleep for a long time."

"Steve," she gasped. "I kind of like this side of you. Can we get some of that medicine to go?"

He laughed heartily. "If that's what it takes."

"I heard from Chaise today. They're back home, settling in to married life like they've been married for years," Sara told him. "Colton talked to me for a little while, too. I can see why Chaise loves him so much. He's really a great guy."

"It'll be nice to have everyone over for birthdays, holidays, and Tuesdays," Steve replied wistfully.

"Tuesdays?"

"Yes, Tuesday doesn't get enough attention. It's the forgotten weekday, and it needs to be celebrated. We'll have all the kids over every Tuesday," he decided.

Sara stared at him dumbfounded for several seconds. "Who is this man, and what have you done with my husband?"

"I've replaced him with the new and upgraded version. We'll have Super-Steve-Tuesdays from now on. It's part of my new leaf. So, what else did Chaise have to say?"

"She asked about you, of course. I still didn't tell her that you're in the hospital. They won't be happy when they find out," she replied.

"We'll tell them one way or another when my labs come back. We'll know more then. Is Silas still home?"

"Yes, he is. I've never known him to stay put for so long. When he comes home between cases, he's usually there no longer than two or three days before leaving out again."

"Maybe he's getting out of it and planning to stay home for good now. It's time for him to settle down anyway. He's been on so many undercover operations, he has to be risking crossing paths with the same people again," Steve replied, worry etched in his expression.

"Wouldn't that be wonderful, Steve? To have all of our kids and grandkids close to us?"

"It definitely would be."

"I'm never speaking to you again, so don't even start," Chaise yelled at Silas.

"I've apologized a hundred times. What more do you want me to do?"

"Well, I don't know, Silas. I've never used my sister's wedding to spy on my siblings and see what they're up to. I haven't put my family's lives in jeopardy without even telling them. And I've never hurt my brothers the way you've hurt me. So you tell me, Silas. How do you make up for something like that?"

"Baby girl, I'd never let anything happen to you."

She whirled around to face him with fire shooting out of her eyes. "That's the difference between us, Silas. I'm not thinking of only myself. My husband was there. Noah and Brianna were there, too. She's pregnant, Silas. And everyone else who I love and who has helped me through some really hard times was also there. You used all of us. How could you do that?"

His lack of response only infuriated Chaise even more.

"You're not my brother. I don't know you anymore. Is this what years of pretending to be someone else has done to you? Is the Silas I love dead and gone, only to be replaced by someone who treats his family the same way he treats criminals?"

Chaise walked away and left Silas standing alone on Noah's deck. Her words cut him to the quick, and he realized that was the first time he'd felt anything in a very long time. He turned to follow her, to try to talk to her again, but stopped when he realized he wasn't alone.

"Did Chaise ever tell you how we met?" Bull asked.

"No."

Bull nodded and his gaze drifted to just over Silas's shoulder as he remembered that day. "She was in trouble, and she was looking for Noah. She came to his wedding, lurked in the shadows, and we cornered her as soon as Noah and Brianna were safely on their way to the airport.

"She was in trouble with some very bad men who were running drugs and selling girls as sex slaves. They wanted her to join the ranks of women who had disappeared. After meeting her, I knew there was no way in hell I'd let anyone hurt her. The leader of this group had her brought to his island home. He was determined to make her his personal sex slave for a while before he disposed of her. One of his guys roughed her up pretty good on the way to deliver her to the boss. Then, the guy's father wanted to take his revenge out on me by killing Chaise.

"You're probably wondering why I'm sharing all of this with you right now. I'll be glad to tell you." Bull took a step toward Silas. "I don't give a flying fuck if you're her brother, Noah's brother, or Steve and Sara's son. If Chaise gets hurt because you're too stupid to realize that even undercover cops get tailed, I'll kill you just like I did those other bastards."

Bull stared him down, willing him to make a move or say the wrong thing, but Silas looked too shocked to do either. "I never knew she was in trouble like that."

"Can't say that I'm surprised about that," Bull replied bluntly.

"How did she get dragged into that?"

"She was trying to find a missing girl."

"I need to talk to her. To apologize."

"You've done that. Now you need to leave her alone. You hurt her when you brought this to our wedding but didn't have the balls to tell us you're still working undercover. She trusted you. Saying you're sorry doesn't build that trust back," Bull stated and walked away.

Silas walked into the house and found Noah and Shadow in the office. "Can I talk to you for a minute?" Silas asked Shadow.

"Sure."

They walked back to the deck and closed the sliding glass door behind them. Silas walked to the edge of the pool and stared down into the water as he spoke. "I don't know how to be myself anymore. I think I lost myself to the job years ago. How did you make it back?"

"I never totally lost touch with the people who keep me

grounded. Even if they didn't realize I was watching them, living vicariously through them. With every decision I made, I asked myself how it would look if I had to explain my actions to them one day," Shadow replied.

"Who are they? The people who keep you grounded?" Silas asked.

"Reaper, Bull, and Rebel," Shadow replied. "Brianna has been like my little sister for years, and I also watched over her when she didn't know."

"How do I turn this around?"

"Start by telling them the truth about what you know."

Silas looked up at Shadow and immediately knew he was right. He also knew that Shadow had an uncanny ability to see through him. He was as transparent as glass to this man. "You know what it means when I do that."

"I know what it means if you stay with the CIA any longer."

Silas started to deny his involvement with the agency, but the *"spare me"* expression on Shadow's face convinced him otherwise. "I'll be lost forever," he confirmed.

"It's not worth it, man. Trust me," Shadow counseled him. "It's much better to work on this side of the fence."

"What happens when I leave?"

"You never really leave the CIA, Silas."

"I've heard that saying for years, but I finally understand what it means."

"Now, don't you have some news on Turan that you need to share with us?"

"Why do I get the feeling you already know what news I have?" Silas narrowed his eyes at Shadow.

"Why do you answer my questions with a question? Why is the ocean salty when fresh water flows into it? Why do women need so many shoes? These are the questions that keep me up at night," Shadow responded.

"Fine. Let's go talk Turan," Silas agreed as he rubbed his head. "It's easier to keep up with than your line of thinking."

"Both of you boys could take lessons from me," Liz stated from behind them. "You're far too gabby to be a spy. I wouldn't even have to give either of you any sodium pentothal to get you to tell all your secrets. Take me, for example. My mind is a steel trap, an impenetrable fortress. You'd never get me to spill all my secrets."

"Liz, for the last time," Shadow spoke slowly. "I'm not falling for your bait and teaching you the tricks of the trade for you to use on some poor, unsuspecting soul."

"Shadow," Liz barked. "I need to be trained. It's a matter of national security."

"I'm positive that it's safer for national security if you're never trained in our methods. Ever," Silas replied.

Liz stood from her chair, straightened her clothes out, and looked Silas in the eye. "Young man," she started. "I can make your life hell in ways that you've never imagined. Don't test me."

With that, she walked back into the house and slammed the sliding door shut behind her. Silas and Shadow burst out in laughter and followed in her footsteps. When they reached the door, they realized that Liz had locked them outside.

"We can either bang loudly on the door and admit that Liz locked us out," Shadow said. "Or we can go over the fence, around the house, and back in the front door."

"Front door," Silas replied quickly.

"Agreed," Shadow said. "Then we never speak of this again."

"Never."

"So good of you boys to join us," Liz yelled as Shadow and Silas walked in the front door. "What took you so long?"

"We just took a walk," Shadow replied nonchalantly.

"Over the fence, around the house, and to the front door?" Liz asked. Snickers came from every direction around the room, but no one would make eye contact.

"I have some information to share with everyone," Silas announced and changed the subject.

"We're listening," Noah replied.

"Turan was found dead in his cell today," he announced. When it was obvious that he had the undivided attention of the room, he continued. "The medical examiner is doing an autopsy, but there were no obvious signs of injury reported. With his age, it's highly unlikely that it was from natural causes."

"Do you think someone took their questioning techniques too far?" Brianna asked.

"From what I've been told, that doesn't appear to be the reason. There were no marks on his body."

"Waterboarding doesn't leave marks, and people can die from it," she retorted.

Silas looked at her with a newfound respect for her boldness. "That's true," he said. "But waterboarding is illegal now."

"I'm sure those little technicalities stop you from using that form of questioning," Brianna replied sardonically.

"You have a point," he admitted. "He could've died from that, but I have no reason to think that. My gut tells me it's something far worse."

"Like what?" Noah asked.

"I think his cell turned on him and killed him."

"His cell turned on him?" Liz asked incredulously. "Are you one of those agents who the government did all those crazy tests on? His cell couldn't come to life and kill him."

"What? No. I meant his terrorist group, the other members of his terrorist cell," Silas replied. "Not his holding cell."

Liz gave him her evil smile to remind him of her cleverly veiled threat.

"How would they get to him in there?" Rebel asked.

"Their arm is very long. I know they have agents on their payroll, but I haven't been able to find out who they are yet."

"Why do you think it was his cell?" Rebel asked.

"Because the man I worked for in my undercover role was named Rashad. He spoke of Turan frequently, usually to curse the day he was born because Turan kept pursuing his own goals instead of the group's goal," Silas replied. "The group is geared more to causing anarchy and terror in the masses. They want to bring America to her knees."

"What did Turan want?" Noah asked.

"To bring one man to his knees."

"Me," Rebel replied.

"I believe that's correct," Silas replied. "For killing his father."

"So that was his father." Rebel nodded. "He looked a lot like his dad. They didn't have the same name, though."

"His distant uncle took him to Turkey and raised him. Hid his Iranian descent as much as he could. He taught Turan everything he knew—kid was like a sponge when it came to computers. The cell loved that because most everything in this country is managed by some kind of computer now," Silas explained. "He used 'Ali' because it means exalted. Babek and Turan are areas of Turkey and Iran that he associated his heritage with; the names meant something to him."

"Do you know who and where the other members of the cell are?" Bull asked.

"No. I'm obviously American, so there's a lot of information that Rashad wouldn't trust me with. I was supposed to come here and get close to all of you and then report back to Rashad with your weaknesses, where he could hit you hardest," Silas admitted.

"So, I hopped on a plane and showed up at Chaise's wedding, with the approval of the CIA. I've since realized that they must have known Shadow was part of this group, he'd see straight through me with his training, and that he'd set me straight. That's the story I choose to believe anyway.

"Telling you all of this means I now have to leave the CIA and this undercover life. And that actually puts all of you in even more danger. When Rashad figures out who I really am, he'll come after all of us."

22

CHAPTER TWENTY-TWO

"When he comes after us, he'll have one hell of a fight on his hands. We don't go down easily," Brianna said as she stood. "You have our back, we'll have yours, Silas. We're a family, and there's always room for one more."

"I'm relearning what it means to be a family, Brianna," Silas replied. "Hell, I'm relearning what it means to be *myself*."

"I don't remember you having a hard time assimilating into real life, Shadow," Rebel replied.

Silas and Shadow chuckled. "Yeah, I asked him about that," Silas admitted. "Seems he had some pretty damn good reasons to keep his head on right."

"What reasons, Shadow?" Brianna asked.

"You," Shadow replied. "And Reaper, Bull, and Rebel. You didn't know it, but I had my ways to stay close to all of you while I was undercover."

"Even while I was in Boulder?" Brianna asked.

"No, not then. But I was at your funeral," Shadow replied and cut his eyes to Reaper. "I was always there."

"Since you were able to help Shadow so much, I have every reason to believe you'll have no problem putting me in my rightful place." Silas smiled.

"Of course," Liz replied. "Especially now that I'm here. I'll be glad to put you in your place every damn day."

"I have no doubt about that, Liz," Silas laughed. "I want to be the best brother, uncle, and friend I can be."

Chaise had been silent through the entire discussion and that worried Silas. He was concerned that she wouldn't forgive him, regardless of what he did. He'd betrayed her trust and used her love to help his case. He couldn't blame her for being upset with him because he was furious with himself over it.

"Chaise?" His voice held the sadness his heart felt. He'd never considered how much his actions would hurt her.

She stood and rushed into his arms. She hugged him tightly and her tears flowed down her face. "I love you, Silas. I've missed you so much."

"I've missed you, baby girl. I didn't even realize how much until I saw you. It's been way too long. I'm so sorry. Please forgive me," he pleaded.

She nodded and squeezed him tighter. "You're forgiven."

"So what's the plan to draw Rashad out?" Rebel asked.

Silas released Chaise and looked at Rebel. "I don't think it'll take much once he realizes I'm not coming back."

"What makes you think he hasn't already followed you here?" Bull asked.

"He may have; that's a very real possibility. He obviously already knows who you guys are because of Turan, but he doesn't know about my relation to Noah and Chaise. If he had known about that when I worked for him, I'd already be dead," Silas replied.

Chaise's cell phone started ringing and she glanced at the display. "It's Mom," she announced. "Hey, Mom... Yeah, we're all here... Sure. Just a second.

"I'm putting Mom on speaker so she can give us all the news at once," Chaise told the room. "Okay, go ahead, Mom."

"Hello, everyone. Sorry to interrupt your team meeting, but I thought you'd want the latest update on Steve," Sara said.

"Yes, we do," Noah replied. "Tell us what's going on."

Sara explained that Steve had been in the hospital for the past couple of weeks and why. The group wasn't happy with them for not sharing that information earlier, but they had to agree that they understood why.

"So that brings me to what's happened now," Sara said. "Dr. Stanton just came in with the lab results and…"

She paused deliberately for dramatic effect.

"Mom!" Chaise yelled. "Tell us."

"The new treatment is working," she shrieked. "His blood work looked good, so they took him down and did an X-ray. The tumors are shrinking!"

"That's amazing," Noah replied. "Mom, that's incredible news."

"It really is," Sara sniffled. "We still have a long way to go to finish the treatment, but we'll take every piece of good news we can get."

Sara put Steve on the phone, and they talked for a while longer. The good news was very welcome, especially in light of the topic they'd been discussing. When they hung up, Noah and Silas faced each other.

"I'm sorry I wasn't a better brother," Silas began. "Our family has been torn to hell, but now we're coming back together."

"Don't think you're alone in that," Noah replied. "I have my own failures as a brother to answer for. But one thing I know for sure—our family is definitely worth fighting for."

"I'm afraid we'll have quite the fight on our hands," Silas replied. "Rashad is vehement about seeing this through to the end."

"So are we," Rebel replied. "What do you need from us?"

Silas looked around the room, and each of the men signaled that he was in with a single nod of his head. "Okay. Let's take them down, then. First, we need to identify the agents and how they've been compromised."

Noah typed out a message to Brad, instructing him to track down Joe and Bill, the CIA agents, and check their bank account records. "I've had a bad feeling about them since the start of this case."

"Do you have Rashad's last name?" Rebel asked. "The one he uses now."

"Samir," Silas replied.

"On it," Shadow replied. "Looking for known accomplices and any frequently dialed numbers."

"Burner phones can't be traced, though," Liz replied.

"Sure, they can't," Shadow replied with a smile.

"Shadow, you have to teach me these tricks you know!" Liz pouted.

"I'll start checking airline records to see if Rashad is in Miami now," Bull said and walked off to the office.

"I'm going to look through that mission file again. See if anything else about Turan stands out," Rebel said.

"I'll put out some feelers with my CIA buddies," Silas replied. "See if we can cast a wide enough net to catch a bunch of terrorists."

"Sounds like we all have our marching orders," Noah said.

~

JANUARY

"I have the names and bank records for both Joe and Bill," Brad announced. "Finally. They were buried so deep, I didn't think I'd ever find them."

"Let's hear it," Noah replied.

"Joe appears to be clean, but Bill has numerous deposits in various multiples of $10,000 over a very short span. It looks like the payments were split up in differing amounts to avoid calling too much attention to them. But when you add them all up, it comes up to exactly a quarter of a million dollars," Brad explained.

"He's our guy. We need a tail on him at all times," Noah replied.

"I'll take it," Rebel volunteered. "If he leads us to Rashad, I want to be the first one there."

"Find him, tail him, and let's end this," Noah replied. "Don't engage alone if you can avoid it."

Rebel nodded. "I hope he leads us to another cell member."

"Rashad Samir is traveling as Sam Rash and he's in Miami," Bull reported. "Let's go find him and Bill."

"I'm ready," Rebel replied. "Let's go."

Rebel and Bull left to find Bill and hoped they'd also find Rashad nearby. They staked out the address listed for Bill and waited for him to arrive. When he pulled into his driveway several hours later, he walked inside without a backward glance.

"Arrogant, isn't he?" Bull asked.

"He's definitely sure that he's getting away with murder," Rebel replied. "He doesn't even check his surroundings to see if anyone's watching him."

Bull pulled out his phone and hit the speed dial. "Brad, you got that tap going?"

"It's up and running. As soon as I get a hit, you'll be the first to know," Brad replied.

Bull and Rebel continued to stake out his house, monitor his online activities, and wait for a phone call to come in. After a week and a half of driving different cars, tailing Bill everywhere he went, and monitoring his online activities, they finally got a break in the case.

"This guy really leads a boring life to be a terrorist wannabe," Bull quipped. "He has the treadmill at the gym, checking on his elderly mother at the nursing home, and a daily trip to the grocery store. He's boring me to death."

Bull's phone chimed and he looked at the text. "Huh. Brad said Bill isn't employed by the CIA anymore. He recently took a personal leave of absence for family reasons. Wonder if that's because of the mother in the nursing home or the quarter of a million dollars burning a hole in his pocket."

"I'm going to go with the latter," Rebel replied.

Thirty minutes later, Bull received another text from Brad with the phone number that Rashad was using, compliments of Shadow.

"How does he do that?" Rebel chuckled.

"It's all in those tricks he won't teach Liz about," Bull replied. "So, shall we call Rashad now?"

"Yes, let's," Rebel replied.

Bull called out the number while Rebel dialed. It rang several times before Rashad picked up. "Hello." The irritation of being interrupted was clear in his tone.

"Hello, Rashad Samir, Sam Rash, whoever you are," Rebel replied.

"Who is this?" Rashad emphasized each word.

"I'm the man who's going to put you away for life. And then I'll watch from the front row when you get the lethal injection," Rebel replied. "Ask your CIA friend Bill who I am."

"By the time you find me, it'll be much too late," Rashad replied with confidence. "But you can have Bill. I'll even help you out with that."

Rashad disconnected, and Rebel told Bull what he'd said. "What the hell does that mean?"

The explosion was so loud and violent that it blew out the glass in Bull's truck windows. Rebel jumped out of the truck and called Shadow as he ran across the front yard. "Shadow, tell me you have a list of names and numbers from Rashad's phone."

"Of course I do," Shadow chuckled. "What's all the commotion in the background?"

"Bill's house just exploded," Rebel said as he approached the raging inferno that had been Bill's home.

"Was he in it at the time?" Shadow asked.

"Yes, he went inside about thirty minutes ago," Rebel replied.

"Rashad is covering his tracks, then. He's getting ready to leave town," Shadow said. "If he hasn't already."

"He said by the time I found him, it'd be too late," Rebel said.

"He's put his plans into motion, then," Shadow replied. "I just received word that Joe has been reported missing to the agency. I don't know if he is hiding, dead, or if he's in on it and has already left town because of that. Let me make a few more calls. This just got a little harder to manage and a little more serious."

Rebel and Bull stayed until the fire department and police arrived. They explained the circumstances and as much about the case as they could provide. When they finally left the scene, they both felt defeated and like they were still several steps behind Rashad.

"Shadow thinks he may have already left the area when I talked to him," Rebel said.

"I have APBs out at all the major transit points," Bull replied. "But if he used a private charter at a private airstrip, he could bypass all of that."

"We need that info from Shadow," Rebel said. "The names

and numbers of the people he's been talking to. And Joe is missing. He doesn't know if Joe is dead, hiding, or in on it."

When Bull and Rebel walked into the office, Shadow had the lists ready for them. "I've been looking into some of these names and have a few locations we need to scout out. There's a high volume of call activity to people in New York City, Atlanta, Houston, Denver, and Los Angeles. This could take some time, boys."

"I'll take LA," Silas replied. "I've done quite a bit of work out there and still have a number of undercover contacts."

"I'll take Atlanta," Noah replied. "The baby is due in a few weeks, so I'd rather not be far from home if I can help it."

"I've got NYC," Shadow replied.

"Houston," Rebel replied and ignored the glances from Bull and Noah.

"Guess I'll take Denver." Bull smiled. "Chaise can go with me if it turns out there's something to investigate there."

"Everyone set? Research these names and phone numbers. Get Brad to run background checks, searches on bank records, credit cards, and known accomplices if anyone looks suspicious," Noah instructed. "We'll have to partner with the local LEOs if we pinpoint a location."

"What does 'local LEO' mean?" Liz asked, her pen and paper ready to take notes.

"Local law enforcement office," Noah replied. "LEO so we don't have to say the whole thing every time."

"Well, aren't you clever," Liz remarked with a chuckle.

"Liz, I'm going to need your help while I'm working on this case," Noah replied.

"I'm your woman," Liz replied. "Do I get to carry a Glock?"

"No," Noah replied. "I need you to help take care of Brianna, watch out for her, make sure she's taking care of herself."

"You need me to be her bodyguard." Liz nodded. "Got it.

Keep the bad guys away from her, escort her to the doctor, check the security system."

"Something like that." Noah smiled. "Can I count on you?"

"I'm on it. Don't you worry," Liz replied. She walked out of the office and began calling through the house. "Brianna? You and I are about to become even closer than we are now. Don't be embarrassed, I have all the same body parts you have."

Shadow barked out a laugh and looked at Noah. "You are a dead man. Brianna will have your head for this."

"She'll understand. I had to think of something to keep Liz busy and out of our hair," Noah laughed.

"Liz, close the door," Brianna's voice carried through the house.

"What are those? I don't have those," Liz answered.

Several minutes later, Brianna stopped in the doorway of Noah's office and glared at him. "I know what you did. You owe me, Noah Steele. When this case is over, you owe me. Don't think I won't collect either. I'm talking diamonds. *Big* diamonds."

"Anything, babe." Noah smiled. "It's worth whatever I have to pay."

The five men spent the following weeks combing through countless records in their attempt to pinpoint the people Rashad was in league with. When they'd narrowed their sights to a few people in each city, they started coordinating with their local contacts for stakeouts.

"Atlanta turned out to be a bust," Noah said. "The people Rashad called were employees of a news organization who ran an unfavorable story about terrorists. He was harassing everyone involved with the broadcast—the anchor, the producer, even the cameraman. None of the people on that list warrants further investigation."

"At least we can cross one city off the list. That's a relief," Silas replied. "LA isn't as fortunate. There are several indications it's a hot bed. One of my contacts out there has warned me against returning, though. Apparently, I'm to be shot on sight by one of the organized crime families I infiltrated out there. They don't want a massacre in the streets, so they're doing the hard work for me. It's kind of nice to be the boss instead of the grunt."

"Houston is buzzing with activity. If you two have time on your hands, there's plenty of work to be done there," Rebel replied.

"Denver is worth looking into closer," Bull replied. "Definitely a cause for concern."

"NYC is out. The numbers he called there stemmed from a phone-sex hotline. He got the girls' private numbers and began calling them directly. Our boy is mentally unstable," Shadow replied. "I can take LA for Silas. It's been a while since I've been there. Plus, no one in LA is looking to kill me that I know of."

"Sounds good, Shadow. Sounds like Silas's contacts will have your back and get a lot of the preliminary work finished for you. The rest of us can split up and help the others cover more ground working in teams. I'll go to Houston with Rebel. Silas, you can go to Denver with Bull and Chaise," Noah replied. "Any questions or comments?"

"Yes, I have a comment," Brianna said from the doorway. Noah looked up and met her gaze. "Before you rush off to Houston, I need you to do something with me, Noah."

"Sure, babe. Whatever you need," he replied.

"I need you to take me to the hospital. My water just broke," Brianna replied.

"The baby's coming? Now?" came Noah's shocked reply.

"Right now," Brianna answered. "I've had a dull ache in my

lower back all day, but I didn't think anything about it. I thought contractions would be stronger and announce their presence."

Noah's brain and ears finally caught up with each other, and he rushed to Brianna's side. "I'll grab the suitcase upstairs, and we'll go to the hospital right now."

"I've got it, Noah." Chaise smiled as she walked up with the suitcase. "I'll call Mom and Dad and Brianna's family to let them know it's time. Go ahead and take your wife to the hospital. Colton and I will be right behind you."

"Brianna, we're having a baby." Noah placed his hands on her face and lowered his mouth to hers. "You're having my baby."

"I know," she whispered. "I'm scared and excited and can't wait to meet her."

"Oh, shit," Noah hissed.

"What?" Brianna asked.

"We never picked out a name."

23

CHAPTER TWENTY-THREE

The contraction slammed into her like a locomotive and made her gasp for air. "I'm ready for it to go back to being a dull ache now," Brianna said through gritted teeth.

"I'm afraid there's no going back now." The nurse smiled. "The anesthesiologist will be in soon to start your epidural. You'll be able to relax and enjoy it then."

"Can you go drag him in here now?" Brianna requested.

"Let me see where he is," the nurse answered. "Don't forget to breathe through the contractions. It really does help."

"Okay. Got it," Brianna replied. "Breathe."

The nurse walked out of the room and Brianna turned to Noah. "Breathing doesn't help the pain. What a crock of shit."

Noah laughed out loud. "No, I've never found it to help my pain either. What can I do?"

"You're here with me. That's all I need." She smiled.

"It must be subsiding. You're Brianna again. In a few minutes, you'll have that evil, contorted face again," Noah chuckled.

"I'll remember that comment when the next one hits," she threatened playfully.

"Don't scare me like that," Noah retorted.

An hour later, the anesthesiologist still hadn't made an appearance, and Brianna's contractions were much stronger and closer together. Her skin was flushed, her hair was damp, and her fingers appeared to be permanently attached to Noah's hand. When the needle on the monitor redlined, her fingers clenched around his hand so she could share a small portion of her pain with him.

Bull and Chaise watched the scene play out in front of them and exchanged dubious glances. "Do you want us to leave?" Bull asked.

"Of course not. You're her aunt and uncle. Why would we want you to leave?" Noah asked.

"It looks uncomfortable," Silas answered. The muscles in his normally handsome face were drawn and contorted as if he'd felt sympathy pains.

"It is," Brianna and Noah replied in unison.

Noah hit the button to call the nurse after one especially painful contraction nearly broke his hand. The nurse promptly appeared and checked Brianna's progress. "You're very close to being fully effaced and dilated now. It won't be long before your baby arrives. Do you know what you're having?"

"A girl," she panted.

"Have you decided on her name?"

Brianna cut her eyes to Noah, and they both smiled. "No, not yet. Hopefully when we meet her," she replied.

"You'd be surprised how many people change their minds after they meet the baby for the first time," the nurse said.

A quick rap on the door caught their attention, and all heads turned to watch the anesthesiologist sheepishly enter the room with a red-faced Bull close on his heels. "I understand my presence has been requested in this room."

"Yeah, like an hour ago. Have a nice nap?" Brianna snapped.

"So, you're ready for your epidural, I presume." The doctor smiled.

The nurse anesthetist followed the doctor into the room and began assembling the items to start the epidural. "Can everyone except Dad step outside the room for a few minutes, please? We'll get her fixed up, and you can come right back in."

When everyone had left, the medical team helped Brianna sit up on the side of the bed and waited for the contraction to ease. "I'll be as easy as I can," the doctor explained. "You just have to be as still as you can possibly be. We'll have the good stuff going for you in just a minute."

The pain-numbing medicine kicked in almost immediately, and Brianna released a deeply contented sigh. The anesthesiologist checked the placement again before he left the room and wished them both the best for their delivery day.

Brianna's obstetrician then walked in and checked her progress. "Your baby is almost crowning now. I'll be back to check on you in a few minutes."

On his way out, he sent Bull, Chaise, and Silas back into the room.

"That's much better. Now I love you again, Noah," Brianna said sweetly.

"You quit loving me today?" Noah asked.

"For just a minute. When the pain was really severe. And I contemplated castrating you," Brianna joked. "Of course, I didn't really quit loving you. That could never happen."

"Let me unplug this medicine and see if you still say that." Noah pretended to search for the valve to stop the flow of medication into Brianna's epidural line.

"Don't make me have to kill you today, Noah," she retorted.

He laughed in response and leaned over the bed to kiss her. "I love you, too, babe."

"So, let's talk about a name now that I can think straight again," Brianna suggested. "Do you have anything in mind?"

"I really don't," Noah admitted. "Something unique to fit our life together."

"There's a name that's been stuck in my head," Brianna admitted.

"What is it?"

"Amelia Grace Steele," she replied.

"Why Amelia?" he asked.

"Because we've been around the world just to be together," Brianna explained.

Noah repeated it several times and played with how it rolled off his tongue. "I love it," he finally said. "I'm sold on Amelia Grace."

"I love that name," Chaise replied. "It's beautiful. I can't wait to meet my niece. Can you hurry up already?"

The family laughed and talked for the next half hour. Another knock on the door alerted them to more visitors arriving. Brianna was thrilled to see her parents and her three sisters arrive in time to be there for the delivery. "Mom, Dad! I'm so glad you made it.

"Missy, Jessie, and Ashley, get over here," she demanded as she extended her arms for a hug. They all readily complied and found a seat on her bed, surrounding her with love and support.

"We're so sorry we weren't here to give you a baby shower," Missy said solemnly. "But we're going to do one immediately after she's born. We already have it all planned out and everything's arranged."

"That's okay, Missy. We've all been very busy, and it's not easy to plan a baby shower from Atlanta," Brianna replied. "But I really do appreciate it."

"We have more good news, too," Diana quickly added.

"What? Tell me!" Brianna replied.

"We're moving to Miami!" she squealed. "The new hotel

construction is well underway. We've all talked about it, and we want to be together."

"That's great news," Brianna exclaimed. "I'll be so happy to have all of my family here."

The doctor and nurse came back in the room and smiled at all of the visitors. When the doctor reached the foot of Brianna's bed, he stopped and grinned at her. "Are you ready to have a baby, young lady?"

"I am." She nodded enthusiastically. "I'm so ready to see our daughter for the first time."

Everyone left the room to give her some privacy as the doctor checked her again and confirmed that it was time. "The baby's head has completely crowned. She's ready to get out of there," he laughed.

The nurse quickly converted the bed to a delivery bed and set up everything needed for the delivery. With Noah by her side, Brianna began pushing on command. She held her breath, pushed to the doctor's count, and then lay back to rest. They repeated this process several times until the baby's head emerged.

Noah looked at Brianna with amazement when the baby's head first appeared. "Oh my God. It's our baby, Bri. That's Amelia."

"One more good push and she'll be officially delivered. You ready?" The doctor smiled.

"Yes," Brianna replied on bated breath. "I'm so ready."

Noah helped her sit up, and she pushed one last time with all of her might. She felt the immediate relief of pressure and watched as the doctor cradled the baby with one arm while he clamped the umbilical cord with his free hand.

"Would you like to cut the cord?" he asked Noah.

"Yes," Noah said and took the scissors in his hand. With one snip, he cut the cord that had connected his wife and daughter for the last nine months. "This is all so amazing."

The nurse took the baby from the doctor and cleaned her up.

When she'd been weighed, measured, and monitored, the nurse placed the baby in Noah's waiting arms. The strong, alpha male, who could face bullets flying at him without so much as a blink, was completely brought to his knees by a seven-pound, twenty-inch-long baby girl.

"Amelia Grace Steele, you are so very loved," he whispered and kissed her rosy cheeks. "You look just like your mommy, my beautiful baby girl."

Noah walked to Brianna, carefully carrying his precious girl in his arms, and peered at Brianna with love brimming in his eyes. "Momma, I have someone here who would like to meet you now."

Brianna held her arms out as tears streamed down her face. "My sweet baby," she cried.

The nurse watched as Noah lovingly placed Amelia in Brianna's arms and then wrapped his muscular arms around them both. The nurse snapped pictures of them, but they were completely oblivious to anyone else in the room. She switched the camera to video mode and captured the entire moment for them.

"For as long as I have breath in my lungs, I will love and protect you both," Noah whispered. "Nothing is more important to me than my wife and my baby. You've never failed to amaze me, Brianna, and today is no exception. My life, my heart, my whole world—is right here in my arms. I love you." He kissed her softly on the temple when he finished.

The doctor and nurse finished with their tasks and left Brianna and Noah alone to spend time with their newborn. They were so completely wrapped up in everything about their daughter that they lost all track of time. They looked up when they heard a light knock on the door.

"Is everything okay in here? We're dying to meet the baby out here," Diana said.

Noah and Brianna both laughed. "Yes, Mom, everything's

fine. Everyone can come in now," Brianna replied. Everyone started filing into the room, standing anywhere they could fit.

"Sorry, everyone. We got a little lost in our baby girl," Noah chuckled. "Come here and meet Miss Amelia Grace Steele."

After everyone had sufficient time with the baby, meaning Noah allowed them thirty seconds each to hold her and give her back, Missy brought in the baby shower party items. The cake was beautifully decorated with pink shoes and strollers. The gifts were wrapped in matching paper and bows. The iPads were prominently displayed so Noah's parents could participate virtually. Nothing was left undone, and Brianna felt loved beyond measure.

It was the best day of Noah and Brianna's life together. The perfect culmination of their love slept against her mother's chest, wrapped in a pink swaddling blanket.

~

FEBRUARY

"Shadow and Silas have been gone for quite a while," Liz stated. "When will they be back?"

"I'm not sure," Brianna replied. "They've been working so hard on this case for the past few weeks. Rashad hasn't left them many clues to go on."

Brianna picked Amelia up from her bassinet and sang softly to her while she changed her diaper. "I can't believe she's almost a month old now. How do does time fly so fast? It just seems like yesterday when I was still pregnant with her."

"Wait until she's grown. You'll swear that you only blinked

once," Liz replied. "It's the way of things, I suppose. My mother always said the same thing, but I never understood it when I was a kid."

"I completely understand now," Brianna replied. "It's scary how life is so short. I always thought we had all the time in the world."

"Haven't we all," Liz agreed.

"Brianna," Noah called from downstairs. "Can you come here, babe?"

"On our way," Brianna replied.

When Noah saw Brianna approaching with Amelia, he had to stop and smile, just as he'd done every other time over the past several weeks. His wife and his baby together was the most beautiful sight he'd ever seen.

"Do you need something?" Brianna asked.

"Will you and Amelia be okay here if I go to Houston with Rebel?" Noah asked. "Or, would you two rather come with me? You can stay at the same hotel as my parents and visit with them while I'm working."

"We want to go with you," Brianna replied with a bright smile. "Sara and Steve have only seen her over the Internet. Besides, your parents need a break from being so focused on cancer treatments. It'll be good for them."

"I agree." Noah smiled. "Liz, you in?"

"Try to stop me from getting on that plane." She winked.

"Good. It's settled then. We all go together. Go ahead and get packed. We're leaving in a few hours."

Rebel's phone chimed, and he absently removed it from his pocket while his attention was focused on the intel he'd gathered.

"You bastard," he growled loudly.

Noah, Brianna, and Liz openly gawked at Rebel's outburst because it was so unlike him. "What is it, man?" Noah asked.

Rebel held out his phone, and Noah took it from him. Rebel paced the office while Noah looked at the text.

"Motherfucker," Noah replied.

"What is it, Noah?" Brianna asked. "What's wrong?"

Noah held up the phone for Brianna to see. The screen had a picture of a beautiful nurse as she walked out of the hospital. The bright sun reflected off her short, black hair and made it almost sparkle. Her warm smile was genuine and made her instantly appealing and inviting. Brianna imagined her personality matched her smile, making her a perfect candidate to be a nurse.

"She's gorgeous. What's the big deal? Who is she?" Brianna asked.

"The message that came with this picture says, 'Don't you love my next victim?' and it's from Rashad's burner phone," Noah replied.

"He's after her now?" Brianna asked, and urgency filled her tone. "Who is she? Where is she?"

"She's in Houston," Rebel replied. His voice was like ice—cold, hard, and unfeeling. Rebel stared out the window, his hands on his hips and his back to Brianna. "And she's my wife."

EPILOGUE

Rashad watched the lovely nurse leave the hospital after her shift. She'd been working several days in a row—many more days than nurses normally worked. Three twelve-hour shifts in a row were hard enough, but with the addition of extra days and longer hours, anyone would be worn out. Rashad knew from experience when women were too tired, they weren't as aware of their surroundings as they should be. He'd used this fact to his advantage too many times to count.

If this particular pretty nurse had been watching, she would've noticed the same car following her home over the past few days. She would've seen the handsome, Middle Eastern man who followed her in the hospital halls. She would've felt his eyes on her skin. Fortunately for Rashad, she didn't notice anything out of the ordinary, and that gave him all the advantage he needed.

When he sent the picture to the man called Rebel, he simply wanted to repay an insult at first. But the more he thought about what he'd been forced to do, the more he understood Turan's obsession with revenge. The revenge he'd seek for being forced to kill his own brother wouldn't get in the way of the large-scale attack that was well underway. He decided he'd avenge his father, his brother, and his own actions all in one fatal blow.

But having a little fun by torturing Rebel along the way would definitely be an added benefit.

When he'd torched the rental house, he made sure Turan lost everything he loved and needed to carry out his specific part of the plan in the fire. All of his laptops and equipment were melted. The few articles of clothing he owned were destroyed. The roof over his head was taken away. Rashad had hoped Turan would finally give up on his quest and leave the country. But he didn't.

When their adoptive uncle publically disowned and dishonored Turan, he tried to give his brother time to get out. When he disappeared from the apartment, Rashad had hoped Turan had finally made the right decision. But then he showed up on the CIA's radar yet again after he accepted a contract as a hired killer, on the Internet of all places.

Rashad exhaled forcefully at the thought. "That was such a stupid move, Turan. How could you have been such an idiot? You knew better than anyone that nothing is safe on the web."

Killing Bill had been an added benefit for Rashad. The dirty undercover agent had become greedy and demanding. He expected Rashad to give him more money in exchange for keeping silent, looking the other way, and keeping the other agents off his trail. The fact that Bill's death happened at the exact time Rashad received the phone call was an added bonus.

Heather Reed walked by his car on the way to her car. Without so much as a glance in his direction, she continued on alone through the parking garage.

Remain oblivious to the danger all around you, Rashad thought as she crossed in front of him. *I'll see you soon.*

Ready for more Reaper, Bull, Rebel, & Shadow?
The story continues in Wicked Intentions!

~

Keep reading for a FREE sneak peek
of Wicked Intentions!

WICKED INTENTIONS SNEAK PEEK

Wicked Intentions (Book 4)

PROLOGUE

June 22, 2001

Heather,

I've watched you sleep for the past few hours, and I've racked my brain trying to remember what my life was like without you in it. We've known each other as long as I can remember, and I can't recall a time when I didn't love you. There hasn't been a single day gone by I didn't know exactly how much you meant to me. You've never kept secrets from me. Your heart has always been an open book, reserved only for me to devour every word, thought, and feeling.

When we first met as kids, I was only looking for someone to play with after school. The day I knocked on your front door changed me forever. You became my partner in crime, my best friend, and the love of my life. Remember how we were inseparable? Every day, we rushed to do our chores or homework, so we'd have more time to spend together. You were, and still are, the coolest girl in the world. You could hang with me on the bicycle. You'd hold frogs and touch snakes. Every other girl would run away screaming, but never you. Nothing could make you leave my side.

As we got older, those things weren't as important to me anymore, and I saw you in a whole new light. You still had just as much spunk about you. Remember the time at the middle school dance when you punched that girl for flirting with me? I still laugh about that to this day. As if she was ever any threat to you. You said I belonged to you, even if I didn't realize it yet. You said you wouldn't put up with another girl disrespecting what we had. There are no words to describe how turned on I was when you said that. I knew I loved you then, but an awkward thirteen-year-old me didn't know how to tell you.

Then came the high school years. Yes, you remember those well, don't you? Our class schedules separated us, so I didn't see you as much during the day. The first semester of our freshman year, I thought I'd die from being apart from you for so long. Every day after school, I waited for you outside so we could go home together. Absence really did make the heart grow fonder, and I knew without a doubt it was time to tell you exactly how I felt. That day, I waited in the rain for you to come out of the school. I had my speech memorized down to the last syllable.

Then you walked out, and I watched in horror as David Richards put his arm around you and announced to the school that you were his girlfriend. You know me…there was no way I could let that stand. So I decked him. Punched his lights right out. The look on your face was priceless—you were shocked, awed, and dumbfounded all at once. You were shocked that I had finally admitted my feelings for you. Awed that I did it in such a public display. And dumbfounded that it took me so fucking long to realize what you'd always known. When I kissed you that day, you changed me again. You ruined me for any other woman. Your kiss, your taste, and your sweet scent —no one else on earth could compare to you.

So began our dating experience. We defied the odds, didn't we, babe? We showed everyone in this one-horse town that our love was real and lasting. Neither of us has ever even been on a date with anyone else. Never kissed another person in the intimate ways we kiss. Never made love to another and shared the special bond that we have together. Even after more than four years of officially dating, I can honestly say that I don't regret one minute of the time I've spent exclusively with you. Four years of football games, school dances, junior and senior proms. Weekend dates, weeknights sneaking out my bedroom window just to make out with you. Making plans and dreaming big —together.

Sometimes I look back and miss the "us" we used to be, even just a short year ago. The things we've been through have taken a hard toll on you, and I blame myself for that. You can blame me, too. I can take it, and I deserve it. More than anything, I wanted to be the one to always protect you, love you, and provide for you. Our life together was supposed to be perfect. Wonderful. Magical. Beautiful.

I failed you. I failed us. I'm sorry, baby. I'm sorry I couldn't be the man I should've been, the man you needed me to be. Because of my failures, you're all but estranged from your family, especially your dad. The stress of everything has just been too much on you, and my presence here is only adding to it.

We fight every day now over things we'd normally laugh about. We're slowly tearing each other apart, bit by bit, and I'm afraid there will be nothing left of the Heather I fell in love with before much longer. When he died, I think he took the best part of us with him. I can't keep putting you through this hell every day, baby. It's killing me to watch you slowly die right before my eyes. When you look at me, I know you blame me for not being able to protect him like I should have.

Saying all this to you in a letter is a really shitty thing to do, I know. I openly admit that I'm a coward when it comes to losing you. On one hand, I'm afraid that if I tell you I'm leaving, you'd cry and ask me to stay. And I would. For you, there's nothing I wouldn't do. On the other hand, I'm petrified that you'd tell me to go, because then I'd know that your love for me has truly died. Love that has been alive and growing since the day we met. That means I'm taking the coward's way out, so I can keep your love with me.

I'm apparently also selfish, because I can't stand to think of doing this any other way. But I'm not so selfish that I don't want you to be happy. I want you to find someone who makes you the Heather I once knew, before I brought so much pain and suffering to your life. Find someone who puts that spark in your eye, the spring in your step, and the smile on your face. Give him all of you, everything you possess, and hold nothing back so that you can be whole again. Put me in the past, where I belong, and don't look back.

Know that you have my love—all of my love, all of my heart, and all of me. Forever.

Until death do us part,
Braxton Reed

Braxton placed the folded letter on the empty pillow beside his wife's head and stared at her intently one last time. Over the years, he'd memorized every line, curve, and tiny freckle on her face. He knew her better than anyone else did. Better than her family members who'd done everything in their power to drive them apart. Better than her friends who'd tried to convince her to date other people before settling for him. Better than their teachers who thought they knew everything but had no idea how deeply Braxton and Heather's love ran.

Part of him wished they'd listened to at least one of the naysayers before they'd reached such a low point. Maybe if they'd broken up, dated other people, or just took a break from their all-consuming relationship, the sorrows they'd experienced wouldn't have ever happened. Maybe if they'd actually waited until they were adults, instead of pretending to be grown-ups, everything would've turned out differently.

But that wasn't the way of things. Being young and foolish, they'd made mistakes and tried to fix them. In doing so, Braxton realized they'd only made their follies worse. In his mind, the only way either of them would make it out alive was if they did something they'd never tried before. They had to split up and never look back.

In the weeks leading up to that day, Braxton had talked secretly to a recruiter about his choices and completed all the steps to enlist in the Army. By the time Heather awoke that morning, he planned to be long gone, far away from her so he couldn't hurt her again.

He paused at the door, and his hand gripped the knob as his heart shattered into a million pieces. "Eighteen, married, and divorced." He shook his head in disbelief. "How did we come to this?"

When Braxton walked out the door of the tiny, one-bedroom apartment they had briefly shared as husband and wife, he reflected on how it was the second hardest thing he'd ever done. He closed the door behind him quietly, ensured it was locked, and walked away from the woman who held his heart in her hands, who had been his best friend for as long as he could remember, and whom he'd failed in the worst way. He tried to block the visions of Heather waking and finding the letter on his pillow rather than seeing him lying there. He didn't want to think about her reaction when she read his words, regardless of what it was. The thought of her crying, brokenhearted, and feeling abandoned hurt him as much as the thought of her being relieved that he was gone.

As the bus pulled away from the station, he leaned his head on the seatback and closed his eyes. "I love you, baby. Until death do us part."

A MESSAGE TO YOU

Dear Reader,

From the bottom of my heart, I want to thank you for spending your time reading this book. Whether you loved, liked, or hated it, your time is precious and I appreciate you spending it with the characters I love so much.

If you will take just a few more minutes to leave a review, I would greatly appreciate it. Even just a few words helps more than you know. Your review doesn't have to be a long book report. :) A simple, "Everyone needs to read this book," or even, "This book wasn't really for me," is more than enough.

Again, thank you for your time and support.

Lots of Love,
Angel

BOOKS BY A.D. JUSTICE

Steele Security Series

Wicked Games (Book 1)

Wicked Ties (Book 2)

Wicked Nights (Book 3)

Wicked Intentions (Book 4)

Wicked Shadows (Book 5)

Crossing Lines Series

Fine Line

Blurred Line

Hard Line

The Vault Series

Precarious: Warning, Part One

Insidious: Warning, Part Two

Treacherous: Warning, Part Three

A HOMETOWN NOVEL

Intent

All I Want

All I Need

Entice (coming soon!)

The Crazy Series

Crazy Maybe (Book 1)

Crazy Baby (Book 2)

Crazy Love (Book 3, Free Short Story)

Dominic Powers Series

Her Dom (Book 1)

Her Dom's Lesson (Book 2)

Covis Realm, Easthaven Crest Series

Cloaked

Deceived

Unveiled

Stand—alone Books

Saving Grace

Completely Captivated

Immortal Envy

Mistletoe Not Required

Just One Summer

ABOUT THE AUTHOR

A.D. Justice is the award-winning, *USA Today* bestselling author of several series and stand-alone romance novels in various romance genres, including romantic suspense, contemporary, and paranormal.

When she's not writing, she loves spending time with her alpha male husband in the Northwest Georgia mountains. They're living out their own HEA, frequently on horseback with a dog in tow.

She is also an avid reader of romance novels, a master of procrastination, a chocolate sommelier, a twister of words, and speaks fluent sarcasm. An avid animal lover, she has two horses, two cats, and two very spoiled dogs.

She loves chatting with her readers. You're welcome to stalk her across all social media!

Connect with her online!

Newsletter
Facebook Reader Group
Website

ACKNOWLEDGMENTS

First and foremost, I want to thank my Lord and Savior for His continued forgiveness of a sinner.

To my husband: I love you! Thank you for putting up with the late nights, long weekends, and the less-than-stellar kept house. Writing the book didn't help much with any of that, either. :)

To my street team: Y'all are the best! Thank you for being my beta readers, my sounding boards, my biggest supporters, and the best all-around people in the world. Love all of you!

To my readers: Thank you for taking a chance on a new indie author! I love hearing from everyone, so stop by my page and say hello.

To my assistant: Tabitha Charisse, thank you for all your help and support. You are very much appreciated.

To my BFFs: I don't know how I managed to do anything right before I met the best friends anyone could ever ask for. T.K. Leigh and Michelle Dare, I love both of you!

To the bloggers: None of this would be possible without your help, support, and tireless pimping! I love everyone in this great group of people! I can't name one without naming everyone because you've all been so helpful and wonderful friends.